THE QUEEN OF DISCORD

TEMPORAL ARMISTICE #4
MATTHEW S. COX

A WASTE OF A FINE AFTERNOON

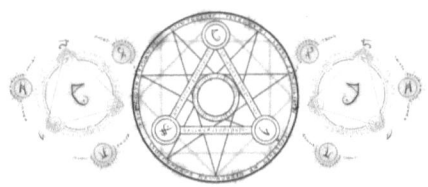

Boredom is the root of all evil.

Some people like to think it's money. Others blame lust, or one of those other 'sin' things the humans added to their various mythologies. Truth is, almost everything humans do, good or bad, is a product of boredom. Leave someone sitting around long enough with nothing to do and the brain gets to work. Leave someone with nothing to do and access to spray paint... teenage girls who aren't fully human end up in the back seat of a police car.

However, busy people don't have time to come up with schemes or daydream. When hands are idle, strange things happen. For example, someone got bored... and decided to try eating lobster. Well, maybe the lobster thing happened out of desperation. Seriously—how hungry did the first guy have to be in order to look at a giant sea bug and think 'dinner'?

Humans of antiquity got bored and invented all sorts of stories to explain stuff they didn't understand. Oh, look. There's a sun in the sky. Must be a giant flying phoenix or there's a man in a flaming chariot pulling it around. Oh, look, this naked girl has bright feathery wings—she's an angel and here's exactly what she's like. Aha, the other naked guy has wings, but they're all dragon-like and not pretty. He's gotta be evil. Must be a 'demon.'

Sorry, bud. Not that simple.

Anyway, I know boredom is the root of all evil. I'm kind of an expert on the subject. It's responsible for roughly sixty percent of the bad stuff I did growing up. The remainder came from sudden inspiration. You know, like I'm walking down the hall at school and spot a freshman wearing his pants down a bit too far. Telekinesis let me get away with *so* much shit back then. Unlike mages, it's not obvious when I do something.

In the interest of full disclosure, I will admit a small percentage of my nefarious deeds *were* the result of pre-planning. Those usually involved revenge pranks, like the time I covered the police chief's unmarked car in dozens of spray painted penises. So what if I'd deserved to be arrested. I wasn't mad at the cops for picking me up. The chief didn't have to be a dick to me. Seriously, what kind of asshole leaves a kid handcuffed in a solitary holding cell for hours because she's got a little attitude and 'didn't respect him' enough? And it's not like I disrespected cops. Whenever they picked me up, I'd always be all respectful and shit. But this prick didn't want 'respect,' he acted like some kind of tyrant king who held my entire future in his hands. I knew they didn't have any real serious charges against me, but the guy kept trying to scare me with threats of twenty years in prison if I didn't rat out my friends. He didn't believe me telling him I didn't really know them. Didn't matter I lied. Beside the point. I'm not a snitch. Dickhead figured he'd get the truth out of me if he left me alone in a little cell long enough. Think I spent six hours there. Bastard even put handcuffs on my ankles, lying about me trying to run away. He did it to basically torture me into snitching. Fortunately, Mom showed up and got me out of there before I cracked.

Ooh. He's so damn lucky my powers had been dormant back then. Mom totally should have sued them, but she was afraid of retaliation and didn't. So... the spray paint happened.

But, yeah. The humans have a saying about idle hands being the Devil's playthings. If they're talking about a literal father of evil, they're totally making shit up, though I don't necessarily put it past a Shaar'Nath to pretend to be Satan to dick with humans. Yeah, neither side has a big boss, so no God or Devil. Also, neither side is what humans think them to be. Shaar'Nath (demons) aren't evil as much as impulsive. Elestari (angels) are definitely not paragons of right-eousness. Talk about sanctimonious and arrogant. Grr. Although... I suppose in terms of an abstract concept of some people's ability to do bad things, the general idea of a 'father of evil' works. As long as no one takes it literally.

Case in point... I'm presently sitting in the vilest cauldron of evil known to humanity.

No, not Wall Street.

I mean the grand temple of boredom: the DMV.

Yeah, yeah, rub it in. The rebel is finally surrendering a piece of her soul to the government and getting a driver's license. A few of the guys at the firehouse are baffled at how I even made it into the ranks without one. It's amazing what a little charm can do. At the time, no one—including me—knew the truth about my father. Or how I'm half-demon. No, we're not really 'demons' in the true sense of the way humans think of the word. It's merely easier to say 'demon' than Shaar'Nath. The differences aren't terribly huge. Mostly, we aren't ghastly ugly monstrous creatures, nor are *we* evil, really. More chaotic with more-than-minor impulse control issues. One could argue the Elestari are technically more evil than us. Humans think of them as angels because they're all fabulously pretty with beautiful feathery wings.

The truth is uglier.

Elestari are generally elitists who look down on humans the way most people regard an unwanted infestation of cockroaches. Okay, maybe it's redundant to say 'unwanted infestation.' Does anyone really *want* roaches? So far, I've encountered one exception to the rule of Elestari being insufferable: Laniah. She is nauseatingly sweet. She's kinda like the kid sister who went vegan at age nine and cries when-ever someone eats meat nearby.

Not being literal there about the meat thing. More talking about her highly sensitive personality. For all I know, she swallows chickens whole when no one is looking. But, she's super nice to humans, if a bit condescending.

Maybe I am calming down a bit in my old age, so to speak. Is it bad twenty-three feels like old? I still remember being thirteen and thinking of high school seniors as boring old people. Now I'm older than them and *still* feel like eighteen is over the hill. Honestly, it's not like my body hurts or I've developed a weird need to go to bed early. Nor is buying a new kitchen gadget the height of my week... it's the stupid 'consequences' thing. As a kid, I could do almost anything from skateboard naked down the street to stealing cars for joyrides or breaking into places, graffiti-ing up walls and such—and people would brush it off as cute or be concerned about my home life.

Okay, maybe not so much the car stealing bit. Out of maybe sixteen times riding in stolen cars, I'd only initiated the theft once. And it's not like I hotwired a stranger's car or truly *stole* one. I took Mom's keys and drove to get myself ice cream when I was like seven. Back then, I was small enough to get away with being caught. The rest of the joyriding happened in my teen years, and one of my friends or some rando always did the stealing part. I had my whole teary-eyed 'I told him to stop but he wouldn't pull over' act rehearsed well in advance.

By some miracle, I never got busted in a stolen car. We usually got away clean. However, twice I wound up leaving the car before the joyride ended, and both times, the cops got my friends. Guess bringing me along really was a good luck charm. Once had been a pickup truck where a speed bump—or maybe a curb, night's kinda blurry—launched me out of the bed into a ditch on the side of the road. My friends didn't even realize I'd been catapulted. At the time, I thought I'd been seriously lucky to walk away without a scratch. Now knowing what I am, it's way more likely my ass *did* get bashed up a bit, but I healed before waking up. Somehow none of the cops chasing us saw me get ejected from the truck.

The other time I survived a joyride without arrest, the guys stopped at a gas station for snacks. Cops hadn't been chasing us at the time, obviously. We were crazy, but not stupid enough to stop for chips in the middle of a high-speed pursuit. Anyway, gas station bathrooms are filthier than the outermost layer of Hell. I decided to water the bushes behind the building. Just so happened to be two cops in the gas station convenience store, and they recognized the stolen car. Both of my then-friends got picked up. Mad props to them, though. Neither one ratted me out. Granted, I didn't actually do much other than be with them. Had a long ass walk home, but it beat being arrested.

So, yeah. Cars and I have had an interesting history.

It's going to be a weird feeling to drive and not worry about getting in trouble for it.

Damn, if only I'd known about my other powers back then, it would've spared me a lot of bad experiences with the police. Not saying the cops—except the chief—had been nasty to me or anything. Usually, they treated me fairly well. I wasn't 'stupid proud' as a kid. I dropped the 'tude after they caught me. Acting demure and respectful worked in my favor. Still, I really effing hate handcuffs. Not big on locked rooms either, but chains freak me out.

Maybe it's a good thing I didn't understand myself back then, or I'd have snapped them off.

Yeah, my half-human half-Shaar'Nath body is a skosh stronger than normal humans.

Being in handcuffs unnerves me in a way like how normal people would feel if someone tied them to train tracks and they could hear the horn coming. Not to say I liked holding cells, but at least I could more or less sit still in one. Cuffs? I couldn't stop fidgeting and struggling to escape. Basically, torture. Hence, why after Chief Dickhead left me cuffed hands and feet in a tiny cell, his car got a covering of spray painted penises. I *almost* blew it up, but knew they'd come after me hard for that. At least the dickpaint made other cops laugh. Considering my hatred of confinement, it's kinda strange how the secret about me being half Shaar'Nath stayed in the bag so long. Maybe it required me *knowing* my strength? Now? I can snap steel handcuffs like plastic toys.

As far as memory serves, the first time I ever did anything super-human had been lifting the burning debris off Jason during the hotel fire. Not wanting to watch a fellow firefighter die right in front of me carried a tad more emotional weight than being pissed off at hand-cuffs. Or maybe the warmongers did something to me to keep my abilities suppressed until adulthood? For the longest time, I thought I killed a perv who tried to abduct me as a child by telekinetically smashing his brain. Turns out, my father did it.

I grew up thinking my dad was an ordinary asshole who raped my mother and disappeared. The way Mom always got spacey whenever I mentioned him, never spoke of him, kept no pictures of him, and so on, made me assume the worst. In truth, Dad didn't do anything bad to Mom. She spaced out so much whenever I asked about him because of magic. No, not any magic Mom did, even though she's a luminare herself, a sorta half-mage not terribly powerful. She's what they call a seer or diviner, the genuine version of a fortune-teller. She'll never throw fireballs, but she can read a mean tarot—and be accurate.

Yours truly is a damn bomb.

Not in the sense I'm going to explode someday, but the warmon-gers—a group of Elestari and Shaar'Nath working together to bring about the end of the world—arranged for my existence. They charmed my mother into summoning Dad and throwing herself at him. Dad, obviously, is a full-blooded Shaar'Nath. As a result of the charm, my mother didn't remember how she ended up pregnant with me. Every time someone brought up my father, she'd get all foggy because her brain tried to look up data someone erased.

See, the problem is, Elestari and Shaar'Nath generally don't get along with each other. We think the Elestari are elitist snobs, and they regard us as slovenly, impulsive, and wanton. I object to the slovenly part, but can't argue the impulsive. Elestari hate Shaar'Nath the way Puritans hate anyone who can have fun and not feel guilty about it. They think our lack of elitism makes us inferior.

So, the two groups had a little bit of an argument. Yeah, under-statement. They didn't have an argument. More like a genocidal war. It didn't last *too* long, only like 10,000 years or so until it got to a point where both sides had ground each other down to teetering on extinction and none of them could really remember what started the war or why they'd been fighting so long. In a remarkable feat of intelligence, Elestari and Shaar'Nath worked together to declare a truce. To ensure no idiots broke the truce and brought about the complete extinction of both sides, they created the Armistice.

'Armistice' is a fancy word for reality. Or the physical world humans know as home.

Our world serves as a barrier between the Elestari and Shaar'Nath realms, Aesinor and Imbreleth respectively. Pure-bloods can travel freely between their home realm and the human world, but can't go past it into the other team's space. Before the physical world existed, nothing stopped invasions but walls of bodies.

Their plan had been to stop the war. No one on either side expected life to develop in the supposedly 'dead' space between their worlds. Moss growing on it (life) came as a surprise. Elestari have about the same attitude toward humans as people would have to algae growing on the walls of their fish tank: it's alive, unsightly, didn't plan on it being there, don't want it there, and really aren't bothered if it dies. Shaar'Nath find humans amusing. As in, they're an endless source of amusement, often as a result of playing games on them. That whole demonic temptation deal has some basis in fact, but it's not about souls—purely shits and giggles.

Given the energy used to create the Armistice came from both sides, humans have attributes of both Elestari and Shaar'Nath, albeit way watered down. It's also why they kind of look like us, without the wings, tails, horns, or self-aggrandizing beauty. A few sneaky bastards involved in the creation of the Armistice didn't want it to be a temporary cease-fire so forces could build back up before resuming war. They wanted to stop fighting for good. Consequently, they made it so the Armistice couldn't be 'turned off' or destroyed by a Shaar'Nath *or* an Elestari, or even them working together.

Only a being with the powers of one side or the other, but also native to the Armistice can access—and theoretically destroy—the Pillars of Creation, thus bringing about the end of the physical world and the removal of the barrier. This would allow the Elestari and Shaar'Nath to once again act like complete morons and chop each other apart. I don't know if the ones responsible for the caveat knew humanity would develop or if they tried to be sneaky by requiring a being native to a place where nothing lived in hopes it would establish permanent security. Maybe life developed here as a response to the requirement.

And seriously, I don't understand why the idiots want to wipe each other out so bad. If they're only craving a bloodsport to watch, they should do what a few bored Shaar'Nath did years ago: invent Beanie Babies and make them have a supply problem—or just go hang out in the Middle East.

Anyway, the warmongers tried once a bunch of years ago to bring about the end. They arranged for a half-human, half-Elestari child, filling her full of the religious mythology stuff in hopes of turning her into a crusader against 'demons,' then tricking her into destroying the Pillars of Creation by claiming they were evil. Fortunately, Joan of Arc fell *totally* for the myth of an all-powerful god and went off the deep end of virtue. Once she found out destroying the pillars would destroy everything, she refused to do it.

When the warmongers got tired of trying to manipulate her, they arranged for her to be killed. Of course, to half-breeds like her and me, 'killed' only got rid of the human side. She ended up in Aesinor as an Elestari. According to rumor, she's *still* upset over discovering the truth about religion.

Clearly, going all the way 'good' didn't work for the warmongers, so I'm the next try.

As Elestari were involved and they trust Shaar'Nath about as much as people trust Nigerian princes asking for money, they didn't want to try going completely in the other direction from Joan. Hence why they chose my mother. She's so Catholic it hurts, and not in the 'can't wait for the world to end holier than thou' sort of way. She's humble, sweet, would give a total stranger the clothes off her back, and so on. Funny how humans make up this character who's like so caring and humble, then the people who claim to follow him never act like that. If the dude really existed as described, I could totally hang with him.

So anyway, the warmongers figured an influence like Mom would 'tame' a half Shaar'Nath (me) into a bad-but-good-but-bad creature they could control. I should have been their guided weapon to take out the Armistice.

Whoops. Didn't quite work out for them.

Not only are Shaar'Nath *not* truly evil like the Elestari think, our genes are pretty damn strong. I'm called a 'half-breed' because of having two parents, one of each, but Shaar'Nath on human is more of an eighty-twenty or seventy-five percent situation. Hence, my poor impulse control and general 'whatever' attitude. So, yeah. My job—at least according to the warmongers—is to destroy the physical universe and enable a whole bunch of knuckle-dragging morons to club each other over the head until one side destroys the other. I have other plans: my job is saving the world.

I like it here.

Best part? Doing said job requires only sitting on my ass. To destroy everything, I'd have to run back and forth across the universe and do a whole bunch of complicated crap in accordance with prophecy. No, there isn't a prophecy. It just sounds cooler to say. Adding 'in accordance with prophecy' or 'as was written eons ago' to anything makes it sound much cooler. In addition to being sarcastic, random, impulsive, and disrespectful of authority, I'm lazy. *Way* too lazy to run around destroying creation.

My laziness is the stuff of legend. Half the time the cops picked me up as a kid had been for wandering around outside with no clothes or just underpants. I hadn't been a hippie child, messed up in the head, or even particularly fond of nudity. Getting dressed took effort and time. Pure laziness. I suppose it helped to have a complete lack of shame. Comes from the Shaar'Nath side. Granted, Elestari are the same. Clothing as a concept doesn't exist in our home worlds. Kinda hard to make fabric in a world filled with flames. Also, the Elestari are conceited and beautiful, so they adore showing themselves off like Greek statues all the time.

And okay, sure, I do sometimes look.

Anyway, speaking of sitting on my ass... I'm at the DMV waiting for my license, hence my thinking about boredom being the root of evil. Ever wonder why they always have one or two cops hanging around Motor Vehicle Services offices? The government understands the sort of malevolence capable of fomenting here. They *know* what boredom does to people, especially in a setting where people are *forced* to sit around doing nothing while waiting for something too important to say 'oh screw it' and leave. Gets worse when the employees are obviously in no hurry to deal with the hundred or so people in the waiting area and standing in line.

Patience has never been my strongest virtue. It isn't even among my weaker ones.

Two police officers being here is enough to keep most people from having wild meltdowns of frustration or exacting some manner of revenge on the DMV for being slow. Fortunately, I suffer no such hesitation. What the cops can't trace back to me is fair game.

For the first hour, boredom made me amuse myself.

I telekinetically knocked over random small objects on the clerks' desks whenever another worker appeared to be wasting time and shooting the breeze with them. Made it look like they bumped it. This one dye-blonde cougar decided to pull the 'do you know who I am' routine, holding up a line when the clerk insisted she still had to show proof of ID. Her yoga pants experienced explosive decompression. She totally didn't have anywhere near a big enough ass likely to rupture fabric, but no one questioned it, too thankful to have her run out of the building.

A toddler chased a mysteriously self-moving toy car for a little while until I got bored with it. I totally get why cat people buy laser pointers now.

Around the second hour of my DMV sentence, a guy helped himself to the seat next to mine. No, not to be a creep; the place is full. He gave me a slightly longer than passing glance—probably due to my unusual skin color—but otherwise has been polite. Most people have a little bit of a reaction to my pigmentation (or lack thereof) since it's basically inhuman. I'm white as chalk, and literally, not like an Irish girl. It used to get me yelled at in grade school as a kid sometimes if a teacher thought I'd put on face paint.

Mom started off trying to send me to Catholic school.

Yeah, didn't last long.

First problem: she couldn't really afford private school, so she'd made some kind of deal with the nuns, either volunteering to work for them or appealing to their sense of charity. Either way, I climbed up on my desk and mooned my third grade teacher who accused me of wearing banned 'devil goth' makeup to turn my face white. If I remember correctly, nine-year-old me yelled, "Do you think I painted my ass, too?"

For three glorious minutes, I'd been the absolute queen of cool students in St. Bartleby's. Guess who finished third grade in public school? I wasn't trying to be rude, honest. Just wanted to prove I hadn't lied about not wearing paint.

Some people say they were 'born goth.' For me, it's more than metaphorical.

Suppose I lucked out, really. Shaar'Nath come in several colors, and of those, white is the one most easily passed off as normal when mixing up a demi-human. Full-blooded Shaar'Nath visiting the physical world can make themselves look more or less however they want as long as it's basically human. Tall, short, fat, skinny, any coloration or hair... whatever. Half-breeds get stuck with skin the same color as their 'demonic' side.

My skin could've been crimson, jet black, blue, dark grey... or even pink. It's hereditary, so in addition to his being old and powerful, coloration had to play a part in the warmongers selecting my father, Baal'nethiel, as my mother's target. No way could anyone have passed me off as normal if I looked like a crimson succubus.

I think Dad is still upset at not realizing what happened before he'd already been seduced. My father would bend over backward to protect me, but he definitely would have preferred *not* to sire the potential destroyer of the human world. He's totally on the side of peace. The man loves a good time, but doesn't see any point to fighting an endless war merely for the sake of fighting. He'd even kill me to protect the Armistice if necessary, in the most loving way possible, of course. And no, it's not as bad as it sounds. If I die here, I'll end up being flung into Imbreleth and becoming a Shaar'Nath. The same way Joan of Arc landed on the other side. Well, maybe. It's not guaranteed my soul energy would re-form. Not sure exactly what the odds are, but it's possible I'd cease to exist. The odds must not be good or the peaceful Shaar'Nath would have tried to kill me already.

Reincarnated me wouldn't be the exact same as Joan. I wouldn't spend the rest of my supernatural existence pouting over wasting my mortal life serving a deity who didn't really exist. Makes sense why she's upset. She never got much of a chance to be a child as a kid. Never had fun. Always penitent, trying to be 'good,' desperately afraid to do anything even remotely wild or thrilling.

The odds of me meeting oblivion have to be more than trivial. Otherwise, why wouldn't Dad have killed this version of me already and eliminated the risk to the Armistice? Guess Dad's more of a softie than he acts and couldn't do it. Plenty of others could have tried, and haven't. Wonder if there are more complications than merely destroying me permanently?

Whatever.

I'm not about to destroy the world and there isn't anything the warmongers can do to change my mind. Fortunately, the opposition isn't exactly smart. For example, they tried kidnapping my mother and threatening to kill her if I didn't destroy the world. Like, hello? Destroying the world also destroys my mother. Did they honestly think I'd kill my mother to save her? Ugh.

"… origins of the fire deemed suspicious."

One of the television sets facing the waiting area takes a break from mind-numbing daytime pablum for news. The word 'fire' catches my attention.

"The plant, in operation since 1964, is still burning. Firefighters in Camden, New Jersey are working to get control of the blaze, which is believed to have broken out early this morning around two," says the news anchor, Michael Sandoval. "Teams of Hydromancers have joined the effort to mixed success. Sources on the scene indicate the authorities suspect it is another in a series of arson attacks targeting industrial sites over the past few weeks. With me now, please welcome our panel: Ladonna Steele from The Academy, Sidney Stafford representing FRUM, or the Foundation for the Responsible Use of Magic, and Rachel Feuerstein from the Society for the Prevention of Cruelty to Magical Animals."

The screen cuts to a three-box view showing a lawyery-looking black woman in a grey suit, an uptight white fortyish dude with tragic-curly blond hair, and a magenta-haired woman in her mid-thirties. Either she's got some elven blood or it's dye. The grey tiger cat curled around her neck is a nice touch, though.

"What are your thoughts on these attacks?" asks Michael.

"It's obvious there's a little bit of bias going on here, no?" asks Sidney.

Ladonna's smile becomes forced. "We're discussing magical events. Why wouldn't the panel consist of people who are experts?"

Rachel glances sideways at Sidney. "Remind me what a guy from the Foundation for Useless Contrarian Kvetching can contribute to a discussion about magic?"

Sidney glares. "It's F-R-U-M, not F-U-C-K."

Rachel laughs. Ladonna snickers. I burst out laughing.

Michael coughs to cover a chuckle.

"Sorry, didn't quite catch that," says Rachel with a small, victorious smile.

I swear, her cat laughs, too.

Ignoring having made a fool of himself, Sidney adjusts his tie. "Do you see the sort of things we have to put up with from the magical community?" Beige works for him, but not in the form of a three-piece suit. He's got a punchable face, as they say. "At FRUM, we believe those who possess the ability to use magic must be responsible with it."

"And by responsible, you mean you wish they would stop existing," says Ladonna.

Sidney's face reddens. "You are exaggerating. There is a time and place for magic, but it's not everywhere and whenever they damn well feel like it."

"Oh, come on." Ladonna rolls her eyes. "Some of your members make no secret of their contempt and fear of mages. You've been trying to lobby the state legislature to outlaw magic inside city limits for decades. In fact, your group is responsible for the state law prohibiting magical creatures inside any township with more than 10,000 residents."

"Those beasts are a menace," says Sidney.

"Magical creatures are no more dangerous than any other animal. Not *every* creature is unsuitable to be near humans," says Rachel. "Your group is quite obviously biased against magic. We don't ban people from having pet cats or dogs because lions and bears exist."

"Cats and dogs don't breathe fire!" snaps Sidney. "Why is she even on this panel? What does she do?"

"Some people claim to have seen a magical beast at the sites of these fires," says Michael. "She's here as an expert on magical creatures."

Rachel sits taller. "Our organization protects and cares for all magical creatures struggling to co-exist with humanity, especially in cases where industrialization has destroyed natural habitats."

"Your group helped two dangerous cockatrices escape after they turned several workers to stone!" yells Sidney.

"Well, those workers shouldn't have invaded the birds' territory." Rachel examines her fingernails. "Everyone, even magical creatures, has a right to defend themselves."

Michael clears his throat. "Yes, well, what are your thoughts about the series of fires at industrial sites? Could this be an act of magical terror? Some witnesses have described seeing a large flying beast in the area shortly before the fires broke out. Others describe unnatural lightning."

"These attacks are quite clearly an act of magical terrorism," says Sidney. "Natural lightning does not strike out of clear skies and target only refineries, chemical plants, and logging operations."

The panel on TV goes back and forth, discussing the various

'attacks.' They mostly come to the consensus it's the work of an anti-technology magical eco-terrorist. Even Rachel's cat gets in on it, mostly hissing whenever Sidney says something.

"You don't think a creature is responsible?" asks Michael.

"It seems unlikely to me." Sidney shakes his head. "No, I don't believe this is the work of a creature."

Rachel regards Sidney with a surprised eyebrow lift. Yeah, it's weird seeing someone you can't stand say something you agree with.

"There's too much intelligence at work here," says Sidney. "The attacks are occurring on facilities all connected to industrialization or logging. Stray creatures would merely attack whatever happened to be in their way."

The surprise falls out of Rachel's expression. She frowns. "Many magical creatures are as smart or smarter than humans. For example, manticores would never wear a beige tie with a beige suit."

I swear the darn cat snickers.

"I see." Michael blinks. "Ladonna?"

"Creatures," blurts Sidney, talking over whatever Ladonna tries to say, "have been around for hundreds of years without this sort of behavior. It has to be the actions of a crazed mage. It's well known mages have contempt for technology and want to drag society back into the past."

"We absolutely do not, as a group, wish to reverse progress," says Ladonna, glaring at him. "Acts of violence or eco-terrorism are not endorsed by the Academy or the magical community at large."

"Then you agree the abominations should be put down?" asks Sidney.

"Abominations?" Ladonna leans back in her chair, giving him a 'bitch please' face.

"Put down?!" Rachel glowers. "Oh, hell no."

Dayum. Wish I had some popcorn. This is getting good.

"Not you people." Sidney shakes his head. "I mean creatures with no proper place in nature should be culled."

"*You people?*" Ladonna raises her voice. "What's that supposed to mean."

"Mages, obviously," says Sidney.

"The only thing with no proper place in nature is your hair," snaps Rachel. "I don't know whether to comb it or have a funeral for it. How dare you say some animals should be arbitrarily destroyed because they don't fit your definition of normal?"

Michael covers his mouth, seemingly holding in a laugh.

Ladonna appears to assume Sidney's idea of 'creatures with no proper place in nature' also includes humans who use magic. The panel erupts in a three-way argument. Michael, the anchor, tries to butt in and pull everyone back on topic, but it's about as effective as holding up an umbrella to stop a falling boulder. Sidney finds himself saying increasingly stupid things about mages. When he suggests the enchantment responsible for keeping magical beasts (like cockatrices) out of Philadelphia be changed to annihilate them instead of merely being a wall, most of what Rachel says gets bleeped—and I think she's holding the cat physically back from attacking him.

After another two minutes of completely uncontrolled screaming back and forth, a thin red beam comes out of the cat's eyes and ignites the man's ridiculous hair.

Ladonna gestures at him, putting the fire out—and the network hastily cuts to a weather report.

My sudden eruption of laughter in the relatively quiet waiting area startles people and causes one cop to fumble his coffee. The guy sitting next to me decides to strike up a conversation while gesturing at the TV.

"You think it's an eco-terrorist, a creature, or a foreign power?"

I shrug. "No idea. Don't really do the magic thing."

"Neither do I. Scary stuff, right?"

"It can be."

He nods. "They ought to come up with a place for them, mages I mean, to go and live peacefully apart from normal people. Nothing against them, personally, I just don't think it's a good idea to have that stuff near ordinary folks."

"Uh huh." I smirk, giving him side eye. Alas, he doesn't have a drink I can dump in his lap. It's beyond tempting to let my horns out and shift my eyes to their Shaar'Nath form—glowing pools of sapphire energy—but I have somewhat more impulse control now than I did as a teenager.

While I'm sure seeing my other half would totally make this guy shit his pants, outing myself as a magical being might cost me my job with the fire department. They probably wouldn't kick me out of the city, but I'd end up living under a microscope, no longer able to get away with stuff. So, as much as I'd love to see this guy flip out, I keep my cool.

He continues rambling about how unstable and dangerous magic is despite me no longer responding to him.

I stare at the screen showing the last tag number: 264. My ticket reads 333. Ugh. The Universe has a twisted sense of humor. This is getting old. Time to cheat. All I have to do is find a manager or something, use a little charm, and get them to fast-track me. Honestly, how long does it take to print out a damn card? I've already finished all the paperwork. Do they have one little old lady in a back room grading everyone's written exam?

Dammit. I hate losing a Saturday, but really should've expected a trip to the DMV would devour the whole afternoon.

2

MELTDOWN

A most bizarre noise comes from the area by the doors to the parking lot.

It's part balloon slowly losing air, part electric buzz, part bucket of pudding being dumped on the floor. Definitely not the sort of sound anyone expects to hear in a DMV office. Some screaming also comes from my right.

I peer over at a flashing orb of greenish-pink energy. One of the cops rapidly expands into a fleshy blob, turns lime green, and takes on the form of a six-legged giant iguana with milky white eyes. Aww, shit. Basilisk. Not good. Those things are seriously bad news. The lizard promptly projects a magical beam from its eyes into the second cop, turning him to stone.

A middle-aged, somewhat frumpy, guy in a brown corduroy blazer and khaki pants stomps past the basilisk, raising an amber wand in the direction of the employees behind the counter. A blue bolt flies off the tip of the wand, striking one of the clerks, abruptly shapeshifting him into a six-foot winged azure serpent.

Oh, this should be good.

The guy with the wand walks by in the emotionless, methodical manner of the *Terminator,* zapping any DMV worker he can see who hasn't ducked for cover or run into doorways out of sight. Each beam from the wand is a different color, its victim transforming into a random, monstrous creature. One dude ends up as a bipedal alligator-like beast with blue antlers. The woman who took my paperwork and handed me the 333 ticket vanishes in a cloud of yellow-green fog and emerges as a cockatrice.

People in the waiting area run in a wild mob for the doors, screaming, panicking, and trampling each other in their haste to get out. I remain where I am, arms folded, legs crossed, thoroughly amused by the chaos. The guy next to me doesn't run either, only he doesn't appear to be amused. Might be a bit of an assumption on my part, but since the guy spent the past twenty minutes bitching about mages and how they ought to be rounded up and shipped off to their own country, he's probably too terrified to move.

Another man, one row in front of me and like ten seats to the right, also stays where he is, seeming annoyed.

"Run!" shouts a woman on the way past him.

"Are you kidding?" The annoyed man waves a scrap of paper at her. "I'm 266! They're on 264! I've been sitting here for three hours already. Not losing my place."

Creatures—formerly DMV employees—scurry around biting, zapping, or trying to maul people. Not too much of a change from normal, really. Damn. I'm kinda with Mr. 266. I've been here a little over two hours and this creature BS is going to make it take even longer. For the most part, I watch the spectacle, grinning. However, I do give two little kids a telekinetic boost away from a giant, toothy lizard and a werewolf, respectively. A few adults get pounced on, bitten, and dragged to the ground, turned to stone, or covered in sticky gunk.

Hilarious.

I'm fairly sure the basilisk's petrification isn't permanent. It's how they hunt. Turn stuff to stone, then eat the stone. If not eaten, the victim usually goes back to normal in like an hour. Basilisks are one of the 'super dangerous' creatures they teach children about in school.

The winged serpent opens his mouth to toss lightning my way, but

I telekinetically slap him upside the head, sending the bolt into the desk beside him. Bundles of paperwork go up in flames, ash fluttering around like apocalypse snow.

"Hah! Lay me off, will they!" shouts the guy holding the wand. "Where's Brian hiding? Come on out, Brian! I got something for you. I'm going to show the world what you really are inside!"

As the number of available munchies in the room lessens—due to people running outside—the creatures turn on each other. The lightning snake nails the basilisk in the butt with a zap, enraging it. The giant six-legged lizard charges at him, smashing through the long row of service stations separating the waiting area from the employee area, sending mangled cubicle wall parts and desk kitsch flying. The winged serpent easily zooms over the basilisk, and zaps it in the rear end again. Alligator thing chases the cockatrice around—for a few seconds anyway, until the big green chicken stares at him and he ends up paralyzed.

Mr. Anti-magic next to me screams.

"Hey!" The disgruntled former employee finally seems to notice the two of us *not* panicking or running for our lives. He points his wand in our general direction, more at the screaming guy than me, but we're right next to each other. "Why are you just sitting there?"

"He's too scared to move. Me? Long wait," I say. "Thanks for making it take even longer. Are you done feeling sorry for yourself yet? Can the rest of us get on with our lives?"

"Bitch." He points the wand at me.

I grab Mr. Anti-Magic and yank him in the path of an amber energy bolt heading for my face. The guy I'm holding shapeshifts into a smallish manticore—only about the size of a mountain lion with dragon-like wings and a long tail. A furry pod at the end of the tail holds a cluster of venomous quills. He swings his feline head around, giving me an almost 'do you mind' stare. Probably objects to me clutching a fistful of his fur—used to be shirt. I glance at him, shrug, and throw him at Wand Man, who's too stunned at seeing me one-arm-toss a big cat to move.

The baby Manticore hits him dead on, tackling the disgruntled former DMV worker to the floor and sinking his fangs into the dude's shoulder.

"Aaah!" screams Wand Man. "I'm bleeding!"

"Looks like a case of justifiable nom-icide to me."

A woman by the front windows wails in pain. She's flat on her back while a gremlin in a DMV polo shirt too big for it chews on her arm. Darn. Okay, Mom, fine. No, my mother isn't here or even aware of this, but the weight of her disapproving gaze is still crushing me. I telekinetically yank the wand away from the dude, tossing it into the back of the employee area, then leap over the bank of chairs and run to grab the gremlin off the woman.

Wand Man throws the manticore off to the side and scrambles around, trying to stand.

The little critter in my hands is small, only about forty pounds. Gremlin fastball! It emits this hilarious high-pitched scream as it flies across the room.

And... bounces right off the face of Wand Man, knocking him over.

Three pointer!

Snarling, the manticore pounces on the guy again. Terrified of the manticore, the gremlin shrieks and zooms off, only to end up making eye contact with the cockatrice and freezing, paralyzed.

The basilisk gives up on the lightning serpent and comes after me apparently out of sheer randomness. Following the stop-and-drop procedure they taught us in grade school about these things, I fling myself to the floor as soon as it faces me, allowing its petrifying eye-laser beams to go over me. The magical attack strikes a flying chicken-sized creature, turning it to stone in midair. In an instant, it changes from flying to being a hurled boulder, embedding itself in the wall like a giant dart. Basilisks have notoriously poor eyesight. Not realizing it missed, the huge lizard keeps running in to eat me, believing I'm stone.

I spring back to my feet. School didn't give us much detail for what to do after the stoning beam missed except for advising us to run like hell. I've got twenty seconds before its eyes have recharged and can generate another petrifying beam.

A kick to the jaw knocks it senseless and sliding, taking out half the chairs in the waiting area. Ow, hell. I hop on my left leg a few times. Feels like I kicked a statue. Shit, that hurt. I hobble over and grab the last two people being chewed on—except for the guy who did this—and lug them to the door. Plenty of survivors outside are already on the phone with the police. Good, since I'm not sure it's possible for me to actually bring myself to call them. I've mellowed somewhat as a so-called adult, but some things are still going too far.

Society will have to settle for me standing in the doorway playing goalie. DMV employees are dangerous enough in their own environment.

I can't let them loose on the city.

Oh, and containing the magical beasts is a good idea, too.

3

HERE WE GO AGAIN

C ould have been worse.

At least the pissed-off former employee didn't show up with a rifle. Luckily, only one person died. Some poor bastard had the misfortune of ending up polymorphed into a one-foot-tall anthropomorphic hamster type critter in a room with at least three large cat creatures.

Yeah. Didn't end well for him.

He turned human again upon death, which confused the big cats trying to eat him, except for the manticore, who laughed. Manticores are smarter than the average human, deviously tricky, greedy, and power hungry. Rumor has it, they're actually running the governments of some small countries predominantly covered in jungle—from the shadows of course.

Eventually, mage cops showed up and got things under control, dispelling the polymorph effects. Mr. 266 unfortunately did not get called and, like the rest of us, needs to go back another time. He walked away with only a manticore tail quill stuck in his butt. Okay, 'walked away' isn't entirely accurate. They wheeled him out on a stretcher. The guy will be paralyzed for a few days.

Fortunately for me, the police believed my story about being a mere telekinetic. Helps they kinda know me from the fire department and the time I helped Detective Zheng using my psychic talents. Only the temporarily polymorphed creatures witnessed me throwing them around like stuffed animals. As far as the police know, I did everything with mental powers. Psychics are much rarer than magic users. No real cat out of the bag there, since the FD brass already knows I'm psychic. They think I'm clairvoyant, and maybe I am to a degree. After all, the crystal used as an arson device *did* give me a vision the instant my skin touched it.

The worst part of today is my prediction coming true. The entire afternoon went to hell.

I didn't get home until after dark.

So, here I am sitting on my sofa after showering creature drool, blood, ichor, and plaster dust out of my hair. A long T-shirt happened to be in arms reach on my way out of the bathroom, so I put it on. Still feels like I'm sitting in a cloud of steam. Showering in 100% hot water is wonderfully relaxing. Bit unsettling to other people. Not quite as unsettling as strolling casually into open flames, but I think the manager of my building would object to a roaring inferno in the apartment.

Hmm. Blank TV in front of me. PlayStation ready and waiting. Alternatively, not a whole lot of fabric between my hand and parts below. The great conundrum of what to do on a day off work when Jason's busy. I could watch *Dead Like Me* again—no I'm never going to get bored with it. The series, I mean. My DVD set also has the direct-to-video movie they made a few years after the show got cancelled, but, meh... Nice to see the characters again but it would've been better if it had an actual story. Hmm. Could flip channels to see if anything's on. I could play video games, or I could play with myself.

Decisions... decisions.

Suppose I could go out for a random fly. Weird how little time it took me to go from being afraid of heights to enjoying flight. To be fair, most people—myself included—aren't afraid of heights as much as they're afraid of falling. Having wings makes it far less likely I'm going to fall. I used to *loathe* going up on the ladder truck during training. Now, I'm the idiot who doesn't hold the hand rails. But nah. Jason wants to go on a hang-gliding date tomorrow.

Hmm. Flying would involve going outside—at least if I want my apartment to continue having walls and not give myself a concussion. Going outside is going to require pants. The long tee covers my naughty bits, but only by two or three inches. I don't really feel like moving; the couch is comfortable. Don't have the energy to go get changed, either. Pants are for losers. Screw it. I'm in for the night.

I lean back, put my feet up on the coffee table, and summon the remote to my hand using telekinesis. After flicking the TV on, I levitate the first season-one DVD for *Dead Like Me* out of its box and float it over to the PlayStation.

Before I can switch the TV mode, the screen fills with an image of fire—which catches my attention.

The news is showing another report of a suspicious blaze, this one at a paper products company in Albany. The on-site reporter mentions witnesses spotting giant birds in the area, which supposedly spat lightning into the building to start the inferno. Say what? Giant birds? Lightning starting the fire makes me think of the natural gas blaze not long ago. I'd suspected a mage capable of throwing lightning bolts started it, but birds? I'm no expert on magical creatures, but mixing the idea of lightning and enormous flying creatures goes to one of two places for me: dragons or thunderbirds. Considering we're not in the southwest part of the country, it'd be pretty freakin' weird for a thunderbird to be around here. Either someone misidentified a dragon, or the huge bird is unrelated. Also, even I'm tempted to agree with that clueless FRUM idiot on the news. A magical creature wouldn't have the planning power to specifically target chemical plants, petroleum-based facilities, or lumber mills—basically, all stuff someone might consider to be 'destroying' the environment. Exactly the kind of places an eco-terrorist would attack.

On second thought, dragons definitely would be smart enough— but why would they blow up only industrial sites? If dragons seriously got pissed at humans, they'd burn entire cities. Well, maybe small towns. Concrete megalopolises like Philadelphia are a bit hardier than medieval peasant villages. Dragon fire is hot, but they're not going to burn down a high-rise too easily.

Thunderbirds have all sorts of folkloric connections to Native Americans. I could kinda see one of them getting angry at humans for poisoning the earth or some Greenpeace level thing, but I also don't know if those birds are legit 'smart.' Maybe they can simply smell polluters or something.

Bleh. Not my job.

Gotta be an eco-terrorist mage of some kind who is striking all over the country in multiple states. This isn't even police now. Totally an FBI case. Sucks to be them, right?

Glad he isn't my problem. I put fires out. It takes far too much energy to chase criminals.

I switch the TV to HDMI-1 and hit 'play.'

Honestly, I'm not so much anti-fire as I'm anti-people-being-burned. And no, it doesn't make sense how a dude being creamed by a bus makes me laugh but I'll go to any length to save total strangers from a fire.

Hmm. If I dragged a guy out of a burning building, but *then* he gets hit by a bus, would it be funny or feel like a cosmic f-you from the universe?

Ashley's scream of terror comes from next door.

Speaking of cosmic middle fingers from the universe.

No, not the kid. Her life situation. Reminds me of my childhood somewhat. We both kinda got the flying double bird from Fate. Both of us are daughters to poor single moms barely able to afford to feed and clothe us. It's kinda worse for Tracy—Ashley's mother—since everything is more expensive now. Scary part is I'm only twenty-three. My childhood wasn't *that* long ago. Also, gotta say, Fate gave it to Ashley worse than me. My mother is a saint. The only thing in the world to truly make me feel guilt is my mother, and she never tried to do it on purpose.

Somewhere around the time I hit twenty or so, it finally occurred to me how much my mother busted her ass and sacrificed for me—and most of my life until then, I'd been an oblivious, selfish little brat.

Though, I never really fought with her or turned mean. Even as a seventeen-year-old, I sounded embarrassingly like a small child whining whenever we argued. Something about Mom could suck the flames out of my sails in an instant. We got along great even if I did push the boundaries. Mostly, I went on about my day focused entirely on amusing myself or having fun while my Mom worked two—sometimes three—jobs and barely slept.

So yeah, little bit of guilt.

But really, what kid truly comprehends parental sacrifice? Okay, not many first-graders steal their Mom's car to go make an ice cream run, but still. Children are children.

Speaking of kids, my neighbor's eight-year-old is screaming like Freddy Kreuger's conducting a home invasion. Maybe it's sick of me, but I'm relieved to hear her shrieking in terror. The last time I heard her scream through the wall, Tracy's then-boyfriend was trying to molest her. Good thing the kid's smart. She never trusted him so she hesitated getting close to him. He hadn't managed to do much more than rip her dress before I kicked in the door.

You might think such an attack would trigger screams of terror as well. In a sense, it does, but terror comes in different flavors. People, especially children, scream slightly differently depending on if the source of their alarm is a mortal person or something worse. When Frank attacked her, she clearly screamed in 'fear.' This sounds like 'terror.'

This is straight up 'a monster's trying to eat me' type screaming—so I'm sure Tracy doesn't have a new creepy boyfriend.

Still, the kid's in danger.

Tracy isn't shouting at all... so, guess it's my turn to intervene.

I roll off the couch to my feet and jog out into the hall. Fortunately, I don't have too far to go. They live in the next apartment. I grab the knob and turn, but the door's locked.

"Ash, you okay?" I yell.

"Help! It's trying to eat me!" shouts the girl.

Called it.

"Should I kick the door in or do I have a minute?"

The child grunts as if trying to lift something too heavy for her. "Umm. Mom will be mad if you break the door again."

Okay, whatever is trying to eat her isn't *too* dangerous.

"Can you unlock it?" I yell.

She grunts again. "No. I'm tied to the chair."

"Say what?"

"Noodles!" shouts Ashley.

Oh, good grief.

I run back into my apartment and grab the spare key Tracy gave me for emergencies. Ashley's stopped screaming, but the grunts and growls of a kid struggling continue. I hurry back to their apartment and let myself in, racing across the living room to the kitchen, the source of the noise.

Ashley's nearly mummified by the noodles of a living chicken lo mein creature. It's wrapped her to the chair so she can barely move. Peapod-tipped noodles appear to be acting like Venus fly trap mouths, snapping at her face. She squirms, straining to break loose, but the noodles are abnormally tough. The monster has left a few scratches on her cheek, but I've seen kittens do more damage. A peapod mouth goes for her nose; she ducks her head out of the way, then bites the noodle off.

"You're not supposed to play with your food," I say.

"It's trying to eat me!" she yells. "Help!"

I walk over, shaking my head. "Ashley... you know better than to put Chinese leftovers in the rune oven."

She looks down at her lap. "Sorry."

I extend my claws, gingerly slicing the pasta away from her so she can escape the chair. As soon as I've cut enough of it away, she wriggles clear of several lingering strands trying to hold onto her arm and scoots around behind me. Her sky blue top is a mess of stains, a few wriggling bits of stray noodle cling to her black tights.

The lo mein monster gathers into a bundle and starts whipping at me. Oh, like it's going to hurt. The saying hits as weak as a wet noodle is true.

"Seriously?"

It growls.

Ashley grabs a pair of chopsticks, holding them up like a cross.

Despite me slashing at the flailing mass of carbs, no matter how tiny the noodle fragments become, the entity continues trying to attack us. Dad taught me how to summon a stream of fire, but the stuff is much hotter than normal Earth fire. Can't use it in here or there won't be a floor left. So... I need to relocate the blob. I telekinetically levitate the noodly bits into a sphere, walk it across the apartment to the patio door, and outside. While hovering the undulating mass in midair over the alley, I project a stream of dark crimson flame at it, reducing the lo mein beast into a charred orb of ash in two seconds. A green specter rises from the smoldering ruin. It stares at me for a moment before careening off down the alley, shrieking and setting off a few car alarms. A handful of windows explode as well.

Ashley leans out the door behind me, watching it go. "Oops. Mom did tell me not to put Chinese in the rune oven, but I thought it's because it doesn't cook evenly. I didn't know it summoned elder horrors."

"Ehh... I'd call it more of a tormented spirit, but yeah... Chinese food and rune ovens don't mix."

"Why?" She peers up at me.

"Do you think food as yummy as Chinese is made without using magic?"

"Oh." She gives a slow nod, realization dawning at last.

"Exactly. The ancient traditions don't play well with cheap modern magic." I step inside and shut the sliding glass door. Damn. The whole place smells like lo mein now... and I'm hungry. "Where's Tracy?"

"Out," says Ashley, trudging to the kitchen.

I follow. "She left you alone?"

"Yeah." Ashley opens the fridge—which contains one can of diet soda, a bottle of milk, and a pack of American cheese slices. She grabs the cheese.

"And she left you alone?"

"Yeah." The kid grabs a bag of bread from the counter. "Mom said she'd be right back."

"How long ago did she leave?" I walk up behind her.

Ashley turns to face me. "Like an hour."

"Damn." I poke the loaf of bread in her hand. "Cheese sandwich gonna do it for ya, or would you rather have fresh Chinese?"

"Fresh Chinese, definitely. I want revenge." She narrows her eyes in playful anger.

4

KINDA LAZY

We head back to my apartment.

Wearing a top covered in oil, sauce, and bits of scallion doesn't bother Ashley. Again, reminds me of my childhood. An outfit lasted all day—sometimes two or three—no matter what grime happened. After our trailer burned to the ground, I'd go a whole week in the same clothes sometimes (except for sleeping) since I didn't have too many left. Yeah, it got me teased and picked on, but I was never an easy target for bullies. Break a nose or two and mean kids leave you alone. Even better whenever I got suspended. Bully problem fixed plus vacation. Win-win.

I let Ashley take over the PlayStation. *Dead Like Me* is a bit over the head of an eight-year-old. I'll start her on it in a couple years. Real damn shame it only went two seasons. Maybe I'm wrong about the whole Satan and God thing being myths made by humans. There could actually be an overarching evil intelligence running all things bad in the world. How else does anyone explain networks always cancelling the great shows too early?

Anyway, she sits on the floor in front of the TV, occupying herself with a kid-friendly game while I order Chinese. Sometimes, poor impulse control isn't a bad thing. I hadn't eaten dinner yet and a hungry person simply cannot smell Chinese food without ordering some. Ashley's both guilty and thankful. Not having money sucks. It's embarrassing. On some level, she's ashamed of having to rely on charity to eat, but also not about to refuse it. Tracy's going in a slightly different direction than my mother. She tries to get Ash new-looking clothes rather than focus most of the money on food. Probably concerned with bullying. No one at her school knows Ashley is 'poor.' She looks ordinary. Tracy's also a little body-image obsessed, so *she* doesn't eat enough either.

Speaking of Tracy.

I call her next—and go straight to voicemail. The instantaneous transfer means she didn't see the caller ID and decide to ignore me. Her phone is either off or dead.

I sigh.

Ashley twists around, peering past the edge of the sofa at me. "Mom's in trouble, isn't she?"

"Probably. One sec."

I head to my room while calling the Chinese place back, changing the order from delivery to pick-up, and add a second quart of lo mein. Hopefully, Tracy will be with us by the time we're eating. If not, I doubt Ashley's going to want food tonight. After pulling on a pair of jeans, I grab a phial of Tracy's blood from my drawer. What? People aren't supposed to keep blood samples from their friends on hand? It's not much, only like ten drops… but it's enough to find her. Again, thanks, Dad.

Blood in hand, I return to the living room. "C'mon. Let's go find your mother."

Ashley pauses the video game and stares at me in shock. "You're taking me with you?"

"Yeah. You're too little to leave home alone."

"Wow, burn," mutters Ashley.

I glance at her. "Burn?"

"You're like the queen of rebelling and *you* think it's bad to leave me home alone. Kinda burned my mom pretty hard." She stands and walks over.

"Didn't mean it that way. I'm sure your mother intended to come right back. You're eight, not three. I might leave you on your own for a five-minute run to Kwan's. But, even with the mesmerizing power of a PlayStation to keep you out of trouble, you're still too small to be home alone. They made an entire movie franchise about why it's a bad idea."

She laughs, looking down at her feet. "Should I put shoes on?"

"Yeah. We're probably going to end up somewhere dirty."

"Umm." She squints at me. "Is it worse to bring me someplace dangerous and dirty or leave me here alone?"

I pat her on the head. "It's less me worrying about what you're going to do if left unsupervised and more worrying you'd have no one around if something weird or bad happened."

"Okay. Be right back."

She still has the protection amulet Natalie made for her, which will encase her in a magical box if someone tries to hurt her or she ends up in a dangerous situation. I'm less worried about bringing her to a bad part of town because of the force field. Rather keep her in sight.

While she grabs the key and runs next door for shoes, I trade my long tee for a racer-back halter and step into my older pair of shit kickers. Got 'em at seventeen, and they've done a fair share of trespassing. Nothing too bad, mostly exploring abandoned malls or houses. They've only walked on three faces though. Participated in a gang fight once. No, I've never been in a gang. Can't say you hate people telling you what to do and then join a gang. Being in a gang only changes who's telling you what to do.

So yeah, I wound up in a gang fight for a couple reasons, the main one being I'd never done it before and had curiosity issues. Second reason: the brawl just kinda started up around me. For a third reason, by then, I kinda had some suspicions of being weird. Used to have this little voice in my head whispering at me all the time whenever things got too quiet. Kinda freaked me out, so I did my damnedest never to be in a calm, quiet situation. The voice belonged to my subconscious and had basically been trying to tell me I wasn't fully human. As soon as I realized what I was, it stopped bugging me. Anyway, in fifth grade

—which happened a few years before I turned seventeen, hence before the gang fight—I kicked this kid Vince Milligan in the balls so hard his pelvis broke.

I'm no genius, but even I understood several things about the situation made no sense. One, a small eleven-year-old girl should not be strong enough to break a large boy's pelvis in one untrained, spontaneous kick. Two, a kick hard enough to break his bones should have smashed all the bones in my foot—and didn't. I walked away without so much as a bruise. Can't say the same for poor Vince. Never saw him again after our 'fight.' Word is, his parents transferred him to a different school once he could walk again. Lucky for me, most of the kids in the schoolyard and several teachers saw him punch me in the nose first and knock me on my back.

Everyone thought I'd had one of those super adrenaline moments like where a mother lifts a car wreck off their child. No one really questioned how I'd been able to do so much damage to a boy significantly bigger than me—I was kind of a short, scrawny kid for my age and Vince was huge. Not fat, more like he had the body of a fourteen-year-old a few years early. Looking back on it, I wonder if my father had something to do with making everyone ignore the oddity of little ol' me ruining a boy twice her size in one hit.

Whatever. Either way, I knew *something* about me had to be different.

The gang fight didn't last long, nor was it particularly fun. Honestly, the sudden eruption of creatures at the DMV reminded me a bit of it. Mostly, I stood there watching and only got involved if someone came after me. Didn't kill anyone. One face stomp apiece knocked the idiots out of the fight.

Tracy used to be involved with a few local gangs prior to ending up pregnant with Ashley. As far as I know, she never officially joined any of them, merely dated or hung out with some guys who belonged. Me thinking about gangs has to be some kind of psychic read. I've worn these boots tons of times before tonight and never once reminisced about the gang fight.

Ashley runs in, having put on her sneakers.

I lead her down the hall to the stairs, then up to the roof. It's nice and quiet up here, solitary even. Occasionally, it makes for a good place to sit and veg out while staring at the sky. The walls here are thin, so the roof is the only true quiet available. A couple of stray beer bottles litter the black stuff covering the roof. Guess I'm not the only one who likes to 'meditate' up here. As we approach the edge, I extend my wings and scoop her into my arms. She clings, but is unusually calm. Her lack of visible worry is probably only strange to me since I used to be scared of heights. Seeing a kid her age unfazed by me carrying her a couple hundred feet in the air is odd.

Once we go up high enough to escape casual notice from people on the ground, I pull the phial of Tracy's blood out of my pocket and concentrate on it. Elestari tend to have magic and Shaar'Nath are more psychic. However, we do have a few magical tricks. Mostly, they involve fire, even if it's in a cosmetic sense.

Less than a minute after I start focusing on the blood with the intent to find the person it came from, the liquid begins to glow bright red-orange. A sense of direction gnaws at the back of my mind, pointing the way to Tracy. It doesn't give me any indication of distance, only which way to go. Obviously, I can't fly at full speed while carrying Ashley. Children are much happier when they have skin on their faces.

Ashley keeps her eyes closed due to the wind whipping her hair around. We're not on a sightseeing cruise after all. Our dinner's going to be ready in like fifteen minutes. Also, Tracy's probably not in a good situation. Hopefully, she's merely stranded somewhere, but a bus accident wouldn't make her cell phone stop working.

In less than two minutes, the feeling pulling me toward Tracy abruptly swings downward and begins pointing to the rear. I slow, rolling into a dive while circling back and dropping to an altitude of about 150 feet. My magic is pointing out a spot only like four miles from our apartment building, in Fairhill. And bingo… gang territory. Been awhile, but my memory says this is Front Street Bastards territory. As gangs go, they're not too large, but they are involved in drug trafficking, prostitution, and probably burglary. Not the sort of thugs who go out looking for cops to shoot as an initiation rite, but they're most likely armed.

Damn. Maybe I should have left Ashley home alone.

Doubt they'd hurt her, but stray bullets are a thing.

Hopefully, the protection necklace works, but better not to risk it. Can't let this escalate.

I circle for a few seconds to get a feel for Tracy's location, a small mechanic's garage on the corner. Doesn't look abandoned, so maybe the gang's only borrowing the building. Seems odd for ordinary people to bring their cars to a street gang for work. Some gang-bangers like to trick out their rides. Maybe they only work on gang members' cars here. Meh. Don't care.

We land in the gap between the garage and the next building, a four-story apartment even worse-looking than mine. A lovely aroma of beer, piss, and gasoline competes with the scent of someone cooking hot dogs. Good bet half the people inside the building are high. No one's screaming like they're being fed feet-first into a wood chipper or trying to kill us, a sign they aren't using e-meth around here. Nasty stuff. Mixing magic and drugs, bad idea.

Tracy screams, "I'm sorry!" from inside the garage.

"Mom," whispers Ashley.

I set her on her feet. "Okay. Gonna try to keep this quick and tame."

"If you have to rip someone's head off to help Mom, I give you permission," says Ashley.

Heh. She still thinks she summoned me. "Thanks. I'll keep it in mind, but you still shouldn't watch such violence."

She shrugs.

A meaty *slap* comes from the garage, followed by Tracy screaming in pain.

"You will hit that guy back." She narrows her eyes.

"Yeah, sure. C'mon. If it gets ugly in there, you run outside, okay?"

"Sure."

I walk across the driveway, passing two service bay garage doors, and let myself in the office door. One dude, who can't be older than twenty, sits at a desk in a room wallpapered with Sports Illustrated swimsuit pictures, watching TV on a tablet. He jumps at me entering, starts to give me a 'who the f are you' look, which shifts to an 'oh, nice tits' expression. The girls aren't out, but the racer back top doesn't hide much in the way of shape. Still, my wings won't rip it off as it bares most of my back, so… compromise. He continues to gawk at me as I walk straight on past him like I live here. Upon noticing Ashley, he furrows his brow like 'what are you, crazy?'

Continuous shouting leads me to a door connecting the office to the service bay. Six guys stand in a horseshoe around Tracy, who's backed up against a giant metal cabinet. Her clothes are a little disheveled, as is her hair, but no blood has been spilled yet. Seems as if they'd only been roughing her up a little. One guy holds a fistful of her shirt, pinning her shoulders to the cabinet. He looks like the oldest, creeping up on the big three-zero.

"I'm sorry," whispers Tracy. "I'll get you the rest of the money back as soon as I get paid again."

"Mommy!" yells Ashley.

Tracy and all six gang punks stare at us. The guy from the desk steps into the door behind me, thinking he can block it off. It's pretty obvious I don't have a weapon on me—tight jeans and a halter top— but the dude's still holding a 9mm. Not pointing it at us, but he's trying to be intimidating.

Three of the guys in front of me have pistols stuffed in their belts. A little telekinesis to the trigger will make one of them an instant eunuch, but I resist the temptation for now. Any moron who stuffs a gun in the front of their pants is going to end up neutering themselves soon enough, anyway.

"What's going on?" I ask.

Tracy stares at me. "Why did you bring *her* here?"

"Sorry. Should I have left an eight-year-old home alone?"

She cringes. "Didn't mean to be gone this long. I just needed to talk to Manuel about the money I owe him." She indicates a brown-skinned Hispanic guy, not the man who's been slapping her around.

"This is talking? Please tell me you didn't take drugs from them."

"No. Not drugs." She shies back from the guy holding her shirt. "Just borrowed some money from Manuel to make it to the end of last week. We ran out of food. They cut my hours at work, so I didn't get as much as I thought I would."

"Who is this bitch?" A skinny punk in the group pulls a Glock out of his belt and points it—generally—toward me.

Never did understand why these fools hold guns sideways, high up, and angled down. Not only does it look stupid, it's inaccurate.

Ignoring him, I step closer. "How much?"

"I'm talkin' to you, bitch," says Glock Boy.

I smirk at him. "No you're not. You asked 'who is this bitch?' If you were talking to me, you would've asked 'who are you, bitch?' or maybe 'who do you think you are, bitch?' 'Who is this bitch' is clearly directed at Tracy, since none of you know me."

A few of the other guys chuckle. Glock Boy makes a series of constipated faces and tries to shove his gun into my nose.

"Put that thing away or it's going up your ass." I narrow my eyes.

"Chill out, Jojo," says the guy pinning Tracy to the cabinet. "Don't waste a fine piece of ass."

Jojo—a.k.a. Glock Boy—shifts his stare to him, still sniffing and twitching. He, and most of the crew here, probably took a threat coming from a girl my size as some crazy *chica* talking tough with no true intention of doing anything. They're right in one way. I wouldn't have bothered stuffing the Glock in a body cavity. It's much cooler to *say* than do. Actual firearm proctology is really messy, takes too long, and is wholly unsatisfying. Kinda like trying to get a cake to come out like it looks on Pinterest.

"How much?" I ask.

"Borrowed a hundred," says Tracy. "Gave him eighty when I got paid."

I blink in disbelief at the guy holding her shirt. "You losers are seriously roughing her up over twenty bucks?"

"She still owes us eighty," says Manuel. "We suggested"—he eyes Ashley—"umm, alternate payment options, but she don't wanna cooperate."

Jojo waves his Glock in my face again. "You got a mouth on you b—"

I grab his wrist in one hand, pushing the gun high, grip his shoulder in the other, then introduce my knee to his groin. The *crack* of his pelvis breaking is loud enough for everyone to notice. Jojo emits a brief, pitiful squeak, and passes out. I let him crumple into a heap, taking the Glock from his hand as he goes down and chucking it to the back of the room.

"Okay. Here's what's going to happen. Either you guys are going to let Tracy leave and forget she exists... or I'm going to kill all of you."

"Brook, you don't have to do this..." Tracy eyes the man holding her shirt. "I'll get them the eighty by Friday. Just didn't wanna bl— umm, yeah."

Manuel and the others chuckle. The dude behind me in the door points his 9mm at my head.

"Luis, take the little girl outside. We're about to have some fun with Tracy's friend," says the white guy holding her, in Spanish.

"Oh. Sorry. Maybe you boys didn't understand me." I reveal my horns, shift my eyes to glowing pools of blue energy, and sprout claws. "Let me try Spanish"—I swap languages. Yelling in Spanish conveys anger in a way English can't match. "You morons are gonna let her leave, forget she exists, and eat a $20 idiot tax... or you can all spend the last two minutes of your lives wondering why you don't have any skin left."

Five of the seven thugs begin praying rapidly in Spanish.

In the ensuing moment of confusion, I mentally yank door guy's gun away from him and send it flying into a shelf of oil filters on the right side of the garage. Catching and crushing it would've been cooler, but fingerprints. Shit, I touched the Glock. Oh, well. Not like these fools are gonna call the police.

The men exchange glances, little trace of bravado left in their eyes.

I shift my appearance back to fully human. "Do we have an understanding?"

"You have to slap the guy who hit Mommy," says Ashley.

Three of the guys look at the dude who'd been holding her shirt, but none overtly point him out.

I step over Jojo and approach the guy. "Sorry. Condition of the summoning ritual. Gotta listen to her. I don't know my own strength sometimes, so if I break your jaw or neck, it's entirely an accident."

"Wait!" He leans back, raising his hands.

For a second, I consider letting him bribe his way out of it, but this asshole didn't hesitate to hit Tracy when she refused to get on her knees for them. Totally lied about not knowing my strength. I slap him hard enough to knock him stumbling and leave a red mark, but not break any bones.

He cringes, apparently somewhat confused at still having a jaw.

"Just had to satisfy the command. Doesn't require me to tear your head off. Seeing as how I've taken over this mortal once, it's a pretty simple matter to grab her again if I need to. You guys are going to forget Tracy exists, and I'll forget you exist."

"It's not their fault," says Tracy.

"Asking you to pay back $160 on borrowing $100? Even banks don't screw people that bad." I take Tracy's hand, pull her away from the storage cabinet, and lead her past the men. "Oh, and you guys might want to get Jojo to a hospital."

Door guy backs out of our way as I approach. Tracy and Ashley follow me outside. We walk about a block to an ideal secluded lot. Great place for sprouting wings unnoticed.

"What did you mean about taking over a mortal?" Ashley scrunches up her nose.

Heh. "I kinda got a little pissed and showed my horns. Tried to play it off like I'm some sort of magical creature who took over a random body so if they see me again somewhere, they won't freak out."

"Oh." The kid grins. "Nice."

"Gee. Again you bail my butt out of a bad situation." Tracy fidgets.

"I could've loaned you money for food. Or you could've sent Ash over to eat if you want. Why'd you go to those losers?"

She glances off to the side, unable to look me in the eye. "You keep doing stuff for us. Got me a scholarship, always watching Ash. Feels like I'm taking advantage. Used to sorta know those guys. Dated Manuel before I had Ash. Didn't want to do anything illegal, just a small loan between friends."

"You have a weird idea of friends."

Tracy exhales. "Yeah. And, wow. I'm surprised you didn't rip them apart."

"Ehh. Would've been faster, but... not in front of Ash."

"Thanks."

I smile. "And I'm kinda lazy. C'mon. I got Chinese on order. Hope it isn't cold by now."

5

A LITTLE EXTREME

Jason arrives at my place a little after seven on Sunday morning.

Yeah, sure we're breaking international law by being out of bed this early on a weekend, but we've got like a four-hour ride ahead of us. Go figure, a fireman's a bit of an adrenaline junkie. He's been hang gliding for a few years already, though he doesn't own a glider. The place he goes to, Hyner View State Park, has rentals. Since I've never gone gliding before—with a mechanical set of wings—we're planning on going tandem: one glider, both of us. The rental place won't let anyone who doesn't have instructor certification rent a glider solo.

Doesn't bother me. I prefer being next to him on the same glider, anyway. Hard to talk in separate ones. Well, radios maybe, but still. Hmm. I wonder... how much of my ability to fly is physically coming from my wings as opposed to 'magic.' Honestly, there's no way dragon-style wings should be able to propel me at 350 MPH. It's even crazier to think Elestari and their feathery wings can go faster than me. Yeah, something more than pure physics is at work here.

Question is, do I have to extend my wings to fly at all or can I pull a Supergirl?

If so, having me on a hang glider is basically like adding an engine.

I might surprise Jason.

We swing by a little place, grab some egg sandwiches and coffee, then begin the ride northwest.

My navigation app predicts the ride will eat three hours and forty-one minutes. It takes me a bit of effort to not suggest flying out there. However, we're taking the trip as a date, so there's no need to rush. Also, I can't exactly cruise at full speed while carrying a grown man. Even if he could tolerate the wind force, the extra weight slows me. Plus, I'd have to fully shift into my armored form in order to have the power to carry him without being in a continuous descent. Also, by the time we got there, my arms would be spent.

So, while *I* could get there in less than an hour by air, doing so would defeat the point of this being relaxing and fun.

Normally, Jason should have been working today since it's his weekend rotation, but he swapped with Herlihy. He had the kind of Saturday shift I dream about on rotation: nothing happened. Spent the whole day at the stationhouse doing maintenance or watching television. Love those days, and not only because I'm lazy. No fire alarms means no one's hurt.

Says the girl who smashed a guy's pelvis last night.

Hey, waving a gun in my face is not the best way to get me to care about your life.

I tell Jason about it. He's in on my secret. In fact, he found out about my true nature the same time as me. If not for my being half 'demon,' he'd be dead. A normal human could not have moved the debris off him or survived jumping out a window so high up on a burning hotel. Immunity to fire, wings, and body armor come in damn handy.

At first, I worried his interest in me came from a weird obligatory sense of gratitude for saving his life. But it eventually hit me he hadn't run away screaming after seeing the real me. No, I'm not like hideous or anything when I 'fully shift.' My face doesn't change much at all except for the glowing eyes and my skin hardening to armor. Sure, the armor is basically a shell, but it looks like I'm wearing a suit somewhere between fantasy plate armor and something out of a science fiction story. I'd compare it to Storm Trooper armor in *Star Wars*, but mine actually stops damage sometimes. It also fits better and has something of an 'organic' aesthetic.

Strangest feeling to armor up, too. I simultaneously have a sense of touch, but the plates are tough. Someone brushing their hand over it feels like they're caressing my skin, but a knife slash would only hurt if it penetrated.

Anyone watching a little five-foot-nothing Latina who'd intimidate nobody grow into a seven-foot horned critter with dragon-like wings and a bladed tail would probably soil themselves and pass the hell out. That 'look' is mostly why humans mistook us for evil demons. Elestari didn't help matters by encouraging it. It stroked their ego to have humans think of them as holy protectors or agents of some powerful deity, even though the average Elestari wouldn't bother to inconvenience themselves six seconds for a human's benefit.

So, yeah. Jason Dunn saw me at my most inhuman and didn't run for the hills. I decided to give him a chance, knowing his interest in me was more than curiosity, adrenaline-seeking, or some sort of Viking-esque 'you saved my life so it's yours now' deal. My telepathic abilities are still pretty limited, so straight-up mind reading is a pain in the ass if it works at all. However, as long as I can remember, I've had the ability to know a person's heart by looking at them.

No big deal there. It's like wings, horns, and a tail. Every Shaar'-Nath gets it.

Ever wonder why there are so many stories about demons tempting humans with their heart's greatest desires? Yeah. We know. Sometimes, the read is kinda vague. Most of the time, as soon as I look at someone, I get a good feel for what kind of person they are and what drives them. Like the creep in the car who tried to lure me when I was little. The instant I made eye contact with him, I totally knew he lusted after me and intended to kill me afterward to keep me quiet. In school, I always knew the teachers who adored their jobs and the ones who hated kids but liked paychecks. Same ability let me gravitate toward the nicer cops who felt sorry for me.

With Jason, I sensed love. He didn't have any ulterior motives when he approached. Just wanted to be with me.

So here we are, in his giant red pickup truck, cruising down the road early on a Sunday morning. Jason doesn't drive as fast as I would. Honestly, he's fairly normal behind the wheel, five to ten over the speed limit depending on conditions.

We eventually leave Interstate 476 behind, heading past a small rest area toward Interstate 80. As we approach the end of the on-ramp, a jackass in a blue Honda shoots past us on the right shoulder and damn near sideswipes us while cutting in front. Jason swerves left, putting two wheels on grass for a second or two. We get bounced around and he hits the brakes a little hard. Fortunately, our coffees are both empty by now. The only damage is some of his tools banging in the steel toolbox out in the bed.

I probably would have ignored the idiot, but he has the nerve to flip us off—so he gets a telekinetic whammy. My shove spins his car around in a fishtail and almost sends him careening into the center ditch. He recovers, narrowly missing a Chevy van, forcing it to brake hard and nearly go into the guardrail. Whoops. Sorry dude in the van. Didn't see you.

Honda Moron stomps on the gas, racing off down I-80.

"Unbelievable," mutters Jason. "Guy jumps into the shoulder, goes around two other cars and us, then has the nerve to give *me* the finger."

"How dare you do forty on a ramp." I roll my eyes.

"Seriously. Crazy idiot's going to get himself killed."

"Hope he doesn't take anyone else with him." Grumbling, I fold my arms, annoyed the Honda's too far away to push again.

In addition to a steel guardrail on the right, there's a fairly severe drop-off to trees. Jason accelerates, but he's not trying to chase the guy, merely resume traffic speed. Maybe twenty minutes later, we catch up to the idiot in the Honda because he's trapped behind a small snarl of traffic. Honda Man weaves around a few straggler cars before he ends up riding the bumper of an Escalade leading the pack in the left lane, who's keeping pace with a Corolla in the right lane. Jason tends to drive in the right lane whenever possible, unless he needs to pass an old person, so we end up behind the Corolla.

I can't see the Honda driver due to us being a little higher up and Jason blocking my view. However, feeling petty, I give a mild tele-kinetic boost to the Corolla, making it accelerate and overtake the Escalade. The woman driving it doesn't seem to notice anything unusual until I help her make a lane change out of our way in front of the Escalade. Predictably, she begins wigging out.

Jason chuckles to himself, shaking his head, but takes the opportunity of an open lane to pass the Escalade. Honda Idiot yanks his car into the right lane—but I shove the Corolla in his way amid a screech of tires. Dude starts flashing his high beams and blaring his horn at the Toyota driver who is screaming her head off. Can't blame her, really. It's scary being in a car moving around by itself.

"You're going to cause an accident," says Jason.

"I'm fine with that as long as it's only the idiot in the Honda who eats dirt."

He sighs.

The woman in the Corolla appears rattled from her car making two abrupt lane changes apparently on its own, so she slows. Dude in the Escalade apparently shares my opinion of Honda Idiot. He slows down as well, trapping the guy, who keeps going back and forth from lane to lane behind them as they fade into the distance of our rear view mirrors.

Heh.

Okay, spiteful vengeance resolved. Resume date.

We encounter a little more traffic, a few cars, a semi-truck or three, and continue driving while Jason mostly tells me about hang gliding. Apparently, they don't have flaps or anything for controls. The pilot shifts weight around to steer. We'll be dangling in harnesses and need to move together in order to make the glider turn.

He's in the middle of explaining the concept of thermal updrafts—which I've experienced before but didn't know they had a name—when Honda Man reappears. He overtakes us so fast he's gotta be doing like 120. Rather than pass us, he crawls up our back bumper, flicking high beams and honking.

"What the hell is his problem?" asks Jason, peering at the rearview. "Does he have any concept of vehicular weight? If I have to stop short, he's going to end up in a body bag with my rear differential up his nose."

"I could bounce his face off the steering wheel a few times, hon."

"Nah. Ignore him. If you knock him out, he could crash into someone else. He'll eventually get bored, take off in the left lane, and feel the big dick energy of outrunning a factory stock pickup truck."

I laugh.

Idiot sits on our bumper for eight minutes despite the left lane being wide open. A relatively slow big rig finally encourages Jason to change lanes. The Honda again aggressively swerves—not sure if he tried to get around us to keep us stuck behind the big rig—but he nearly goes into the center ditch. So, so tempting to give his car a little twist. Jason's right. This guy *is* going to hurt someone.

Once we get far enough ahead of the tractor-trailer to return to the right lane and not be rude about it, Jason does so, staring at his side mirror. Sure enough, Honda Man flies past us giving us the finger. The instant he swerves in front of us, Jason makes a rapid lane change left, anticipating the idiot intends to brake check us. Honda Man does slam on his brakes for a second until he realizes we're no longer behind him.

"Shit," mutters Jason. "This guy's off the deep end. Gonna pull over and let him think he won."

"Okay."

The Honda zooms past us on the right, swerving into the left lane ahead of us and slamming on his brakes. Again, ready for it, Jason makes an evasive maneuver into the right lane, dodging the brake check. The Honda speeds up, coming after us like a police car trying to force a pursuit suspect off the road. Jason veers into the shoulder and slows to a stop.

Rather than flip us off and keep going, Honda Idiot stops in front of us and gets out. He's an average sized white dude with a beard, little muscular, but nowhere near an ogre.

"What the hell is this guy's problem?" asks Jason.

"Jersey plates," I say.

Jason opens his door. Most girlfriends at this point would be pulling on the guy's arm trying to talk them out of violence. One: I'm not most girlfriends. Two: if violence is going to happen here, I know it won't be Jason starting it. It also won't be Honda Idiot starting it.

I also hop out of the truck.

Honda Man launches into a diatribe of cursing, accusing Jason of driving like an asshole. The semi we passed blows by us, honking. I saunter over to the Honda, using the amulet Natalie gave me to magically absorb my clothes and replace them with an illusion. Anyone looking at me would've seen my grey sweater, jeans, and boots flicker into a frilly goth girl dress. Of course, I'm naked at the moment even if I don't look it.

This idiot isn't worth putting a hole in my jeans.

Casual as can be, I extend my tail and wander around the car as if I'm checking it out for damage. Did I mention the onyx blade on the end of my tail is capable of cutting concrete and metal? Yeah. Magic is cool, right? Guess what it does to tires? Like pushing a butter knife through Cool Whip. Jason and the idiot are yelling at each other so loud neither one of them notice the bursts of air.

Not my first time slashing tires, but it's the most satisfying—also by far the fastest.

Once all four are flat, I retract my tail and activate the amulet to swap back to real clothes. The guys haven't quite gotten to the point of hitting each other yet. Mostly, Jason's talking down at the man about his aggressive driving habits, stuck on a repeating loop about being a firefighter and this idiot's a public safety hazard. Honda Man's wittiest retort involves verbal acrobatics with the F-bomb.

Screw this.

I peer back over my shoulder and telekinetically nudge the car off the road into the ditch. The little Honda would never be able to drive out of there on its own, even with intact tires. It bounces down the grass and rolls into the trees at the bottom with a *bang* loud enough to get the idiot's attention.

"Guess you forgot to put it in park," I say, then burst into laughter—harder than necessary since it really irks guys like this to look foolish.

"What the fuck?" yells the guy, running to the spot where the car went over.

I can't help myself. Another TK nudge knocks his feet into each other, sending him into a pratfall on the grass. Screaming obscenities, he slides down the embankment out of sight.

"I'm amazed at your self-control." I smile at Jason. "You didn't hit him."

"I'm not amazed at your lack of it." He chuckles.

"C'mon. Let's go."

"We can't leave..."

"It's not an accident. No contact occurred between our vehicles." I playfully shove at him. "Go. Get in. Drive. Before this jerk escalates things even more. He might have a gun or knife in the car and then I'm *going* to kill him."

Honda Idiot, still down by his car out of sight, starts shouting. Sounds like Pavarotti warming up for a performance if every word in the opera started with an F and rhymed with duck.

"Wonder if he noticed the tires yet or if he's merely reacting to being stranded in a ditch."

Jason reluctantly gets in the truck. I run around and climb into my side.

"You slashed his tires? A bit extreme, no?" He hesitates for a second, but starts driving, using the shoulder to get up to a safe speed to merge into the traffic lane.

"Nah. Extreme would've been burning the car."

He gives me side eye. "No, that would've been crazy."

"Nope. Crazy would've been killing him, then slashing the tires, then burning the car with him in it."

"I'd call that psychotic, not crazy."

"I'm going to stop here before you think I'm mental." I grin.

He raises an eyebrow. "Do I even want to know what you'd define as 'psychotic'?"

"Probably not. You'll have to settle for me simply saying I've seen some messed up horror movies. It's nothing I've done, thought about doing, or ever will do... but eek."

"Oh, like *Hellraiser* type stuff?"

"Yeah, I'd consider carving someone up to look like one of those guys pretty psychotic."

"You'd never do anything like that to a person, right?"

"Of course not."

He exhales in relief.

I examine my fingernails. "Way too much effort."

He laughs.

Good, he knows I'm kidding.

6

TERRITORIAL

We arrive at Hyner View a little after noon.

Lunch happened on the road, a little early so we wouldn't be stuffed by the time we arrived. Except for the moron in the blue Honda, our day date has been fun so far. Road trips alone can be entertaining. Just spending a few hours talking while the scenery changes is pretty cool.

A guy—Clayton—from the hang gliding place insists on helping Jason check my harness. I'll be suspended below him, both of us dangling from the frame. Both harnesses have leg shrouds, which we'll use after we're up in the air. Clayton demonstrates how to zip and unzip the leg wrap by pull ropes, and has me practice a few times in a demonstration rig inside the shop.

Easy enough.

Forty-five minutes later, we're carrying a big green wing and aluminum frame to the takeoff point. Excitement radiates from Jason enough to get me feeling vicariously excited as if flying wasn't something I did all the time. Beyond simply flying for fun, it's thrilling in a 'flying for the first time ever' way.

A few months ago, before I knew anything about Shaar'Nath, having wings, or what I am, the idea of hang gliding would have terrified me. No way in hell would I ever have let anyone talk me into doing it. I'm not really impressed with myself for getting over the fear —since I have obvious reasons for it. It's more being astonished at Jason. He's done this over and over again, trusting his life to aluminum and thin fabric.

Well, and a parachute.

Yeah, the glider has an emergency chute.

"Ready?" asks Jason.

"Is tonight going to end with us in bed?"

He glances at me.

"Yes, dork." I elbow him, then grab the triangle frame. "Let's go."

Grinning, he hefts the glider. "Wow, this one's way lighter than usual."

"Hello," I say. "You're not the only one lifting it."

He chuckles. "Duh. Okay, takeoff is pretty easy. We just race down this hill until we're off the ground. Then legs up and zip."

We hold the glider up and sprint. It's a lot less fun than it sounds while tethered together at the chest. However clumsy it feels, we jump upon reaching the top of a sharp downhill, trusting the wing to keep us airborne. We start off gliding down pretty fast toward the Susquehanna River. Considering only a thin steel cable connects us to the wing frame, I'm nervous about trying to play 'jet engine' and add power to our flight. Telekinesis won't help much as I can't lift myself, or lift an object I'm hanging from. One advantage magic has over psychic powers: magic ignores physics.

Oh heck, might as well experiment.

As gently as possible, I attempt to 'fly' forward and upward at the equivalent of a calm walk. Alas, nothing happens. Damn. Well, at least I know for sure any sort of flying requires my wings being out. We cruise over a small town—seriously small, it's only a handful of streets —and fly over the river.

"Just passed the village of Hyner," yells Jason.

"So small. Like twenty houses... where do those people work? There's nothing out here."

He laughs. "Long commutes, probably. Maybe they're retired."

Jason lets out a cheer when we catch an updraft coming off hills on the opposite side of the river and gain altitude. Since I'm hanging beneath him, I don't really have to do anything to steer. Whenever he shifts his weight, he shifts me, too. The glider's fun, if a bit slow. Again, we're not trying to go anywhere specific, merely cruise around the air to enjoy the sensation of flying.

An amazing view of green hills and rivers stretches out below us. Most of the flying I've done has been around the city, so this is a nice change of scenery. If we didn't have to be back in Philly by tomorrow morning for work, I'd totally suggest we camp somewhere out here. Maybe look for a boat rental place.

Not really sure when I turned into the outdoorswoman. Nah, I'm still a city girl, but everyone needs a brief change of scenery now and then.

Shaar'Nath aren't really into the whole tree-hugging thing. Then again, neither are Elestari.

Jason locates a thermal strong enough to carry us up to maybe 1,000 feet. It's a stationary air current, allowing us to cruise back into it whenever needed to gain altitude. The major problem with gliders is they are in a constant state of descent. Without exploiting thermals or updrafts, flight time has a hard limit. Literally hard, as in the ground. However, we manage to keep it going via looping into the thermal again and again, spending maybe ten minutes each time gazing out over the landscape before having to steer back into the thermal to regain altitude. Jason is thrilled, loving every bit of the adrenaline rush. Not being in control of flying is unnerving to me, but I refuse to allow myself to feel trapped and committed to crashing in a worst-case scenario. If the shit really hits the fan, my wings are coming out even if I have to tow the wreckage of a glider—and Jason —with me safely to the ground.

Out of nowhere, another hang glider zooms by, coming in from high and left. It nearly crashes into us while passing over. Something, maybe the pilot's foot, brushes our wing. I catch a blur of dark blue low and right before our glider lurches into a hard, evasive turn.

Jason shouts, "Hey! Watch it!"

I look around, but can't see much more than our wing above us. "Where'd he go?"

"Crazy damn idiot. I swear, if this is the same guy from the highway…"

"Hah. You said these gliders are kinda unpredictable. Maybe it got away from him and he lost control?"

The other glider whooshes over us again, way close. This time, they don't appear below us, somehow managing to stay higher. Okay, something's not right. He's moving way too fast and… sounds heavy. Also one near-miss is an accident. Two is not. Jason rolls into another turn. As we bank, I spot a patch of fast-moving dark blue coming around on us again… and it's got a face.

It's not a hang glider.

"Wyvern!" I shout.

"What?" yells Jason.

Pointing, I shout, "Wyvern!" again.

He looks, then yells, "Shit!"

I don't know much about these creatures other than they are called 'wyverns' and are distant cousins to dragons. This one's got a body about the size of an average passenger sedan and a dragon-shaped head supported by a serpentine neck eight or nine feet long. A bony cluster at the end of its tail looks like a spiked medieval mace. Might be decorative or it may use it as a bludgeon. The creature's two legs resemble a reptilian version of eagle's feet, complete with talons. I'll assume the tail brushed our glider instead of those talons. If it got us with those scythes, the flimsy membrane would be in tatters and we'd be crashing.

"Is it a full moon tonight or something?" Jason dives, avoiding another strafing pass from the wyvern. "Never saw one of those damn things so close before."

"So close? Meaning you *have* seen them before?"

He shifts our weight left, maneuvering evasively. "Yeah, but they're usually miles away."

"I'm no expert on magical wildlife, but I think if he wanted to kill us, we'd already be smashed."

Jason grunts, swinging us back the other way into another spiraling turn. We are losing altitude alarmingly fast. "What the hell's it doing if not trying to kill us?"

"No idea. I think it might be trying to scare us off. Want me to call Rachel Feuerstein and ask her about wyvern behavior?"

"Who?" yells Jason.

"Some woman they had on the news. Did you know there's a Society for the Prevention of Cruelty to Magical Animals?"

"Some magical animals eat people."

"They protect those, too."

He emits a nervous scream. "What about the society for the prevention of destruction of innocent hang gliders?"

"Oh… that's me. Unhook me."

"What?" Are you crazy?"

"Not the last time I checked, though a few teachers and a cop or two might disagree. I can fly, remember?"

He squeezes my arm. "I… feels too much like trying to hurt you."

"Do you want us *both* to crash? If it *is* doing some kind of territorial bullshit, it's eventually going to attack for real if we don't leave."

"So we leave."

"This glider doesn't go fast enough. Unclip me. I'll be right back." I pull the cord to unzip my leg sheath.

Jason still hesitates, so I sprout horns as a reminder. He finally nods. A few seconds later, I drop away from him like a bomb.

My best friend Natalie is an enchanter. She's a good enchanter. The necklace she made me automatically activates if I shift or sprout extra body parts while wearing clothes. Gaining two feet of height in two seconds, plus bulking up with armor plates is quite destructive to my wardrobe. Even the glider harness went into magical storage. Awesome. As soon as I shift, my body stops plummeting in an instant, hovering.

Okay, game on.

Going from the glider to my wings is about the same as trading a bicycle for a Kawasaki street bike. I pull up into a hard climb, zooming to intercept the wyvern before it can make another harassing dive at the glider. It rears back, the flying equivalent of slamming on brakes, as I get in its face.

"What?" I shout at it.

It roars as we pass in a no-contact joust.

I roll left, accelerating into a climb and overtaking the wyvern after a few seconds. Cruising up alongside its head makes me feel like a bizarre version of a cop trying to pull over an idiot.

"Guess you don't speak?" I shout.

It snaps at me, six-inch conical teeth crashing together so close, spittle hits me.

I swerve out of the way and veer back. "Hey!"

It tries to bite me again.

What the heck; works for sharks. I punch it in the nose.

My armor-plated knuckles leave a dent in the scales at the end of the wyvern's snout and swat its long, sinuous neck down like a limp noodle. Actual dragons have long necks, too, but not nearly as prehensile. Wyvern necks are narrow, the head—and mouth—roughly the size of a large alligator's. Lizards don't get big enough to swallow people whole until we get into full dragons, which also happen to be quite smart. This critter's intelligence feels like an animal's, according to my ability to read people. All I'm sensing from it is territorial aggression.

Unfortunately, I can't tell him to chill out.

Well, the words could leave my mouth, but he wouldn't understand.

He snaps at me again. I swerve to avoid the teeth, and notice the tail swinging at me with only a second to spare. Reflexively, I cross my arms to shield my face. The bony nugget at the tip of the wyvern's tail smacks me pretty damn hard. Even had some whip action going there, too.

The hit cracks my left forearm plate and comes close to breaking the bone inside. Hurts for a moment. Yay for Shaar'Nath genes. Or whatever they have. My body heals quite a bit faster than a normal human. Small caliber bullet wounds disappear in less than an hour. This crack will be gone before I get back to Jason.

Okay, damn thing. I *was* trying not to hurt you. Maybe the punch to the nose already crossed the line. Did leave a noticeable dent, after all. Still, he started it. I roll over to right myself and resume chasing, intending to show him what my tail blade can do. For no particular reason, the wyvern dives for the ground, gaining speed.

Either he sensed me changing my mind and wanting blood or maybe he intended the tail whack as a final f-you before he went away.

Whatever. Looks like he's had enough.

I swing around in a climbing turn, scanning the sky for the hang glider. A streak of neon green draws my attention down and left. Scarily far down. Jason's flying over the hills a bit east of the river, dropping marginally slower than a rock. Fluttering fabric tells me why he's having so much trouble holding altitude—the wyvern *did* slash the glider. Such minor damage proves it had only been trying to chase us off. What would've been a mild 'go away' swat to another wyvern shredded a hole in the wing. If it had been seriously pissed, a tangle of aluminum would've fallen out of the air.

Fortunately, Jason's still got enough control to avoid a hard encounter with trees. He's already too low for the parachute, so he steers toward the Susquehanna. It's as easy for me to catch up to him as a motorcyclist chasing a kid on a bicycle. We're about twenty feet above the water when I settle in above the glider and grasp the front wing spar as gently as possible near the point. Adding a little speed, I pull up, towing him into the air.

"Brook?" shouts Jason. "Is that you?"

Heh. He can't see me through the fabric. My wingspan while fully shifted is about the same as the glider's.

"Who else would I be? A baby wyvern?"

He emits a nervous laugh. "Damn thing ripped the wing pretty good. Least he got both sides, so I didn't go into a corkscrew."

"Gonna head for the trees near the rental place. Hopefully, it'll be enough cover no one gets a good look at me. If anyone asks how we survived, 'some other thing we didn't get a good look at' helped us land."

"Sounds good."

A moment later, a random worry hits me. "Is Clayton going to bill us for wyvern damage or will insurance cover it?"

"No idea," yells Jason. "Never happened before."

It's frustrating to basically crawl along, but flying any faster would bend the glider's frame. I steer us off the river toward a spot a bit east of the rental place so we can basically hide. With any luck, no one on the ground sees me. Maybe they're wondering who has a 'biplane' glider with two wings. Once we're over trees, I drag us to a hover and end up supporting the entire weight of the glider and Jason. It's too heavy for me to stay in the air, but we sink straight down slow enough to avoid injury. Once he's on the ground, Jason grunts and starts fighting his way out of the harness. I land in front of the glider, shifting back to my normal human shape. Jason doesn't even notice me crouching there naked trying to help him escape. Once he's loose, I tap Natalie's amulet to resummon my clothes... and my glider harness.

"You okay?" I ask.

"Yeah... little freaked out. I've seen the occasional wyvern in the distance before, but never heard of them attacking gliders."

I look up past the trees at clear skies, no sign of a wyvern. Also, no sign of other gliders. "Maybe it's guarding eggs in a nest? Clayton didn't give us any warning about recent attacks, so maybe we're the first victims."

"Could be." He hugs me, breathing a hard sigh. "Sorry about that."

"Don't be. Not your fault. I still had fun. More worried about you being okay."

He laughs in a manic sort of way. "Well, nearly eating trees definitely got my heart beating. Thought I was gonna wind up in an ambulance there for a bit."

"So... adrenaline fix achieved?"

"More than." He exhales into a chuckle. "I crave thrills, not near-death experiences."

"Ooh... you've had two of those since we've been together. Maybe I am dangerous."

He kisses me. "But you're an addictive kind of dangerous."

I squeeze his rear end with both hands. "Am I now?"

He grins.

"Later, cowboy. We have another road trip to enjoy."

"Mmm." Jason kisses me again. "Can't wait to get home."

"We could have a little fun right here?"

"The rental place is only a hundred yards away."

I thread my arms around his neck. "Don't you like thrills?"

He looks around in a comical parody of a spy about to do something secretive. "You're a bad influence."

I tug him to the ground. "Oh, I've never heard that before."

7

MOSTLY HARMLESS

I'm relaxing in the fire station late Monday morning, thinking about random shit.

Jason and I didn't go all out in the woods—we saved it for later. Not so much him worrying about people catching us, but he didn't want to rush. We made out for a little while, then lugged the glider back to the office. Clayton had been shocked to hear of the wyvern attack, but didn't dispute it. No one strapped into the glider could have reached the wings where they'd been slashed.

Disappointingly, we didn't see any sign of the road rage idiot on the way back. Jason cooked us dinner and we spent the night at his place. Damn, I hope the Front Street Bastards left Tracy alone. Would it be wrong of me to swing by there on my way home later today and wipe them out?

Yeah, probably. Mom wouldn't approve. Self-defense is one thing, but she'd object to me going on an unprovoked hunt. And yeah, okay, it does feel wrong even to me. Covering their garage in completely un-macho graffiti, on the other hand—totally acceptable.

I text Tracy asking if everything's okay. She sends back ‹In class.› A few seconds later, she sends ‹Yeah.› Okay, cool. The gang left her alone. Hopefully, she stays clear of them. O'Keefe wanders into the squad room, spots me draped over the couch, and lures me to the pool table. I'm not terribly good at the game but I can sink a ball or three. Telekinesis only comes out when money's on the table, which it isn't now. Lieutenant Sims doesn't like us betting in the station house. Besides, most of the guys now know I'm telekinetic, so they wouldn't dare put cash on a game against me.

So weird how I play better when totally not caring who wins.

Around one in the afternoon, a fire call comes in, but it sounds minor. Sims sends out one truck with me, Rich Baker, Don O'Keefe, and Lamar Burke. Next to Burke, I feel like a kid. The man's so damn big he practically intimidates fires out. He and Brian Herlihy are like a pair of giants. Herlihy is beefier, but Burke is a little taller. Didn't stop me from beating Burke in arm wrestling though. He's still trying to figure out what kind of trick I used. His latest excuse is I'm some kind of aikido master of leverage.

Lieutenant Sims is aware of the truth since he's seen me fly and knows fire doesn't burn me. I had to give him some information so he didn't freak the hell out thinking he had a demon running around his station. Not an easy sell, though. He—along with a bunch of the Irish guys—are pretty into the religion thing. It took going with Sims to his church and shoving my hand in holy water to prove to him we're not evil.

As far as I know, 'holy water' doesn't do a damn thing to Shaar'-Nath. No idea why humans think mumbling words over ordinary water is going to change it. All right, to be fair, human mages mumble words and stuff happens… but they're born with the ability to invoke magic. Any random person can't suddenly decide to call themselves a priest or whatever and spontaneously gain magical powers. Not even the ones who go to special schools to 'officially' call themselves priests get magic out of the blue. If it worked that way, you'd see a whole bunch more people summoning food for starving people and so on.

Some Lifemages do muddy the waters. The insidious thing about comfortable lies is they're contagious. A million people believing a lie doesn't make it any less a lie, but if one Lifemage—who has actual power—ends up believing their power comes from a deity instead of from within themselves, they reinforce the misunderstanding among everyone who really wants to believe the nice, comforting story.

I will never understand how ordinary people simply accept anyone who claims to be a clergy at their say so without seeing them do magic. Especially those con artists who are so obviously in it for the money and run mega-churches. Even the Elestari laugh at them and they're the ones who tricked the humans into religion in the first place. Another of their 'great plans' for war. Turn all the humans against us 'demons.' Go figure, humans flipped it around into something they could make money from.

Maybe I shouldn't keep talking about them like they're some other creature. I'm technically half human.

Baker ends up driving. The rest of us pile into the truck.

"What's the word?" asks O'Keefe.

"Smoke coming out a window. Probably a kitchen fire." Burke laughs. "It's gonna be one of us with an extinguisher, the rest standing around."

"Here's hoping," I say.

Being a firefighter has spoiled me on the concept of driving. I love how people move out of the way for us without me having to use telekinesis. Even after I get around to going back to the DMV to finish my license, it probably won't get much use outside of official department vehicles. For personal travel, nothing beats my wings. Between flying and hopping a PEPTA portal, I can't justify the expense of buying a car. The Philadelphia Enchanted Public Transportation Authority has portals all over the place, as well as connections to portals run by private commercial apportation companies. For someone who travels all the time and needs to be independent from other schedules, a car makes sense. Less sense than flying, but being seen driving isn't going to upend my entire world.

Maybe I could steal one... if there's a way to do so and get away with it.

All the kids I used to hang out with who ended up stealing cars either got caught, handed the car over to a chop shop, or ditched them after a joyride. It's *really* damn hard to steal a car and keep it for a long time.

We hook a left turn onto a relatively narrow street of row houses. Our destination is as obvious as the thick plume of bright purple smoke billowing into the sky. Looks like it's coming up from the backyard. Probably leaking from the kitchen window.

"Oh, shit," says Burke.

O'Keefe whistles. "Is it purple?"

"Looks like it." Baker sighs. "Amari, this is all you."

Sigh. "Why is purple smoke 'all me?' I'm not a mage."

"You got the touch," says Burke.

"You got the *powah!*" sings Baker in a horrible attempt to mimic Eighties rock music.

"Ugh... seriously?"

The guys play air guitar and hum the song for the forty seconds it takes us to pull up in front of the house.

"Fine, whatever..." I shove the door open and get out.

A handful of neighbors already outside watch from their stoops or front lawns. Our flashing lights attract even more people out into the street. Since I don't see anyone by the smoking house or on the front lawn, I assume the resident is still inside. I grab a class B extinguisher off the truck, then trudge over to bang on the front door. I'll wait ten seconds before assuming the resident is unconscious, and booting it in. Burke, O'Keefe, and Baker approach. Baker is also carrying an extinguisher.

"One moment," calls a woman from inside, in a singsong tone.

I peer back at the guys. "House is spewing smoke and she sounds like nothing's going on. Might be a psych case."

Baker whistles. The other two nod.

The door opens with a faint squeak. A mid-fifties woman, curly auburn hair, bright floral-print dress, stands there looking at us, her expression one of mild confusion. I brace for the joke about it being too early for Halloween, but she doesn't go there. Or even make a comment about stripper-grams. A legit fire truck behind us is kinda high-budget for trick-or-treaters or singing adult entertainers.

"Oh, someone called you didn't they?" The woman shakes her head. "Can't imagine why."

My read on her is genuine confusion plus embarrassment. "Ma'am. Are you aware your house is on fire?"

O'Keefe points upward. "Probably has something to do with the giant column of bright purple smoke leaking out of your kitchen window."

She waves dismissively at me with a slight blush, as though I noticed she burned the soufflé. "Oh, the smoke? It's nothing."

"Yeah, the smoke." I nod. "It's kinda obvious."

"Bit more than nothing," adds Baker. "Can see the plume for a mile."

I sniff, but only catch a scent akin to raspberry pie. Definitely not the usual sort of stink generated by a burning house. "I'm sorry for the inconvenience, but since we've been dispatched out here—and smoke is clearly visible—we have to at least look around and verify there isn't a threat to life or property going on."

"Of course." She steps back. "Do what you must. Please mind the breakables."

I enter a living room decorated in traditional grandmother, even though the woman's not even sixty yet. A hand-painted wooden placard above the couch depicts multiple faeries holding colorful bottles around the words 'Georgina Rowland – An Elixir for Everything.' It looks like the sort of signboard someone might hang over a merchant pushcart at Silverbough Village.

The 'wall' separating the living room from the dining room is a set of open shelves accessible from both sides. It mostly holds bottles of various sizes, small jewelry boxes, and a few vases. About two dozen small books sit wedged between bottles here and there.

Georgina—I assume—leads us past the dining room to the kitchen. Several inches of dense purple smoke hugs the ceiling, spewing up from a bubbling slow-cooker on the countertop. Dozens of bottles surround it, about two thirds empty, the rest containing purple liquid. The smoke flows along the ceiling to a window overlooking the small backyard.

"What do you make of this?" asks Baker.

"Doesn't look like anything's actually burning." I edge closer to the slow cooker.

Georgina smiles. "It's all perfectly normal. Merely brewing potions."

"No cauldron?" I glance at her.

"Oh, I used to use one… but firewood is such a pain. And my lovely neighbors always call you nice people whenever I used to set up the cauldron in the back yard. The crock pot is so much more convenient. Nice, even heat… not too hot."

"Making potions in a crock pot," mutters Burke. "Somethin' new every day."

O'Keefe gazes up at the cloud covering the ceiling. "You've a kitchen full of smoke."

"Pshaw, it's not smoke." Georgina grins. "It's ethereal fog. Completely harmless."

Splat.

Something quite wet hits the ground in the back yard, close to the house. We all look left at the sudden noise. Georgina sighs, picks up a wand, and hurries over to open the back door. A growling puddle of mutated flesh and feathers a few feet away snarls at us. It's like the 'real bird' version of putting a marshmallow peep in the microwave. By the way, putting them in rune ovens brings them to life.

"Funky," I say.

Georgina invokes the wand at the poor critter. A dark orange magic beam strikes the undulating blob, blasting it back into the shape of an ordinary pigeon. The confused-ass bird sits there for a few seconds before scrambling off into the sky.

"Harmless?" I ask.

"Mostly." Georgina shuts the door.

O'Keefe whistles. "Damn, I hate these weird calls."

"Seems you've got the mutating pigeon thing under control." I gesture at the wand. "Might be a good idea to find a way to contain this smoke, err, fog. But, yeah. Nothing's on fire, so I guess we're not needed here."

"Sorry for the trouble. My neighbors are a pack of worrywarts." Georgina sets the wand on the counter among the potion bottles. "Would you care for muffins and tea?"

The guys exchange glances. I doubt they trust anything coming out of this kitchen—especially if it's been made in the crock pot. We politely decline, citing the need to get back to the station so we can respond to actual emergencies. Georgina sees us out, waves politely, and shuts her door.

We stow the extinguishers, spend a few minutes explaining to the people outside there isn't a fire, then climb back into the truck for the ride back to our station house. A few minutes later, we walk in on Lieutenant Sims and the other guys talking about a giant fire going on at an oil refinery in Texas. Humberto makes a joke about it being so bad they're going to call us down there to help.

"What happened out there?" asks Sims.

"Just a crockpot alchemist."

Humberto glances at me. "Don't you mean crackpot?"

"Nope. Literally crockpot." I explain.

Predictably, the guys laugh their asses off. The diversion doesn't last long before they go back to talking about the giant fire in Texas. Humberto mentions the news interviewed an eyewitness who claims to have seen lightning-spitting birds. I groan internally. It's the same guy. Has to be. But what the heck do the birds have to do with a mage? Dammit, there's no reason for me to feel like I'm doing anything wrong by not hunting him down. We have the FBI. The Academy also has a kind of police force specifically intended to address mage crimes. Between them and the FBI, it's their job to catch crazy people misusing magic. Looks like this nut-job is targeting industrial sites and polluters. They're not exactly trying to be a terrorist, at least, not against ordinary citizens. He or she is even attacking in the middle of the night so fewer people are around. Can't really object to the message, but okay, they're needlessly endangering innocents. I'm all for giving the finger to 'the man,' but hurting people who haven't done anything to deserve it is a bit much.

Says the girl who went joyriding doing 138 miles an hour down the Pennsylvania Turnpike in a stolen Camaro. Hey, I didn't know it was stolen at the time. Found out two days later. Also, I hadn't been driving, though I didn't exactly tell Carlos to stop. Yeah, we could've killed ourselves or someone else. Didn't really think about it back then, living in the moment.

I still don't know how the heck we got away with it.

Carlos? Oh, he's in jail now. Liked stealing cars a little too much. Cops aren't perfect, but roll the dice often enough and you will eventually lose. Especially if you piss them off enough to assign a psychic detective to the case.

Brian Herlihy puts on the TV in the squad room. News, of course, showing the Texas fire.

Argh.

Lightning birds are not my problem. We have cops and shit.

Why does the universe keep throwing this freak show in my face?

8

MY PROBLEM NOW

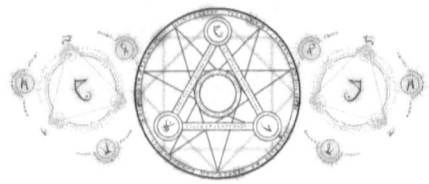

Not sure if I should call the rest of the week good or bad.

Every damn day from Tuesday to Friday, we had at least one fairly serious fire call. The worst one happened on Thursday. Got paged at four in the morning because an office building downtown went off like a Roman candle. I ended up being there all damn day. They suspect arson, but not a disgruntled employee. Rumor has it the whole company was about to be investigated for securities fraud and likely fined out of existence. What better way to destroy a whole bunch of records without appearing to be deliberately destroying evidence than an 'accidental' fire. So, yeah, four days, four huge fires. Surprisingly, despite tons of injuries, only one fatality occurred—the dumbass responsible for starting the Friday fire. A scrap metal worker at a yard adjacent to the Delaware River decided to cut open a big steel tank formerly used to hold gasoline at a service station.

Guess what the first step before taking an acetylene torch to a former gasoline tank is?

Yeah, this guy didn't vent it or check for any remaining gasoline. He went straight to the cutting.

Pity the moron didn't live long enough to understand the price of his dumbassery. We found his charred remains sixty yards away, as flat as a butterfly pressed between the pages of a book. The endcap of the tank blew off and pancaked him against the wall of the salvage company office, which also caught fire. I'd have taken a picture and submitted it to the Darwin Awards, but they'd never print it. Too graphic.

The only truly good thing about the rest of the week is no more stories about the crazy mage popped up in my face. Maybe the universe is finally starting to realize I'm not an FBI agent, superhero, or vapid do-gooder. I'm really freakin' lazy. And, honestly, I'm a fire-fighter. Unless the son of a bitch starts a fire in my jurisdiction, it isn't my problem. And there shouldn't be any guilt about not running all over the place trying to find this whack job.

Shouldn't and is are different things.

Grr. Thanks, Mom.

So anyway, it's Saturday and I'm presently a human (sorta) puddle on my sofa, taking slouching in my seat to extreme levels. I came home from the fire site so exhausted last night I went straight from the shower to bed. Pretty much walked into it and fell flat on my face. Now it's morning. Even after a shower, my hair still kinda smells like smoke. At least it's a fragrance I find soothing.

Dead Like Me is on, my go-to for relaxation. Somehow, despite watching it so often I can literally quote every episode, I still put it on. Since I haven't had the energy to get dressed, I'm being weird and eating my 'screw societal conventions' breakfast of chicken nuggets with my tail. It's a little tricky to spear a nugget on the tip of the blade without putting holes in the tray, but the challenge is amusing. Also, I don't have to move my arms, just lay here like a murder victim while the tail does all the work. Well, most of the work. Still have to chew.

My door flies open as someone barges in.

Ignoring the intrusion, I tail-stab another nugget and bring it up to my mouth, chuckling at one of Ellen Muth's deadpan lines. Damn, I love this show.

"Brooklyn!" yells Tracy from the left end of the sofa.

"Hmm?" I casually glance over at her while chewing—but as soon as I look at her, I sense the desperation of a terrified, heartbroken mother. It's the sort of thing 'demons' in ages past would've used to tempt people into doing crazy things. I may be the queen of 'DILLI-GAF,' but something's happened to Ashley. I jump to my feet, tail swishing like an agitated cat's—throwing a nugget across the living room. (The swishage has to be a normal, subconscious reaction to worry, but the tail's not out often enough for me to have ever really noticed.) "What happened?"

She waves a crumpled bit of paper at me. "They grabbed her! I found this and her book bag hanging on my doorknob."

I take the paper as she's in no state to read it to me. It's written in sharpie marker on the back of a generic estimate form for an automotive garage. Subtle.

Yo, bitch. You lost track of your little brat. Don't worry, we found her. Do what we tell you to and we only gonna break one bone to pay her back for Jojo. Deliver this package, get the cash, and bring it you know where. Take too long, we start sending back fingers or toes. Lose the stuff, go to the cops, or lose the cash, your little freak's gonna have a bad night.

"Dammit," I mutter. Remind me to ask Natalie to make sure the protection amulet she gave Ashley activates in case of abduction, not merely intent to harm. Hopefully, it'll shield her if the idiots go after her with a knife.

"They want me to take this giant package of heroin to an office building in center city."

My tail swishes harder. "Since when the hell do gangs around here abduct kids and force people to run drugs for them?"

She just stares at me. Maybe I escalated the situation by threatening them, though Tracy doesn't appear to be blaming me for this.

"Sorry," I look away. "I'll get her back. They can't hide her from me. Still have a blood sample to use."

"Huh, what?" She blinks, a slight shake to her head as if snapping out of a fog. "You... umm, you're naked."

"Yeah, I noticed. Got out of the shower a little while ago." Last night is a little while, right? "Remember when I said I'm lazy? And I'm not technically naked. I have a necklace on."

"Don't think jewelry counts." She hugs herself, shaking. "It doesn't make any sense those guys would kidnap Ashley. Shouldn't they be terrified of you—or the demon they think possessed you—coming back?"

"I'd been hoping so."

I plod to the bedroom and grab the nearest clothes from the floordrobe: a black ankh T-shirt and black frill skirt. Don't judge. Generally, girly stuff isn't my scene but sometimes, I have sparkle goth phases. Probably not a bad idea anyway. Skirts let me use the tail and not slice my pants off. Speaking of, probably ought to reel in the death noodle until it's needed. Walking around with a tail hanging out of my skirt is going to attract the wrong kind of attention. Either creeps who think I'm into fake body parts stuffed into uncomfortable places, or federal agents wondering what sort of undocumented creature I am.

Yeah, pass on both.

Crap. I like this shirt, but I'm probably going to get into a fight. Don't want any bullet holes or slashes in it. Back to the floordrobe. Out of sheer laziness, it's tempting to go topless, but humans get so damn uptight about it. I pull on a racerback and my shit-kickers, then grab the phial of Ashley's blood from my dresser.

What's creepier: me having a phial of a kid's blood or the child freely giving it to me.

I guess neither really since she knows why I wanted it. Poor kid's probably locked in a closet at the service station biding her time and fully expecting me to kick down a door at any minute. Shouldn't keep the little one waiting, should I? Not going to be irresponsible, promise. I'll kill all the gang idiots *before* I open the cabinet so the child doesn't witness anything.

"Wait… did you say you have Ashley's blood?" asks Tracy from my bedroom door.

"Yeah." I hold the phial up. "Always a good idea to keep a couple drops of blood from people I care about."

"Uhh…" She stares at me.

"To find her, remember. Same way I found you." I walk over and grasp her shoulders. "You are freaking out and not thinking."

Tracy numbly says, "Oh, right. Okay," then breaks down in sobs.

Ugh. She's completely blaming herself for this. Can't really argue with her. Sure I might've made the situation worse, but if she hadn't gone to the Front Street Bastards for a loan in the first place, we wouldn't be here. I can be a bitch sometimes, but not gonna say what I'm thinking out loud. She obviously already said it to herself, more than once.

"Wait here and freak out. Just try not to burn the place down. I'll be back as soon as I can."

She blinks rapidly. "What? Did you just tell me to freak out? Aren't you supposed to say 'wait here and calm down'?"

"Your kid is missing. What mother whose daughter has been abducted would calm down because someone tells her to? I'm only being realistic."

"Sorry," whispers Tracy.

"What those idiots do isn't your fault. Try not to go too crazy."

"No promises…" She paces around the sofa.

"If anyone's hurt Ashley, I'm going to be picking pieces of them out from under my fingernails for days."

She gives me this look like she *wants* me to kill them all while simultaneously being horrified at the idea.

I hurry out into the hall and up the stairs to the roof. No sooner do I set foot outside than the weight of a paranormal stare bores into me from nowhere obvious. Ugh. Stupid Elestari. It's probably Ezriel—a.k.a. David Graf. Prig still doesn't trust me at all. There's no point wondering what it would take to convince them I have no interest in destroying the world, since they'll never believe me. Whatever. If they want to waste time keeping me under surveillance, it's on them.

While standing at the edge of the roof, I stare at the phial of blood in my hand until it glows, surrounded by a dark crimson aura, the interior flickering with the churning red swirl of molten magma. The blood seems to flatten out, no longer a three-dimensional phial but a tiny doorway pulling away from my perception, stretching out into a long, winding flame tunnel leading to Ashley.

Despite it being Saturday and me not vegging out on my sofa, ignoring the world, I didn't for a second even think to blow the kid off as 'not my problem.'

Damn. I'm getting old.

THE FRONT STREET BASTARDS

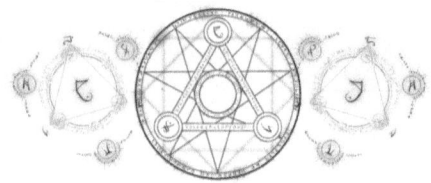

Fair bet, the blood isn't even necessary to find Ashley.

Idiots used a form from the garage for the 'ransom' note. Even though they hadn't bothered getting custom-printed estimate sheets bearing a logo for the place, it's obvious to me where it came from. I extend my wings and let gravity take me off the building. Free fall lasts a story or two before the leathery membranes fill with air and carry me upward. Being lazy is probably going to bite me in the ass eventually. Triple-checking my surroundings to make sure no one sees me do anything 'demony' is a ton of work and effort I can't be bothered with.

Hmm. My best friend is an enchanter. Wonder if people would believe my wings are a toy she made for me? It's a good excuse at least.

Fairhill isn't far from my apartment building and it's only been a week since my last confrontation with these geniuses. Spotting a corner automotive garage from the air is fairly simple. In the interest of speed, I swoop down to land right in front of the service bay doors and fold my wings out of existence. The flying thing's becoming second nature. My skirt didn't flap up due to a rapid descent and landing. I've gotten the hang of it. Trick is staying mostly horizontal until the last second or two, then swinging my legs down.

And the place looks empty.

Grr.

I may have committed a small error by wearing a skirt, mostly because it doesn't have pockets. Oh, well. If I have to toss the phial of blood in order to fight after I find Ashley, no big deal. She won't mind donating a few more drops. Having a being like me infallibly able to find her anywhere on the planet makes abducting her totally not worth it. My only worry is getting to her fast enough to stop a creep. Hmm. Would the protection amulet Nat gave her activate in case of another Frank situation? I really effing hope so. It obviously didn't protect her from being picked up and carried off, which means the person who abducted her didn't intend to cause direct harm. Grr. Magic is like Greek to me. Does the amulet sense a person's intention or merely react to physical things like a knife or bullet flying toward her?

Gaze focused on the phial, I stare into the shifting tunnel—and it goes past the garage. Damn, I should've been paying attention to the spell instead of my assumption. The magic is still active, so it only requires the intent to follow it for a sense of direction to manifest in my mind. I thrust my wings out to either side and leap straight up. Might as well let the tail out, too. The blade does kinda act like a counterweight to make steering a bit easier.

The blood tracking spell guides me southeast toward the Delaware River.

A few minutes later, I zero in on a medium-sized warehouse adjacent to a pier. The place appears in disrepair, probably abandoned for a decade or more. One street-modded Acura in metallic blue sits in the back lot, near a garage door. The gang idiots probably moved their other cars inside so it didn't look too obvious.

Though I fully intend to spare the City of Philadelphia from any future presence of this gang, simply booting in the door and going on a rampage isn't a great idea. They have guns and Ashley is somewhere inside this building. Need to have some sort of plan or at least get close enough to her so my telekinesis can mess up their shots before the punks know they're about to have a really bad day.

I fly up to hover outside the windows on the river-facing side of the warehouse. They're grimy and made out of those thick glass cubes designed to let in light but not be seen through. However, the building is a shambles and the window has enough missing blocks for me to scope out the interior.

It's mostly a single large space containing multiple rows of steel shelves, spaced for forklifts. One small corridor on the opposite side from where I am leads to a pair of bathrooms and a storage closet. On the right, a small supervisor office takes up the corner, but appears empty.

Voices draw my attention to the left, where I can't see past shelves still packed full of abandoned merchandise, or whatever sort of stuff this place held. Hopefully, all those cardboard boxes don't contain hazardous chemicals.

Looks like I'm going in.

I drop to the ground, put the wings away, and tuck the phial of Ashley's blood under my racerback, hoping the amulet considers it part of my outfit when it activates. I hurry over to the only person-sized door on this side of the building and let myself in. Most likely, they didn't lock it since gang idiots wouldn't even think I'd be able to find where they took her.

Once inside, I ease the door closed behind me and shift all the way into my armor. A brief flash of light surrounds me as the amulet absorbs my outfit. Good chance these punks are going to start shooting the instant they see me. I'm also not really in the mood to talk. Still a bit short of a murderous rampage—it's totally not my style —but I'm open to a change of heart should Ashley be hurt. The punks practically shit themselves seeing only horns and glowing eyes. Seven-foot armored me is going to maybe send them running away scream-ing. I can live with that. Getting Ashley out of here intact is all I really care about.

Trying to get in sight of her before the shit hits the fan, I creep across the warehouse toward the sound of people fidgeting about. Most of the big shelves in here are empty, except for the three all the way on the left side packed floor-to-ceiling, becoming veritable walls. I creep up to the end of the first one and peek around at the aisle.

The fifty-foot dead-end passage is empty.

Okay. I move to the next aisle and peek down it.

Also empty.

Third time's the charm, as they say.

Beyond the last shelf, an open area stretches like sixty feet to the far wall, which contains a row of truck dock garage doors. Ashley's in the corner, stuffed into a dog crate on the lowest level of a steel shelf. It's too small for her to stand up in, so she's sorta half sitting, half lying on her side, her face hidden behind a curtain of brown hair. She doesn't appear hurt, or even worried. Except for the book bag the punks left at the apartment, she's still wearing her school outfit, including coat.

Nine men, all the ones from the garage the other night—except Jojo—plus three unfamiliar guys, hang out on folding chairs or crates scattered about the open space, more or less doing nothing but standing there like nameless bad guys in a video game.

This should probably be a clue to me something isn't quite right, but I'm too pissed off at them for sticking Ashley in a dog cage to question it. Four of the men carry obvious guns, my first targets. I step around the shelf, telekinetically ripping their weapons away and launching them across the warehouse. At that, the thugs spot me and come running. Manuel reaches me first, swinging a crowbar at my face. I catch his arm at the wrist, about to crush it when I make eye contact and realize he's blank.

Not blank like one of those empty-headed blonde fascist-Barbie pundits for the Corporatist Party, I mean blank as in he has no radiant intent or desire. Normally, a guy in his situation would be brimming with avarice or anger, and the desire to hurt me would be obvious. He'd either be looking forward to the crapload of money he expected Tracy to bring them for delivering the heroin, or he'd have anger toward her. Maybe even a twisted glee anticipating cutting off Ashley's fingers—and yeah, if I see such desire in any of these losers, they're done.

But, Manuel's vibing like a Shaolin monk high on Khadafy weed. A mixture of total peace with the world and 'screw it.'

Instead of destroying his arm, I throw him aside.

Next guy comes at me with a knife. It's small, and he's skinny, so I let him hit me in the gut, pivoting my body sideways while bashing my forearm into his face. His knife glances off my armor, little more than cat-scratch painful. He, on the other hand, slaps into the floor and goes sliding. Probably broke his jaw. Two more run at me, trying to grab my arms like I'm some ordinary gang groupie they're thinking of dragging off for a good time.

I throw them into the big shelf on my left.

"Brook!" shouts Ashley. "See? I told you losers you were gonna die."

The guys don't react to my appearance or to me chucking them around like mannequins—except for the dude I face-smashed. He stayed down. Not one of them gives off any desire or sense of intent. Broken jaw dude proves they're real people, but they're damn sure not acting like it.

Shit. This isn't what it appears to be.

I need to grab Ashley and get the hell out of here before the real show starts, whatever it is. A radiant telekinetic shove knocks the rest of the gang punks away from me like a bomb blast. Pallets of old merchandise kinda form a gauntlet, but they're not really between me and the kid. I run for the corner, intending to grab the cage and carry her outside—only, I smack face-first into an invisible wall about halfway there. A loud, buzzing magical noise accompanies my cheek rebounding from a surface similar to glass.

Fancy glowing green writing rapidly draws itself in on the formerly plain concrete, defining a ten-foot-wide circular area. Faint energy shimmers in the air, a column around me all the way up to the ceiling two stories overhead. Growling, I attempt to launch myself upward, but a ten-foot circle cramps my wing style. I float upward, far slower than desired, and hit a plane of pale green haze a few inches below the ceiling. It's as impenetrable as the rest of the energy barrier.

I pound on it eight or nine times to no effect before giving up and parachuting down to the floor.

A gang punk jumps on my back.

I reach up over my shoulder, grab a fistful of his shirt, and fling him to the ground. He hits the concrete with a meaty *slap*, gasping for air and staring up at the ceiling. I crouch over him, grab two fistfuls of his shirt at his throat, and yell, "Shut this bullshit field off right now or this guy's dead meat."

"By all means go right ahead," says a smooth, silky aristocratic male voice I recognize instantly as Melisandre.

I peer up to my right.

The blond Elestari man walks out from a golden shimmer, wearing a white loincloth decorated in silver runes. He smiles, his immaculate white feathered wings tucked up neatly behind him. The man is indefinably somewhere between mid-twenties and forty, beyond movie star bodybuilder perfect. Taller and beefier than the last time he showed himself to me. This is his version of 'full shift.' His *true* form without a human disguise. It doesn't impress me. His appearance is entirely a product of his ego, not genetics or hard work.

Hearing his voice makes me want to throat punch him. Seeing his smug smile while I'm stuck inside a magical barrier elevates the hate to daydreaming about ripping his heart out, literally I mean. With claws. Preferably through the stomach.

A silver-haired Elestari woman appears next, her slender body encircled by a garment consisting of a wide, white ribbon coiled around her. It looks like a trendy Paris designer decided to make clothing out of silk toilet paper. The thing defies physics by staying in place despite it having no apparent means of support. Honestly, I'm not sure why she went to the trouble. It's not much different from naked. Then again, neither is Melisandre's loincloth. A third Elestari, another man, appears. He doesn't bother with clothes at all, and answers two questions I never realized I had before. One: why ancient statues always depicted men having such little things… and two: why Melisandre's wearing a loincloth.

A third male Elestari appears. His hair and wings are black, and he is also a fellow member of the 'pants are for losers' club. I'd tell Ashley to cover her eyes, but there really isn't much to see. This guy makes Michelangelo's David seem like Ron Jeremy.

Three Shaar'Nath appear on the other side of my circle, two women (jet black and crimson respectively) and a man (silvery grey). All are fully shifted into their armored forms and grinning at me. Without so much as a word, the seven extraplanars efficiently execute the gang punks, the Elestari using silver swords, the Shaar'Nath relying on claws.

I'm a bit unusual in having *some* regard for human life.

Melisandre goes to drag the man I'm holding out of the circle, but I pull him in past the barrier so the snide bastard can't reach him.

"What the fuck is wrong with you?" I yell. "They're humans, not roaches."

The man jerks violently backward, pulled by strong telekinetic force. He sweeps under me with enough power to flip me over and dump me on my face. Before I can right myself, he slides to a stop in front of the black-armored Shaar'Nath woman, who promptly stabs her tail blade through his face into the floor, then gives it a twist while winking at me.

"If you don't want the same to happen to the tiny roach, you will behave yourself," says Melisandre.

"Bullshit." The crimson-armored woman sashays over, stroking a hand down Melisandre's wing. "The only reason you're leaving that one alone is she's possible leverage over the half-breed."

He sneers at her.

I spring to my feet.

Without his 'human suit' on, Melisandre's also about seven feet tall, so we're eye-to-eye at the moment.

"Do something," whispers Ashley. "Break out and slice their faces off."

"Such a charming little girl," says the crimson-armored woman—sounding entirely serious. "Can I keep her?"

The female Elestari and black-haired male make sour faces at her, but stop short of calling her a 'barbarian' out loud. Yeah, they're not hiding their animosity for each other. Melisandre's presence already confirms they're warmongers.

"Oh, Xir…" The black-armored woman *tsk tsks*. "You're going to have your hands full already. What do you need a human child for?"

"My *dear* Na'az," says Melisandre to the black-armored woman, contempt dripping from the word 'dear,' "We have already determined Ralea and Asztirian will care for the child."

The woman Elestari and the black-haired man nod.

"Bullshit." Na'az jabs a clawed finger at Melisandre. "We saw what happened when you lot tried to raise one." She goes falsely doe eyed, folding her hands and speaking in an overacted, childish voice and French accent. "Oh, dear Lord, please lead me to victory and help me free my people."

The other Shaar'Nath laugh.

Melisandre frowns.

I hurl myself at the force barrier, snarling and clawing. Each time I strike it, the entire column flashes brighter green. My claws leave intense but brief streaks of glow in their wake, but appear incapable of damaging the magical wall.

"We should be the ones to influence the child," says the big male Shaar'Nath in a voice so abnormally deep I feel it in my bones. "To make them into a destroyer."

"Baal'Omun is right." Xir points her tail blade at Melisandre. "Even with Brooklyn, you failed, insisting on no contact from her father. No information at all. Are you so terrified of our people you cannot do what needs to be done?"

"Enough." Melisandre raises his hands.

The others fall silent, ignoring me roaring and smashing at the barrier.

"Perhaps the answer is in more mixed cooperation." Melisandre lowers his arms. "We will ensure she has adequate influence from both of our people."

I stop pounding on the barrier, rasping for breath, staring death at Melisandre. "Sounds like you're planning to brainwash someone else into having a half baby. Just keep the kid yourself. Five hours having to listen to you would make anyone want to destroy the world."

"Let us be done with this." Melisandre steps up to the barrier.

"Done with what?" I lean as close as possible to it, fists balled, daring him to do something. Panic comes out of nowhere at the sudden idea they're going to force me to mother this child—but hang on. They murdered all the human men here. And besides, I'm not an ordinary human. They can't use me as a mother for a destroyer, can they? The mother *has* to be human. What the fuck are they doing?

The others gather around me, alternating Elestari-Shaar'Nath-Elestari around the circle.

"Let me out of here or I'm going to rip your balls off!" I shout. "If I can find them."

Baal'Omun snickers, then clears his throat, resuming serious-face.

All the warmongers gaze upward, their eyes glowing bright white. The barrier responds, intensifying. White light gathers around us all, drowning the world out under a haze of nothingness.

Aww, fuck.

Screaming in rage, I hammer the barrier with all the strength I can find—until the big pain comes.

10

PLAN-B

O uch.
It's a fairly versatile word. Sometimes it's a reaction to seeing or hearing something unpleasant. Like 'I got stuck working every weekend this month' – ouch. Other times, it's a response to a bill. Such as, 'a new transmission's gonna cost $1,800. Again, ouch. Classically, the word refers to physical pain but not too much of it. Humans have a 'threshold of ouch' beyond which other words are used.

Words like holy shitballs.

Words like fuck.

Next is a stage of pain words cannot describe. It's usually expressed by incomprehensible screaming, often resulting in torn vocal cords.

Then there's the kind of pain I'm in now.

It transcends 'holy shitballs,' the big F, or even random screaming, and circles all the way back to a simple 'ouch.' This is mostly due to the sensation being so horrible, consciousness ceases too rapidly for the brain to have the time to think of anything else. I do, however, experience the joyous sensation of being impaled butt-to-mouth on a lightning bolt. This is further interesting because in my armored form, I lack the necessary rearward orifice for anything to invade my personal space.

However, we are talking about transcendental levels of pain here, the sort of brain-stopping agony capable of getting people to do drastic things like change religions or sign up for COBRA. The mere triviality of me not actually having a butthole right now to admit the impaling spike is a minor bit of logic totally irrelevant to what's happening.

Again, ouch.

I open my eyes to a close up view of dirty concrete and a none-too-distant lime green glow of bullshit Elestari magic. Everything is numb, quite a pleasant change from seconds or minutes or even hours ago (I have no damn idea). I feel as worn out as if I'd been the only woman at an orgy with an entire football team and got run over by the team bus as they drove off.

Well, maybe a better metaphor is needed. Orgy puts too much focus on sex. It's way more than my girl parts hurting. Even my claws ache. Imagine a baseball game where the final score ended up being 209 to 208 due to home runs, and they somehow managed to use the same single baseball for the whole game... which, on the last hit, went out of the park and into a wood chipper.

I'm the baseball.

Indistinct voices hover at the edge of my consciousness. It takes me a moment or three to gather enough sense of focus to remember how to make my arms work. I slide one hand out in front of me, happy to see my armor still intact. Pushing myself upright into a sitting position is more strenuous than the time I lifted a car... but I manage it.

The warmongers have moved away from the circle trapping me, relocating a few paces across the room where they surround a little girl. She's tiny, maybe five or six, naked as a newborn, and kinda scrawny. The kid has paper-white skin the same as mine as well as long, straight black hair like mine as well.

She stands calmly, arms at her sides, watching Melisandre and the other extraplanars discuss me, mostly how they screwed up by having a 'super-sweet' woman like Mom raise me. The Elestari thought putting me with a woman so entrenched in religious mythology—and one who actually believed all the selfless, caring, loving parts—would 'save' me from my evil nature. Bear in mind, these are Elestari. They think Shaar'Nath are evil.

We're not the ones responsible for Justin Bieber, beatnik poetry, or Duck Dynasty.

Asztirian the Elestari and Baal'Omun go back and forth regarding the wisdom of not allowing me to know what I was before it happened accidentally in the middle of the hotel fire. In Baal'Omun's opinion, if I had been raised fully aware of my paranormal nature, I'd have been exactly what they wanted—willing to destroy the physical world.

Shit. Did these idiots make me have a baby? I've heard birth is a painful experience, but holy fuck… Something other than childbirth happened here. It's impossible to even consider the agony I experienced however long ago before I passed out came from childbirth. If true, no woman would *ever* have more than one kid.

Na'az slashes her tail at the air. "We need to raise 'this child' to feel alienated from humanity and hate the physical universe. The girl must consider her half-humanity as the corruption it is, something she demands be removed. She will embrace her Shaar'Nath side, break open the Armistice, and join us for glory."

"Join you for defeat you mean," says Ralea, the female Elestari, in a haughty tone.

"This allegiance of ours is one of begrudging necessity," snaps the silver-haired male Elestari. "Do not forget your place."

Xir and Na'az snarl at him.

"Calm yourself, Jenathri." Melisandre raises a hand to him. "These Shaar'Nath are, as much as their kind is able to be, honorable foes. For now, we must work together to seek our proper glory."

I look down at myself. Armor's intact. No blood on the floor. Tail still exists. What felt like an electrified impaling spear must have been pure energy, or something shocking the nerves in my tail and riding up my spine. Doesn't look like anything physically pierced me.

A weak growl leaks past my teeth. I try to stand, but end up falling over into the barrier, blowfishing it like a kid on a school bus window. Ugh.

Ashley's staring at me from the dog crate, her fingers hooked through the bars. It's fairly thin wire, nothing I couldn't shred open easily if I could reach her. At least she also appears unhurt.

"Whatever mistakes we made with the last one, we shall not repeat. This child is our plan-B." Melisandre gestures at the kid, smiling.

"What the fuck are you babbling about?" I rasp.

The little girl twists to look at me. Eyes of rich dark blue, sapphires set in snow, regard me with blasé curiosity.

Oh, shit. It's *me*. Err... me from seventeen years ago. This kid... they somehow freakin' cloned me? Somehow. Magic. Right. Elestari make human mages look like dabblers. They might not have armor or as much superhuman strength as us, but they get magic. Big time magic.

"Holy shit," I mutter.

Melisandre smiles, rather overly proud of himself. "Yes, Brooklyn. We copied you, skipping the nuisance of the first six years."

"No one wanted to deal with diapers," says Xir.

"Or the terrible twos," adds Baal'Omun. "You were an absolute terror then."

I chuckle. "Guess you weren't paying attention. I was pretty much a terror straight through to eighteen. Only mellowed out because the whole 'charged as an adult' thing is a pain in the ass. Are you idiots seriously going to raise her to destroy the world?"

"You say 'destroy' as though it were a bad thing?" Melisandre clasps his hands. "This 'world' you think of as existing is merely an old, crumbling wall we no longer need. Mold growing on the wall is no reason not to tear it down when it is an eyesore."

"Humans aren't mold." I brace a hand on the glowing cylinder for support, and stand. "Do you guys actually want to go back to slaughtering each other to extinction all over again?"

"Only one side will go extinct." Melisandre flashes a condescending smile.

"Damn right." Na'az glares at him. "Surprised you're helping us end your kind."

I sigh. "The same thing is going to happen. Both sides are going to beat each other senseless. Numbers will dwindle. Everyone will freak out and want a truce. They'll make a new Armistice, and we keep going in the same big ol' circle over and over. Why don't you just go back to Aesinor and compose some self-indulgent poetry or something?"

The Shaar'Nath chuckle.

"And let me out of here."

Melisandre dismisses me with a sigh, then turns to face Mini-Me. "Now, dear. I realize it is a lot to take in at such a young age, but you are the bulwark upon which rests our greatest glory. Come, it is time to leave." He offers a hand.

The child peers up at him, head slightly tilted, her expression much like a cat who doesn't know what to make of a new object set in front of them.

"Don't do it!" yells Ashley. "He's lying. If you blow up the world, you're gonna get grounded for like ever."

"He's smiling at you now, but if the Armistice collapses, we'll both become Shaar'Nath, and he'll want to kill you," I rasp, still trying to catch my breath.

The girl looks at me for a few seconds and goes back to staring up at Melisandre.

"Come on, child." He leans down to reach for her hand.

Little-Me punts him square in the balls.

"Oof…" Melisandre doubles over.

She leaps into the air, sprouting wings, tail, and horns, landing an impressive right hook into his nose at the apex of her jump. The kid might be tiny, but she's strong enough to knock Melisandre over backward. Before any of the others can react—the Shaar'Nath are laughing too hard, the Elestari appear stunned—Mini-Me zooms like a missile across the warehouse, crashing out through a window and disappearing into the sky.

I burst out laughing. Watching the overstuffed pompous piece of shit laid low by a six-year-old version of me is totally worth being trapped in a magical cage.

"Find her," bellows Melisandre.

"Wow," I say, finally getting most of my voice back. "I didn't think Elestari had balls. Never thought to kick you guys there."

"They don't." Xir gestures at Jenathri's groin. "Not sure what that sad little thing is, but they're not balls."

He smirks at Baal'Omun, who like any Shaar'Nath in armor, has no visible sexy bits showing. "More than he's got."

Of course, he knows full well its armor, merely taking a cheap shot.

The Shaar'Nath see right through the lame insult and laugh at him.

Melisandre springs to his feet. "Fools. With me. We cannot lose her."

The seven of them rush out the door and fly off, leaving Ashley and me alone with a bunch of dead gang thugs.

"Are you okay?" asks Ashley after a few minutes of silence. "You screamed a lot. Didn't see anything 'cause the magic wall you're stuck in glowed too bright."

"Sore, but I think so." I roll my arms around, tilt my head side to side, and shift my weight from leg to leg. "Everything seems to be where it ought to be."

"You slept for a while. Those buttheads talked to the other kid for a long time. She just stood there staring at them being creepy."

"Damn." I pace around the perimeter of the circle, using my tail to test-stab the barrier. The blade keeps bouncing off with an electric buzzing twang noise, leaving little glowing streaks wherever it hits the field. "Well, this sucks."

"Yeah." Ashley sits cross-legged in the dog crate, resting her chin in both hands. "It does."

11

CIRCLE OF BINDING

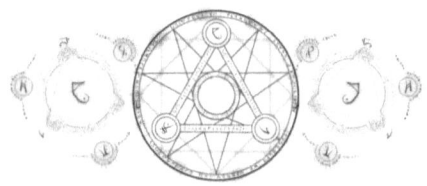

Magic isn't usually perfect.

It almost always has a flaw. All I have to do is find it before Melisandre and his idiots come back. This is one of those times where not understanding magic proves to be an enormous pain in the ass. Not quite as big a pain in the ass as the magic they hit me with. Yeah, it had to be energy grounding out via my tail into the floor. I don't think they forced my body to produce and expel an infant who rapidly grew up to six. More likely they tore my body apart at a cellular level and put it back together somehow.

Hmm. At a guess, my best chance of escape is damaging the florid writing around the circle. I've overheard enough of Natalie's mutterings to guess this is a 'circle of power' type ritual. Maybe a glyph trap.

The Elestari prepared it ahead of time, concealing it under a layer of invisibility until I walked into the circle. Then, like a spring-loaded snare, it snapped closed. I waste a few minutes ineffectually stabbing my tail at the writing around the edge. When it doesn't work, I kneel, grab the tail blade in both hands, and stab it like a handheld shortsword at the ground.

"What are you doing?" asks Ashley.

"Escaping," I grumble, while hammering my tail at the ground.

"Doesn't look like it."

Smartass kid. I can't help but laugh. "I'm trying to crack the floor to ruin the magical writing. If I can, the barrier should collapse."

"Oh."

Unfortunately, I'm fairly sure my cylindrical prison has a 'floor' of energy above the concrete. I'm stabbing a powerful eldritch barrier specifically designed to contain me. According to my father, my combination of human and Shaar'Nath makes me more powerful than full-blooded extraplanar beings, but only in the physical world. If I were to somehow end up in Aesinor or Imbreleth, I'd be noticeably weaker than them. Basically, being partially human gives me a strong home team advantage as long as I remain on my turf.

Fine with me.

Though, I wouldn't necessarily mind visiting Imbreleth. I hear it's warm there. Aesinor is full of stuck up assholes—except Laniah. She seems reasonably nice.

I continue assaulting the barrier for a while, pacing, cursing, screaming swear words, and generally starting to panic at my total inability to escape. Ugh. I hate this. It's like being locked up in juvie all over again, except the cops at least gave me a room with a toilet and a cot.

Ashley shifts around in the kennel and begins stomp-kicking the door. She succeeds only in making a pair of big padlocks dance around.

"What are you doing?" I ask.

"Escaping."

"Hah. Doesn't look like it."

She sticks her tongue out at me, then sighs. "They're gonna leave us here until we starve, aren't they?"

"Don't be so morbid. Once they catch Mini-Me, they'll be back… and probably do something nasty to us."

"Are they going to kill us?" She keeps kicking the door, having about as much success as me attacking the barrier.

"Umm… I don't think so. Melisandre's an arrogant fu—moron, but he's not *so* stupid he'll assume duplicating me is a guaranteed win.

He's going to want to keep me around. And, he's going to want to keep you around because he knows I want to protect you."

"You weren't going to say moron, were you?"

"Nope."

Ashley points through the bars of the kennel. "There are dead people nearby. You can say bad words in front of me. Mom does it all the time."

"Heh. Talk about messed up, right?"

"There's a lot messed up about this." Ashley folds her arms. "Like who puts kids in cages? Seriously? Or kills a bunch of people for fun. Or does magic on you so painful you shout 'holy strawberry eff-bunnies.'"

"I did not say that."

"You did." She folds her arms.

I bury my face in my hands and groan. "Yep. All of it is messed up. But the *more* messed up thing is there are people out in the world who would be angrier at me for cursing in front of you than for those idiots killing people in front of you."

"Wow. Stupid as shit," says Ashley.

I laugh. "You really shouldn't—"

"I'm kidnapped and locked up in a cage!" yells Ashley. "I think being stuck in a dog cage gives me permission to say shit."

"Fine. I can't argue." I kick the barrier. "Dammit. There's one real sucky part to being half human… this binding magic shit works on me."

Ashley snarls, rattling the kennel. "I'm all the way human and still trapped. It's a lot easier to trap me than you, so stop bitching."

"Not really bitching, just complaining to complain without any expectation the complaining will do anything."

She scrunches her nose. "Isn't that exactly what bitching is?"

I blink at her. "Are you sure you're only eight?"

"Yeah. I have an interesting mom."

"So do I… and she'd drop dead on the spot if she heard an eight-year-old swear."

Ashley raises both eyebrows. "So she's undead?"

"No... why would you even think that?"

"Because you're you. I *know* you swore as a kid. A lot."

"Not as bad as you think. Something about Mom. Couldn't do it in front of her."

Ashley stops kicking the crate door and resumes holding her chin in both hands. "Anyone who uses the F word like punctuation cursed a lot as a kid."

I shift to face her, also sitting cross-legged on the floor. "You know why I cursed as a little kid?"

"Is it different from why you curse now?"

"Yes."

Seeming surprised, Ashley lights up with curiosity. "Okay. Why?"

"As a kid, I said those words to be shocking. It made me laugh to watch adults react to hearing rough language come out of little me."

"I understand. Mom was pretty shocked the first time I said the F. She got real mad at me."

I laugh.

"How old were you the first time you said the F?" asks Ashley.

"Nine."

"Beat ya!" Ashley giggles.

"Yeah. You did."

"Why'd you say it? To shock someone?" She grabs the crate door, shaking it and agitating the padlocks.

"Nope. Was on a skateboard going down a steep hill into oncoming traffic. I said it as soon as I realized I had no way to stop."

Ashley facepalms. "All the demons in Hell and I had to summon the stupid one." She thrusts her hands out at me. "Why would you *ever* ride a skateboard into oncoming traffic?"

"Seemed like fun at the time. Figured everyone would swerve to avoid hitting me. Didn't expect to end up going so fast. So why'd you drop an F-bomb at eight?"

"Nothing fun. Hurrying too much not to be late for school in the morning and smashed my toes on the bed post. Kinda yelled the F before thinking about it. Just came out."

I cringe. "Oh, that'll do it." How is it the idea of kicking a bedpost barefoot makes me wince more than being shot in the arm?

"Should we be trying to escape or are we in trouble?" asks Ashley.

Admitting it's futile will only freak me out. The first time the cops actually locked me in a holding cell at eleven, I spent hours fighting the door. Something about being contained pisses me off. I'll sit all damn day in the same spot at home watching TV, but if nothing else changed but the doors being locked so I *couldn't* leave, my apartment would become intolerable.

Filled with anger and contempt, I fire a glare at Manuel's corpse. His head wobbles as if punted.

Oh shit! This barrier isn't containing my telekinesis, only my body. The magic also didn't do anything to stop the one gang punk I tried to save from Melisandre, and Na'az dragged the poor bastard out of it with TK.

I look at her cage and narrow my eyes. "I might not be able to get out of here... but I can get you out."

I focus on the kennel, levitating it via telekinesis and floating her across the open corner of the warehouse, right into my containment circle. The barrier has no effect on the metal or Ashley. As soon as I get my hands on the kennel, I tear the flimsy thing apart like a box made out of dry spaghetti noodles.

Ashley leaps into a hug. She doesn't sob or cry, but I can tell she wants to. She's presently too scared to break down. With the girl obligingly close, I hold her so she can't see any of the dead guys around us, and take a moment to telekinetically fling the corpses out of sight behind the shelf full of boxes. Bet the warmongers moved everything in this warehouse onto those shelves to funnel me straight at the trap. Even the pallets around here form an aisle directing me where they wanted me to go.

Grr.

"Okay, Ash. You need to be brave now. I need you to go find help. You can't be here when those guys come back."

Ashley sniffles, backs away from the hug, and walks out of the barrier. "Screw that. It's scary out there. I'm *so* gonna get kidnapped if I run around alone by the river."

"You already got kidnapped."

"I mean by worse creeps." She runs across the warehouse to the supervisor's office, yelling, "And those buttheads will only grab me again."

Ugh. Not sure what to say back to her. She's got a point. I hate the idea of her being alone around here. But her staying in this building is almost worse. If it wouldn't sound so pathetic, it's tempting to start yelling for Dad. I can't exactly call him any other way but shouting, since he didn't give me a phone number. Don't think Imbreleth has any telephone network. International rates are crazy enough, imagine interdimensional?

Hmm. Now I'm wondering exactly how closely he 'watches' me. He'd been there to protect me from the e-meth lab explosion responsible for wiping out my childhood home. Couple morons in a nearby trailer had been brewing it. He made me lose a joint only minutes before cops busted me for trespassing in an abandoned department store. Why hasn't he shown up here? Does it take a lot of energy for him to jump across dimensions, or is he confident I can get myself out of this mess?

Then again, my mother is the exact opposite of lazy.

Considering how lazy I can be sometimes, it must all come from his side of the family. Meaning, he would need to be convinced I'd be dead unless he intervened. The squeaking of small sneakers on concrete approaches.

Ashley's holding the same crowbar Manuel tried to wallop me in the face with. She kneels at the edge of the barrier, and like some tiny version of Red Sonja wielding a two-handed sword, proceeds to repeatedly hammer the concrete over the glowing writing. The bell-like ringing of a crowbar on stone is kinda annoying, even in the hands of a child. Still, I'm in no position to stop her. Speaking of child... my mini-me must be leading the others on one hell of a chase if they're not back yet. Good for her.

"It's not breaking," says Ashley. "Sorry for being a wimp."

"You're not a wimp. Most adults would have a hard time cracking concrete using a crowbar. Try aiming for the thin parts of the writing."

She pauses a moment to catch her breath, hunts down a nice, delicate spot of the flowery writing, and stands. Like some old-timey railroad worker hammering spikes, she swings the crowbar up and over her head, bringing it down again and again as close to the same spot as she can manage.

All the noise she's making, it's a shock the police haven't shown up yet. Bleh, Melisandre must have enchanted this building to keep people from noticing anything going on here. I cringe each time the crowbar clangs. It's tempting to give her some telekinetic help, but I don't want to break her wrists. As soon as she gets tired and gives up, I'll try levitating the crowbar and stabbing it into the ground. Assuming, of course, this containment spell doesn't have a way to prevent me from freeing myself.

Seconds before my brain turns to Jell-O from the racket, a loud *snap* startles a quick shriek out of Ashley. It sounded like a small firecracker, or a tiny .32 handgun going off. The fancy writing isn't glowing anymore, and the pale green force wall is gone.

"Oh shit! You did it!" I jump out of the circle, scooping her up.

Ashley drops the crowbar, squeezing me back as hard as she can. "The gang didn't kidnap me. One of the angels swooped out of the sky and grabbed me. I command you to punch him in the nose."

"Heh... Technically, I think I already did."

She leans back to stare into my eyes. "Huh?"

"Mini-Me?"

"Oh. Well, I command you to do it again."

"I'd be happy to... a few dozen times. C'mon. Gotta get you home. Your mother's going crazy."

She looks around, then whispers, "Fly fast. I gotta pee."

12

SAVING THE WORLD

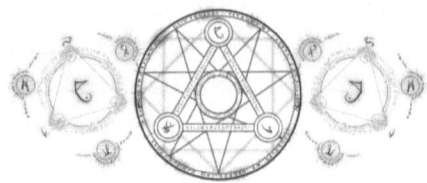

For what it's worth, I hadn't made the situation between Tracy and the Front Street Bastards worse.

Of course, Ashley's abduction was still kinda my fault. If I hadn't gotten involved with her and Tracy, the warmongers would have no reason to go after her. Neighbor with a screaming, abusive boyfriend, not my problem. Other than them ruining my enjoyment of movies and television because I couldn't hear a damn thing over Tracy and Frank yelling at each other, it really didn't matter to me.

At least until Frank had Ashley home alone for the first time and showed his true intent.

Yeah, I might be a lazy, indifferent, impulsive, reckless, free spirit with a side order of selfish, but no way in Imbreleth could I sit there and allow Frank to destroy her innocence. So I did the only reasonable thing possible when one discovers they're living next door to a kid-toucher: I tore him to shreds with my bare hands and burned the remains to ash.

Should've walked away then. But no, I *had* to bark at Tracy about what she almost allowed to happen. I *had* to let this kid worm her way into my guilty conscience. So, shit happened. I kinda adopted them both. Tracy as a sorta friend, Ashley as a sorta daughter. Or little sister. I *am* only twenty-three.

I don't regret it beyond making the two of them targets for the warmongers. Really, it's not as bad as my mind is making it out to be. They can always abduct my mother again if they really wanted to manipulate me. But it makes no sense for them to do so. Their end goal—destroying the physical world—kills everyone or anyone I might care about. What they used Ashley for, luring me into a trap, is about the only possible way to hold a human life over my head and make me dance like a trained dog.

After falling victim to it once, if Ashley, Tracy, or Mom end up mysteriously abducted again, I'm not going to charge in blindly again. My expectation will be it's another trap. I've played enough video games to recognize funneling. The warehouse had been set up to direct me specifically to the rune circle. Straight path to the kennel with Ashley in it.

Will not make the mistake a second time.

The nice thing about the Armistice, or physical world, is I can kill Melisandre over and over here. Ending a full-blooded Elestari—or Shaar'Nath—only sends them back home. Hurts like a bastard, so I hear, but it's not permanent death. They're weak for a while, but can eventually return to this world. The only way to truly kill one of us is to slay them in our native plane. Shaar'Nath who fall in battle while in Aesinor only return to Imbreleth. Sounds like a totally frustrating mess. Both armies surging against each other, trying to push their enemies back into home territory so they will stay dead.

Ugh.

I carry Ashley out of the warehouse and jump into the air.

On the flight home, I debate what, if anything, I should do regarding Mini-Me. On one hand, she's a whole separate can of worms totally unrelated to me. It's not as though only 'the chosen one' could end the world. Basically, any half-Elestari or half-Shaar'Nath can do it if they're motivated and stupid enough. There's no super pressing reason those morons have to come after *me*. Other than my existence. Engineering a half-breed is, from what little Dad explained, a bit of a task. Not every human is a suitable mother, and the mother *has* to be the human partner.

Sometimes, the kid pops out fully human. More often than not, the pregnancy spontaneously miscarries within the first two months. Abandoning me as a lost cause for restarting their war would send them back to square one. Apparently, they'd been trying to make me ever since Joan of Arc died if it's any indication how difficult it is to get a half-breed to 'stick.'

Saving the world from destruction is supposed to involve nothing more than me sitting on my ass. It's prophecy turned on its head. Rather than me needing to scramble all over the place in a desperate quest to fix stuff or stop stuff, it's *me* who can destroy the world. Thus, I simply have to *not* destroy the world.

Perfect. Suits my laziness just fine.

And, as I keep trying to tell Melisandre, I like it here.

I don't want the world to end, even if it occasionally does cruel things like come up with taxes, insurance, or Celine Dion.

No, I'm not going to say something sappy like there's way too much good in the world to focus on the bad. What other universe has so much opportunity to have fun and mess with people? Speaking of messing with people—I can't believe my eyes.

A familiar blue Honda is driving down the street below us. It's gotta be him, since the car's tricked out with custom street racing mods and has a couple of small tree-shaped dents in the hood. I take a slight detour closer for a better look. Yeah, it's the guy. I'm so pissed at Melisandre... and he's nowhere in sight. Gotta vent. This idiot will do.

"This isn't the way home," whispers Ashley. "Go higher. You're gonna get seen."

"Just a moment."

I follow Honda Man for a few blocks until the perfect storm lines up. Oh, thank you, universe. He tries to beat a yellow light, but jams on the brakes at the last second when he spots a police car rolling to a stop on the opposite side, facing him. A nice little telekinetic nudge pushes the Honda through the intersection, 'running' the red light. Damn sure the cop saw him stop hard, too. Running a red light while a cop is looking right at you is basically giving them a double middle finger.

As soon as the police car's lights come on, I laugh to myself and veer back toward home.

Yeah, it's petty, but satisfying.

No sign of any Elestari or Shaar'Nath flying around. Wherever the new me went, she's definitely making them work for it. I land on the roof of our building a few minutes later, set Ashley down, and shift back to normal. My 'chibi succubus' amulet resummons my clothes, including the phial of blood tucked under my top. Cool. Don't have to draw blood from Ash again. Even better.

We hurry downstairs to my apartment.

Tracy's pacing around the sofa as we walk in. She screams like we startled her, then runs over to scoop Ashley into a hug. Both of them end up crying.

"Sorry it took so long," I say. "Things got weird. Be right back."

"Where are you going now?" asks Tracy, staring at me in disbelief.

"Only to change tops." I pluck at the racerback. "Not a big fan of clingy."

Tracy takes Ash to the couch.

I head to my room and put the phial in the drawer, then stare down at my boobs.

Well, not my boobs exactly, but the racerback top, feeling guilty about Mini-Me. I can't let the warmongers exploit a child, even if it is me. Dammit. I grumble on my way back to the living room.

"Weren't you going to change your shirt?" asks Tracy, past sniffles.

"Ehh, yeah. Something came up. I gotta go back out there."

"What? Why?"

I lean on the sofa and give her a quick explanation of the events from the warehouse, especially why it took me three hours to come back. Guilt melts visibly out of her eyes when she hears the abduction hadn't been the gang targeting her, rather them acting under mind control. "The whole scenario was a setup to lure me into a trap. I'm going to try and find her."

"Oh. Umm, what are you going to do if you catch her?" asks Tracy.

"I dunno. Help her hide from those losers? Take her for ice cream?"

Ashley lifts her head off Tracy's shoulder. "If you go for ice cream, can I come?"

"Sure."

"It's okay, Mom. I didn't watch them kill the bad guys. Promise I closed my eyes."

Tracy looks up at me with a pained grimace.

"Truth. She's nowhere near as traumatized as she'd be if she saw it." I tap a finger to my temple. "Trust me. I can tell."

She whimpers. "When did my life get so crazy? Are they going to keep coming after us?"

"I can't think of any reason they would at this point." I pat the sofa. "As much as I want to stay in and veg out for the rest of the weekend, I'm going to hate myself if I don't at least try to find her."

"Heh." Tracy chuckles. "How long can a six-year-old run around alone before someone notices and calls the police?"

"Three hours and forty-six minutes," I say.

Tracy stares at me. "What?"

"My longest run."

"Are you messing with me?" asks Tracy.

"No. But my memory could be foggy. Was only six at the time. Lived in a trailer park near a creek. Felt like about that long, but it might have only been one hour." I shrug. "This is also Philly, not a trailer park outside Allentown. She's probably already in social services by now." Here's hoping she didn't shred any normal human who tried to help her.

"Hope so." Tracy leans back into the couch. "Poor kid's gotta be freezing out there."

"Meh. Clothes don't help much. I'm always cold unless it's in the upper nineties. It's like my body goes into some kind of survival mode when it's less than 200 degrees around me. Being outside in winter bare-assed or in a heavy coat doesn't feel much different temperature wise, just don't have the sensation of the wind on me."

Tracy shivers. "Do you not generate your own body heat or something?"

"I look like a doctor?" How should I know? I've got wings. Like my body is supposed to follow Earth science rules."

Ashley squirms. "Gotta pee *real* bad."

I start toward the door. "Be back soon."

"Okay. I'm too fried to think." Tracy moves so her daughter can get up. "Mind if we stay here?"

Ashley hops off the couch and funny-walks down the hall to the bathroom.

I nod. "Yeah, no problem. I won't stay out there too long. Might as well grab food on my way back."

"Sweet. Thanks. Someday, I'll figure out a way to pay you back."

"Ehh. It's food and babysitting. Hardly major."

I jog out into the hall and go up to the roof. The 'watched' feeling is gone. Dammit. Bet one of the Elestari involved in trapping me had been posted here to watch for me racing off to find Ashley. If it had been Ezriel, he would've helped me escape. Or stopped them from cloning me, then decided me too much of a risk to leave alive. Whatever. Over and done with now. I stretch my wings and jump.

Right. Questions.

How fast can Mini-Me fly? Are child Shaar'Nath slower than adults or might they be faster due to having less mass? How much of 'me' is she? Does the girl know her way around Philly or is she flying randomly looking for a hiding place? I also don't know for a fact Melisandre and the others didn't return because they couldn't find her. Maybe they caught her and decided to leave Ashley and me there as a middle finger. It's also possible they're still out here hunting for her, or gave up and went back to wherever they live when not being a pain in my ass.

Speaking of pain...

I daydream about cutting Melisandre's junk off and stabbing him in the eye with it. No, too small. I'm going to hit him with the fire spell Dad showed me, but only his legs. He is going to know the meaning of experiencing such a massive amount of agony all he can think is 'ouch.' Do I know that inflicting pain on someone won't make the pain I felt any less? Yeah. Do I care? Not really.

Philosophical ramblings about the inefficacy of revenge are for people who obsess about having the moral high ground. I am unburdened by such lofty restrictions. Someone screws with me, I screw back twice as hard. Eventually, they'll leave me alone. Maybe after I kill him five or six times, he'll get the hint.

I do have one advantage over the morons in finding this kid. She's me. Stands to reason, we would think the same way. So... I fly back to the warehouse and land on the roof above the window where she broke out.

Okay. I'm six years old, a bunch of buttheads are standing around me who I don't like. No idea where I am or how I got here. Nut kick, leap, punch to the nose, fly out the window.

I launch myself into the air, trying my best to react in the impulsive manner of a child.

Shut up. I know, not a big stretch for me.

A pair of huge round tanks straight ahead look like a fun place to check out, but I'm being chased. The city past them is relatively the same for a long distance in every direction—no particularly tall buildings or unusual sights beyond the wharf area. I swing left, cruising over a cluster of much smaller white tanks, heading toward the distant skyscrapers of center city. Hmm. To the right of the tanks are a bunch of giant sand piles in various shades of white, brown, grey, and black. Has to be clay, gravel, or some such thing. It also looks like a fun place to mess around. But again, buttheads are chasing me.

Past the tank farm toward center city is a swath of trees and grassland. Maybe a good hiding place, but not really. A couple of artificial peninsulas covered in trees isn't a lot of space to hide in. Guess they used to be piers, but somehow ended up covered in forest.

Oh, the highway... I definitely would have flown in low over I-95 and played chicken with cars. If I'd known about my wings at six, no way would I have been shy about showing them off. Wonder if people would be more shocked at wings or lack of clothing? Either way... at six, I'd have run out the door bare ass naked, wings out and proud shouting, *'witness me and behold!'*

I cruise near the highway. No sign of car accidents, fires, police, or other chaos. If Mini-Me did buzz the freeway, no one noticed or cared. Then again, with the sun setting around then, most drivers would have been squinting into glare if going west. Ordinary people seeing a snow-white winged thing flying at them would probably assume it's a heron or giant seagull, not a small humanoid girl with wings. Come to think of it, she's about goblin sized... but they don't have wings. Imps aren't quite as tall but at sunset and high speed, yeah, someone could've mistaken her for an imp.

The City has been experiencing a mild increase in magical creature sightings, too. The barrier's failing, and as far as I know, no one's been able to locate the crack. Doesn't worry *me* too much. There aren't too many magical beasties around here nasty enough to scare me.

Okay, so a game of highway chicken is a no go. Maybe she did, and got away with it. I bet the warmongers chasing her would have avoided going low enough over traffic for people to see them.

Go me.

Err, go her.

More trees coming up on the left. Still, not much land. Chased by seven buttheads with wings. Even if the kid can fly at the same top speed as me, the Elestari could catch her. Cheating bastards. Yeah, pure jealousy. Not actual cheating. Housecats aren't jealous cheetahs can outrun them, are they? Just the way it is.

Not sure what's making me fixate on center city, perhaps the skyscrapers. I do know center city has tons of places a little kid can hide. Especially a little kid with wings. Even outside the relatively small region with skyscrapers, downtown is surrounded by dense residential areas, hospitals, and schools. Literally millions of small places to crawl into.

My attempt to pretend being the fleeing child leads me to a few spots on skyscraper rooftops or decorative ledges only accessible from the outside. No luck. Hmm. A D-shaped skyscraper with lots of hiding places on the roof catches my eye. It's got a strip of windows around the curved face of the tower, kind of a false story, concealing all the HVAC equipment from view to anyone who can't fly.

Good place to crawl in and stay out of sight.

I land on a flat square in the middle, peering down into the 'pit' of pipes and fan units. "Hello? Hey, it's me. Are you here?"

"Kill me…" says a deep male voice.

Ooo-kay. I turn to the left.

A blob of feathery flesh stares at me. Looks like a pigeon the size of a big dog after it got run over by a Zamboni or five. The poor critter is seriously the Salvador Dali of failed Lifemagery. Its appearance is so WTF it doesn't even register to me as weird the thing spoke.

"Kill. Me," says Mega Pigeon, something beak-like in the middle of its body twitching in time with the words.

"You're talking…"

"So? You're flying. What's the big deal?"

"Did you see another girl like me, only smaller?"

"Nope."

Sigh. "Darn. Can you fly?"

"Freakin' look at me." It undulates, probably trying to raise its wings. "What do you think?"

"How'd you get up here if you can't fly?"

"I live here."

I rub the bridge of my nose. "If you're unable to fly, how did you get from Georgina's backyard to this roof?"

"Everything was normal. I was havin' a great day. Pooped on a couple cars, scored some French fries, came home to rest. Just about to land here for a nice long nap, and—blammo."

"C'mon. I know what happened." Picking him up is weird. Like a plastic trash bag full of raw, warm chicken breasts.

He squawks. "What are you gonna do?"

"Bring you to the person responsible for this. She can put you back to normal. You'll stop talking, but you won't be a blob anymore."

"Blob? Who you callin' a blob? I'll take a dump on your head."

"Fine." I drop him. "You can stay like this."

"Wait. Okay, fine." He strains to look at himself "Yeah, okay. I guess this is kinda blobby."

Grumbling, I pick him up again and jump into the air.

The big baby screams the whole way to Georgina's house. You'd think a pigeon wouldn't be afraid of flying. Maybe he's uncomfortable cruising at 200 miles an hour? I'd go faster, but he started losing feathers. It takes me a few back and forth passes around the neighborhood before I notice purple stains on the siding above a kitchen window. Bingo. This has to be the right house. I land in the backyard, retract the wings, and carry the pigeon over to the door. He's kinda big, so I knock with my boot.

Georgina answers in a few minutes. "What are you doing in my yard, dear?"

I peek around the pigeon. "Hi. It's me. Found this guy. Think he ran into your smoke cloud. Would you mind zapping him back to normal?"

"Oh, dearie. I can try. If it *is* my magic, this should do the trick." She hurries inside to grab the wand she used last time.

I set the pigeon on the ground and take three steps back.

Thankfully, one zap results in the huge blob compressing back down into a normal pigeon. He stares at me for an eerily long moment, emits a coo, and flies off.

"Does he remember being able to talk? Is he still as smart as a person?"

Georgina purses her lips. "Most likely not. This should remove all traces of the runaway magic. Though, I usually dispel them much faster. He's been changed for quite some time. It's not impossible for there to be unintentional side effects."

"Right, umm. Thanks."

She keeps staring at me, not closing the door, not going back inside.

"What?" I look down at myself. No pigeon poo.

"You're in my backyard and the only way in is through the house. The yard's sandwiched between row houses on both sides. How did you get there?"

"Oh… enchanted amulet." I fake-tap it and extend my wings. "Still kinda getting the hang of it."

"Lovely. Oh, it had to be expensive. Well, you be careful with it dear."

"I will. Thanks."

No point waiting for her to go inside, so I take off.

Hmm. Not a bad test drive for the enchanted item excuse. I should probably pick up a cheap ring or bracelet and use it as a scapegoat instead of the necklace. Nat would make me a bracelet with an enchantment so it *appears* to be collapsible wings but doesn't really do anything. Faking it has to be way less work.

Anyway, as much as I hate to admit it… the odds of me finding my little clone aren't good. Does she answer to Brooklyn? I can't really swoop around calling her name. People will look up—and she most likely wouldn't listen.

Hmm. Ya know… if she's basically me and we have the same memories and instincts, maybe she's heading for Quakertown where the trailer park I lived in at the same age is. Also maybe she'll find her way to my place once she loses the buttheads. It all depends on if she has six-year-old me's memory or my current memory. If the former, she'll be hunting for a trailer park. I'd say it doesn't make sense for her to have my memories based on the past, but it also doesn't make sense for a tiny copy of me to exist at all.

Magic, right? Crazy.

Even more strange, none of the buttheads have attacked me or gotten in my face even to gloat. It's not like they want to kill me. Doing so wouldn't help their agenda. It would only send me to Imbreleth as a—possibly—full Shaar'Nath and make me incapable of doing the bad thing.

When I put it in those words, offing myself sounds like a sane option.

Nah. I like it here.

And no, not really. If I die, my 'soul' gets sucked back to Imbreleth, floats around formlessly for several decades, then *maybe* turns into a Shaar'Nath. Unlike a full-blooded extraplanar being killed here, I have a reasonable chance of simply ceasing to exist. Yeah, not rolling those dice.

With a sigh, I reluctantly give up on my search and swing around to fly home.

Good luck wherever you are, kiddo.

13

MOTHER'S GUILT

No sign of Mini-Me on Sunday.

She didn't show up on Monday morning, either. I'd been in kind of a glum mood all day Sunday, unable to find interest in doing much. Jason came over wanting to go out. He ended up sitting with me, watching movies, and letting me ramble. Naturally, he thinks I'm worried about myself. Not actual me, small me. I mean, she looked so damn tiny and helpless and sad. Did *I* look like that back then? Well, obviously I did in general terms, but the sadness in her eyes?

My eyes are a little larger than normal. They've always kinda made me look sorrowful or pleading even if I'm totally calm and happy. Didn't realize they had *such* power though. I mean, a ten-year-old can only have so much pity for another ten-year-old even if it's themselves in a mirror. Kids don't think of other kids the same age or older as being 'just helpless kids' in a bad situation. Seeing six-year-old me with those big eyes and blank face. Ouch. Right in the feels.

For all I know, her mood had been total boredom without a scrap of feeling sorry for herself.

Yeah, I'd been a little out of it after being poked in the rear end by a two-million-volt turkey baster. Metaphorically, I mean. Nothing actually invaded my personal space. At least nothing beyond magical energy.

Dammit, Mom. Somehow, despite my best effort to be a cool, irreverent badass, she somehow instilled me with a bit of a conscience. I've been trying not to pay attention to the crazy mage blowing up chemical plants and refineries—which seriously isn't my problem—but still can't shake guilt for not doing anything. And now I'm feeling even worse about the idea of leaving mini-Brooklyn out there on her own.

I actually called Detective Zheng and asked if he'd heard of anyone picking up a kid fitting her description. For now, he settled for the explanation 'magical weirdness' and didn't press me for my connection to her. Unfortunately, he hadn't heard about any cops in this area picking up an abandoned child, but he's keeping an ear out.

It's not *too* worrying she might run into dangerous humans. Mini-Me leveled Melisandre with a single nut shot. If she kicked a normal human hard enough to stun an Elestari, her tiny foot would be embedded in their intestines. When I punted Vince Milligan's nuts up into his throat—metaphorically—I had no idea what sort of strength my body was capable of. Good chance Mini-Me knows. Okay, maybe I *should* worry about dangerous humans finding her—for their sake.

And, it bothers me to think about her having the mental scars of killing someone.

Okay, I'm being hypocritical here. I grew up thinking I killed a man at ten and it didn't mess me up at all. Really. The only thought ever to surface about the incident had been 'good, fucker. Die.' When Dad told me he'd really been the one to kill the creep, it kinda disappointed me. Yeah, okay. I realize it's abnormal for someone to feel disappointed they *hadn't* killed someone as a kid. Sue me. I'm not fully human.

So, Sunday, despite my inescapable guilt, ended up not being *too* bad. Jason did finally coax me into going out for dinner. We didn't do anything but cuddle and share a bed Sunday night, but sometimes, being held is way better than wall-damaging sex. Right medicine for the right sickness.

Monday, late morning, Jason and I are repacking the hoses on our second pump truck. He's not assigned to my station house, but sometimes people rotate to cover staff shortages. His station is the next nearest toward North Philly. Some people say it's a seriously bad idea to work with someone you're dating or married to. Seeing them all day all the time supposedly drives you crazy. It's probably true for those people. Maybe it will be true for older me. For now, it's nice being around him. Also, we're not married, nor are we living together. So it isn't as though we're in each other's faces 24-7.

I'm having focus issues today. Nothing bad enough to cause injury or accident. My mind keeps wandering off to worry about Melisandre and his idiots going after Ashley again, or Tracy, or my mother... and Mini-Me. Ugh. I am such a tool. A few years ago, I'd wake up in the morning not caring where the day took me. Getting high, spray painting walls, joyriding, shoplifting, sneaking into places I shouldn't be. Every day had been an adventure and not once did any thought of consequences ruin it.

Swear. Adulting totally sucks.

In some respects. Being able to drink legally is pretty cool. As is having my own place, and privacy. Having to earn money to feed myself and keep a roof is pretty lame, but a girl's gotta do, right? Well, maybe not me. I suppose there's always the idea of going fully feral, running off to live naked in the woods and preying on random goats or whatever. I have the fangs and claws for it. But living like a wild thing in the forest would get boring *fast*. Can't watch *Dead Like Me* with a television plugged into a rock. No video games out there either. Or bars. Or Jason.

So, yeah. Gotta deal with the job thing. This half-demonic creature has a certain standard of living needed to keep her happy.

Though, I do miss being able to get high and waste a whole afternoon staring at the clouds. Weekends maybe, but the fire department does random drug testing. I don't trust my mental powers to make a bad test go away yet. Influencing a school bigwig to give Tracy a scholarship had been an interesting experience. There, my stake in it had been nil, so it let me stay calm. If *my* livelihood dangled on the line, I'd probably have overdone it and turned the guy into a lapdog—or choked and screwed up completely. Especially considering I'm not using mind control. My powers aren't like movie vampires where I stare into their eyes, insert a command, and they obey. It's more like repeating over and over again something is a good idea or the person should do it and they eventually start to believe it. The same way 'demons of old' tempted humans to 'sin.'

Hmm. I need practice.

"Starbucks run!" I shout.

I hurry around the station, asking everyone what they want. As the only female firefighter in my stationhouse—honestly, there aren't many of us in Philly to begin with. Something like twelve percent of all firefighters in Philly are women. The day I started here, I became the Starbucks runner. Initially, it had been sort of a hazing situation, trying to make me feel like a secretary assisting the 'real' firefighters. Or at least, it came off as such. But… after a few fire calls where I pulled my weight, the antagonistic tone wore off. Now, I just do it because it's habit. And we all like coffee. And everyone slightly over-pays—by like a dollar each—to cover my coffee as a thank-you for getting it. I keep the extra.

Once I've got everyone's orders—today Lieutenant Sims gave me his department credit card since he's buying for everyone—I head the couple blocks down to the Starbucks. After ordering, I approach Sanjay, the manager, since he won't get in trouble for my little bit of mental influence practice.

I strike up a conversation with him about a $50 gift card, nudging the idea into his head about me buying one the other day. While leaning on his brain, I gradually shift the conversation from a gift card I purchased last week to one I'm purchasing now, to one I've already purchased and he hasn't gotten around to putting it in the system yet. He robotically activates a $50 card and hands it to me.

Okay, nice. Guess we are deceivers after all.

No, I'm totally not above stealing. My only concern is not wanting any low level employee getting fired over it. This card, however, I'll give to Tracy. If I'm going to steal for myself, it's going to be shiny, electronic, or something cool but overpriced in the 'neat to have but no way would I pay for it' category.

A short while later, the order's done. I lug everything back to the station house and set the cup carriers on the table in the squad room. 'Hazing' new girl coffee runner brought everyone their coffees to wherever they happened to be when she got back because she thought it would make people like her. 'Respected colleague' coffee runner leaves it here on the table and lets everyone come get their own shit. Except Lieutenant Sims. Not to brownnose, but he's busy and I need to give him the credit card back anyway.

"... strikes again. A petroleum tank farm along the Raritan River in New Jersey is the latest in a series of attacks by an unknown arcane terrorist," says the TV news in the break room. "Witnesses on the scene described an unidentified magical creature described as an enormous white bird attacking with lightning."

Dammit, Mom.

The universe is seriously going to keep throwing this in my face, isn't it?

No, it's not my mother's fault this mage is doing it or I keep happening to catch it on the news. It's her fault it bothers me not to do anything. Seriously, it makes zero sense. It's like a dentist in California seeing a story on TV about a bunch of bank robbers holding hostages in New York and feeling the need to run over there and help. I'm not a cop. I'm not FBI. I'm not some kind of superhero.

Okay, so I have powers humans don't, but still.

Sigh. Okay, it *is* a fire. It's way out of my territory, but at least it's a fire.

I can practically see Serena Miller—the slightly eccentric crystal vendor from Silverbough, the mage-hippie place—telling me something about how my inaction on the thunderbird guy is the reason other crap is going wrong in my life. As if this shit is all connected somehow. No, I don't believe in that Zen stuff any more than I believe an expensive salt lamp is going to realign my planets or chakra my pressure points.

But, dammit. It feels like Mom is standing here giving me the same look she used to give me every time I arrived home in a police car.

"Okay, fine." I sigh at the ceiling, and go to Sims' office, carrying his caramel macchiato, which I set on the desk next to the official credit card. "Hey, LT, question."

"Thanks, Amari. What's up?"

"They got the news on in the squad room. You know the situation going on with the lightning strikes at chemical plants and such lately?"

"Yeah?" He pulls the green stirrer out of the cup and takes a sip.

"There's another attack in New Jersey... petroleum storage tanks off the Raritan River."

He blinks. "Seriously? Those things are pretty damn difficult to set off. Double layer, thick..."

"Apparently, not thick enough to stop magical lightning. Would you mind if I ran over there real quick? Got this weird feeling the universe wants me to get involved."

Lieutenant Sims chuckles, shaking his head. "Things with you are getting stranger and stranger by the day."

"Don't I know it?" I hook my thumbs in my pockets. "Not super important. Just a hunch. Maybe I'm feeling a psychic warning this guy's going to do something big if he's not stopped in time. I dunno. There's no logical reason for me to feel any urge to get involved here. But it's gnawing at me bad."

"You're going all way to Jersey? What part of that is 'real quick'?"

I look over my shoulder to make sure no one's eavesdropping. "I can fly at like 350 miles an hour."

"It's what, about seventy... maybe eighty miles? Whoever he is will be gone before you get there, even at your speed."

"Straight line, no traffic. If I miss him, I miss him." I shrug. "Ever have one of those hunches?"

"Bring your phone. I expect you to haul ass back here if you're needed. We had one hell of a week last week."

"Understood. No problem."

He nods once, and raises his coffee to drink.

I hurry upstairs to the roof.

SOME GUY SCREAMED IN THE ALLEY BEHIND THE FIREHOUSE WHEN I leapt off the roof.

He probably didn't see much but a blur with wings, and—assuming he tells anyone—it's most likely going to be just another random sighting of an unknown creature. Maybe I should start taking more care to avoid being noticed. If it gets out there I can fly, some politician's going to go crazy trying to legislate it. Make me buy insurance or get a pilot's license.

They might kick me out of the city, too. Stop considering me a 'person' and more of a creature.

Worse, if society thinks I'm the harbinger of the end times, out will come the torches and pitchforks. Then I'll have to kill a bunch of morons or live in a constant state of fleeing. Yeah, I can't go public. But I'm too lazy to turn flying into a ten step project like something out of a spy movie.

So, I circled back, found the guy who screamed, and used him as a mental test dummy.

Now, he thinks he saw an unusually large pigeon. Oh, and he might randomly soil his pants if a jet airplane goes overhead. Oops. He should get over that in a few years. Guess I need more practice messing with people's memories.

One thing they don't tell you about flying 350 miles an hour as a topless woman... stuff flaps around. Feels like an air elemental is trying to rip my boobs off. Maybe I ought to reevaluate my contempt for bras, or at least start wearing a racerback under my uniform polo for situations like this. Meh. Having to fly unexpectedly while at work isn't the issue. It's the long distance pushing me up to maximum speed. The rarity of me needing to fly interstate on a whim is definitely not worth putting up with tit prisons.

I'd fully shift to armor, but if my phone's inside Natalie's amulet, it won't ring should Lieutenant Sims call. Having to be available for him ordering me back to Philly to deal with a fire call didn't leave me much choice but to take my shirt off and fly topless, leaving my pants (and pocket containing my phone) in the real world. Ever wonder why those baroque paintings of angels are always boobs out? This is why. Wings. All those loose, flowing garments they wear don't stay on too well during high speed flight.

Oh, another thing Dad mentioned—the whole deal with religious people being so uptight about nudity? Shaar'Nath did it to mess with the Elestari, who—way back in the day—wandered among humans without even bothering to summon those little ribbon wraps. A bunch of whispering in the right place convinced a bunch of humans to consider exposure somehow 'sinful.' Wow, humans can be gullible. Right? If they're so proud of their mythological creator, why hide his 'greatest work?' It would be like Rafael or Michelangelo keeping their art under sheets, too embarrassed to let anyone see it. Yeah, making humans horrified at the sight of their own bodies cramped our style a little, too, but they considered it worth it to watch the stuck up prick Elestari complain. Religion had been their way to weaponize humans against us, so they had to play along with it.

Supposedly, every Shaar'Nath has the ability to fog humans' minds and memories. Only a handful of Elestari can use the necessary magic to do the same. But again, we're psychic, they're not. I just need a little more practice fiddling around with memories—and hopefully figure out how to do so without inserting random crippling phobias. And sure, their magic can be way more powerful than anything I'll ever be able to do, but whatever. I never wanted power at all—only to have a good time and not be bored. So what if I'll never reshape continents or call down a bombardment of flaming meteors.

Now, if anyone's got a spell to summon a limitless supply of perfect grade-A kush, then I'd be jealous.

I haul ass to the northeast.

Locating the Raritan River isn't too difficult despite me never having been in the area before. It's kinda large. The giant ball of orange fire at the bottom of a miles-high plume of black smoke is a bit of a beacon as well. It's burning at the center of a field of fluid storage tanks, twelve big white ones in two groups of six, a row of five smaller ones north of them, and a cluster of smaller green tanks to the right. The central group of six tanks is ablaze, two of them ruptured. In their energy form, my eyes pierce easily through smoke and flames to the twisted metal beneath. Melt lines look more like a high-energy laser beam hit the tanks than lightning, slicing them open.

Tons of fire crews scramble to contain the blaze to the tank farm. Battling a fire like this is mostly a war of waiting. Provide support to the surrounding area and try to keep the flames from spreading, but short of magic, there's little to be done to stop huge tanks of oil, gasoline or whatever from burning themselves out. Throwing too much foam into the area will raise the fluid level inside the earth retaining walls and let the flaming petroleum seep out into the river—or streets.

I don't see anyone down there in the midst of it. Then again, the fire is so hot, any person trapped in among the tanks would've been vaporized long before I got here. The big threat is the heat reaching the point nearby tanks blow up, too.

Four fireboats on the river throw water on the adjacent tanks as well as properties. A helicopter appears to be trying to go in close enough for some Hydromancers to help. Maybe they're hoping to freeze the oil. Even mages have to know throwing water on a fire like this is a bad idea. They're flying low, close to the fire, not paying any attention to me circling around higher up.

A loud, avian screech from ground level draws my attention two lots left of the burning tanks to a giant paved area filled with rows and rows of tanker trailers. A group of eight people surround an enormous bird trapped under a glowing blue magical net. Strands of pale blue energy run from the hands of two people, empowering the spell pinning the creature down despite its thrashing.

It's somewhere between an eagle and hawk in terms of appearance, mostly white, with a blue head and tail, blue along the front edge of its wings, and a bit of red on the back behind the head as well as the pinfeathers. It's most obvious abnormal feature are the four long streamer feathers extending from the tail, all dark blue. Wait, I take it back. It's most abnormal feature is being the size of a Leer jet. This bird's lustrous sapphire blue beak is big enough to swallow a human whole.

Makes sense to me now why only two tanks suffered strikes. Those mages must have gotten here fast enough to stop its attack from progressing. Pretty damn impressive they managed to ground and contain it. Wonder if they're Academy arcane detectives, FBI, local cops, or civilians who happened to be close enough.

The bird screeches again, the wind blast from its beak knocking over two of the people in front of it. Sparks crackle over their clothes. It pivots its head toward one of the mages trapping it.

A concussive *boom* like a naval cannon firing accompanies a lightning bolt flying from the beak. The mage offers zero resistance to the electrical blast, which passes through him and slices six or seven empty tanker trailers in half. Only a set of charred footprints remains of the guy.

Wow. Sucks to be him. I'm pretty casual about stuff, but in most cases, random animal murder bugs me. Like, seeing a guy French kiss a speeding bus is hilarious. But a cat or dog being hurt? Yeah, *no bueno*. However, in this case, it's really damn obvious these idiots should not have tried to live-capture the enormous monster to study it.

The second mage screams and runs for her life—good plan. Like a neon sign shorting out, the magical net flickers a few times, then dies. As soon as the binding force is gone, the giant bird shoves itself up to stand, thrusting its wings out. People go rolling like tumbleweeds when it flaps downward, launching itself into the air. Tiny arcs of lightning crackle over its feathers.

Damn. So tempting to forget everything and resume ignoring this as not my problem. Not feeling too confident in my armor protecting me from a lightning bolt so big. The heat won't bother me, but I'm not immune to electrocution.

So, yeah. I'm not interested in taking a crash course in wrestling lightning chickens. This critter looks like a thunderbird, but I didn't think they got *this* big. Confronting this thing directly far exceeds my motivation to involve myself here. However, if it's maybe under the control of a mage, I can follow it hoping to find them. Assuming, of course, there *is* a person behind it. Seems a bit odd for magical animals to selectively target environmentally unfriendly places to burn down. Like they said on the news, it has to be an eco-terrorist mage. Or, probably is. I vaguely remember reading somewhere about Native Americans regarding the thunderbirds as something akin to gods. If this is truly some ancient power waking up and sending the birds to give humanity a spanking, yeah, totally over my head. I'm gonna follow the bird. If it leads to a human giving it orders, then I'll consider doing something. If this thing is a primal god sent by the Earth to give us a message, yeah, my ass is going home.

If the birds themselves are making this call, even more so not my problem.

Dicking around with demigods isn't in my job description.

Though, given what I know about the outer workings of the universe, there shouldn't really be anything like a demigod or god out there. There might be entities with magical powers, but calling them gods/demigods is a bit of a stretch. If an isolated tribal human society still in the 'spears and loincloths' stage of development sees someone using modern technology, they'd probably consider them a god. Same sort of situation. A modern mage sees a being of significantly more power, they think 'must be a god.'

Right. Not going to sky joust the electric turkey. Only follow it.

Looks like the bird's lost interest in continuing to blast tanks apart and wants to get out of here before another net happens. I know how you feel, bud. Every time my ass ended up in a holding cell, I couldn't wait to get the hell away from cops.

The bird's pretty damn fast, too. Faster than I can go, but it's not exactly vanishing into a smear of red, white, and blue. It's also oblivious to me or unconcerned about my presence, ignoring me to fly west. I climb higher, pushing myself hard, probably close to 400 MPH. It's not so important to keep up with this thing if I can see where it eventually lands.

A low, rumbling peal of thunder slides off the bird's wings. I'm fairly certain it didn't break the sound barrier as it hasn't left me *way* behind. It's still pulling away, though. All I have to do is keep it in sight to get a rough idea of where it's going.

And... it vanishes in a blue flash.

Shit!

Wormholes? Really? Did the stupid thing teleport on me?

I'm sure some people in New Jersey are wondering why Spanish swearing is falling from the sky. Stupid zap-pigeon. This whole trip was an enormous waste of time. At least Lieutenant Sims hasn't called yet. Nothing more for me to do here. The local fire crews have the site as contained as it can get. One more firefighter visiting from Philly with no equipment other than being immune to fire won't matter. The only thing they can do at this point is wait it out... or maybe call in a Pyromancer to attempt unsummoning the fire. They generally don't like doing it. Much more difficult than making it... you know the whole destruction is simpler than creation deal.

Is there some piece to this I'm not seeing? What does the universe expect me to do to a thunderbird? Sure, I could probably kill one by ambush. My tail blade is totally enough to stab it in the head. If it sees me coming, though, my ass is done. One way ticket to Imbreleth for me. Nah, bird murder doesn't feel right.

Oh, dammit. I keep saying how much I like it here and don't want to destroy the world. Did the world hear me and ask for help? Shit! I meant it in a 'not doing anything bad' sense, not a 'run around doing nice things' way. I've got stuff to do, sofas to sit on, time to waste. Even a little Mini-Me I should probably be out looking for.

This crap isn't my problem.

Okay, maybe I have a kid neighbor who needs a little assist from time to time, too. As a former poor kid, helping Ash and her mom doesn't bother me. Back in the trailer park, I never messed with other people in our financial situation. We're all in the mess together. Well, except for the one or two nosy ones who kept calling social services on me whenever I had a clothing optional day or Mom let me stay home alone a little too young. I might've pranked them a few times. Also, this guy Mr. Kunkler, who all the kids started calling Fuckler once we hit our tweens and discovered foul language. I messed with him big time. Almost got him sent to jail for growing weed. He's a complete asshole to everyone. Anyway, people at the trailer park didn't like calling the cops for various reasons. I mean, an e-meth lab exploded two spaces over from my childhood home if it's any indication of why the residents wanted cops to stay away.

Anyway... time to get back to the office.

So frustrating.

14

WILD THUNDERBIRD CHASE

Inconspicuousness seems to be working for me.

Growing up as a mischievous kid, I'd always had an easy time slipping into or out of places unnoticed or avoiding being caught. Except for situations like the one at the abandoned department store where I crawled out a hole a bunch of cops already focused on. Lately, wanting people around me not to notice me appears to be having a supernatural effect on their minds. Maybe my immature subconscious tapped a little into the same power to help me hide. When I consciously *try* to do it now, I can walk right past someone and they act like I'm not there. The more trust placed in the ability, the more thoroughly it seems to work. Guess 'demonic' powers are like most other things in the world—confidence makes all the difference.

I concentrate on wanting to remain unnoticed as the firehouse comes into view below.

My father managed to prevent an entire city block from noticing me rip Frank to shreds in the alley and subsequently burn him to a cinder. Being a Shaar'Nath—or half of one—is more than wings and having a little more strength than the average human. Our mental power doesn't so much affect reality as it warps the minds of people in my vicinity. No, guy with a Starbucks cup and a ridiculous hipster hat, you did not just see a topless woman with wings fly over you and disappear behind the firehouse.

I can do this.

Herlihy is standing outside in the tiny lot behind the station, vaping. He doesn't look up at me, despite a leathery flutter... so I risk it and drop down to land maybe fifteen feet away from him. Neither my giant wings nor my not so giant boobs—hey they're respectable, just not huge—appear to register to him. In fact, he appears oblivious to my entire presence. I wave at him. No reaction, so I test even further by jiggling the girls at him. Still, no reaction. Okay, gotta be careful. As long as my mind remains focused on *not* wanting to be noticed, it seems to be working. Too much 'hey check me out' might break the effect.

No, I didn't want him to see me, merely testing.

I pull the wings in, slip my polo shirt back on, and hurry in the door. Once in the hallway, I stop wanting to be inconspicuous. As a test, I poke my head out back.

Herlihy looks at me right away.

"Hey, Brian. Sims around?"

"Yeah. In his office, I think. What's up?"

"Nothing. Just got back from an errand. Wanted to let him know I'm here. Anything happen?"

"Been quiet."

"Cool."

I duck back inside, close the door, and stare in awe at myself. Whoa. I totally made someone *not* see me. To get completely technical, he probably *did* see me; his brain disregarded the information coming from his eyes. Oh, the shoplifting I could've gotten away with as a kid if I knew this was possible. Oh, the shoplifting I could get away with now...

Greedy weasel hands last only a few seconds before I think about cameras.

Hmm. This requires testing.

Not now, though.

I head to the LT's office, explain what happened, and try to keep him from freaking out too much over having an enormous avian arsonist running around. Unlike what some of the world's hardcore mages would prefer, technology does exist. A few more thunderbird attacks and it's almost guaranteed the military will get involved. Missiles have a way longer reach than bird lightning.

After I'm done with Sims, it's time to conduct a little test. Before 'Inconspicuousness' can let me take liberties with wings and flying, it needs to prove itself in a situation where the consequences for being caught won't include reclassification as another life form and the potential loss of my job, life, apartment, and pretty much everything.

Streaking seems like the perfect combination of 'people will *definitely* react' and relatively minor consequences. A walk to Starbucks and back is quick enough for me to get out of sight before the police show up—assuming anyone sees me and bothers to call them. They know how guys in uniform can get, so it should be super easy to charm them into thinking I'd been the victim of a bet or dare and everyone will laugh it off.

I head to the locker room, strip, and stash my stuff in a locker. After a moment to focus on my desire to remain supernaturally inconspicuous, I pad out the door and make my way to the front of the garage. O'Keefe and Humberto are polishing the pipe caps on our main pumper truck. Neither of them look up as I go by. At the giant doors, I peer out at the street. A moderate amount of people walk or drive back and forth, not one of them appears to notice a naked woman standing in the firehouse garage door. Okay, here goes.

Acting as normal as can be, I walk the few blocks to the Starbucks and go in, looking around the whole time to see if anyone is staring or trying to take pictures. People don't react or even glance briefly at me, even when I open the door at the Starbucks and walk in. Despite it being afternoon, the place has a respectable line waiting. Not here to get coffee, so no big deal. However, I can't resist another test—me and my impulse control problem, right? I grab a bag of café Verona beans and stand there holding it. No one pays any attention to what might be a bag of coffee floating in the air. Oh, this is pretty damn cool. They still don't react when I walk out the door carrying it.

On the walk back to the firehouse, I hum the *James Bond* theme. This girl has a 'license to steal.' Oh yeah. Grinning like a fool, I return to the station and put my uniform back on. The coffee can wait in my locker until my shift is over. Score one bag of java.

Awesomesauce. If I can streak three blocks, blatantly shoplift a sack of coffee, and casually walk back with my ill-gotten gains, it's pretty much a given I can stop people from seeing my wings. Maybe I've been overly afraid of being caught. Provided nothing knocks me unconscious—or I don't forget to turn on 'inconspicuousness,' there shouldn't be any problems. Sounds like I don't really need a car after all. Just as well. Compared to insurance companies, I'm not even close to being a thief. My larcenous acts are mostly petty and don't hurt anyone.

The rest of the afternoon passes in quiet. No fires. No cats up trees. No overweight people stuck on their toilet bowls. If my imaginary version of Serena Miller the magic crystal vendor is to be believed, me finally showing some effort toward the lightning attacks is the reason the universe isn't throwing a week full of nasty fires at us. Do I think so? No. It would imply genuine sentience on the part of the universe, as well as me being significant enough to warrant its attention. Though I often blame 'the universe' for stuff, I'm only venting, not seriously feeling victimized by a sentient cosmos.

As George from *Dead Like Me* might say, the universe has a fuck-with-me gun and it's not afraid to use it.

The second my shift is over, I snag my coffee, run out back, and think about not being noticed. This time, I let Natalie's amulet eat my uniform and wear the illusionary fancy 'goth faerie' outfit she designed. Basically, a frilly sparkle-goth dress with fancy lace bits and brocade on the chest. More than a touch girlier than anything I'd choose, but Nat's kinda teasing me. Only real weakness with the fake outfit is, despite appearing to wear shit-kicker boots, I leave bare footprints. However, ninety-nine percent of people are way too preoccupied to notice.

I really owe her big time for this necklace. Makes flying so much easier and cheaper. Clothing gets expensive to replace, especially fire department gear. The necklace will even 'absorb' an air tank and mask if I happen to full shift while wearing them.

Speaking of Natalie, her shop is my destination. She's my go-to source for all things weird and magical. I once suggested she name her store 'All Things Weird and Magical' but she decided to go boring with 'Enchanted Evenings.' Sounds like a dating service if you ask me. She'd probably get more business if she gave her store a better name.

I swing by Reanimator Coffee a few doors up the street from her place, and grab a couple mocha lattes. Sure, I'm carrying a sack of Starbucks beans, but brewing it takes effort. When I enter the enchant shop, Nat is not-quite-arguing with a nasal-voiced woman who's trying to convince her to make an enchanted item to silence her two children. The boys, who appear to be around nine and eleven, are presently in the 'kid' section playing with magic toys. Okay, they're chatty and seem to be stuck constantly yelling more than talking, but welcome to being around kids. They make noise. They create random strange odors. They devour food like locust plagues. At least they've both outgrown the worst part. Babies are basically miniature Winston Churchills prone to random explosions of poop or barf. And seriously, this woman should be glad she has loud sons. The quiet ones are more dangerous. Most of my teachers before fifth grade wanted to put bells on me.

Probably because I took great delight in sneaking up on them. All I'd do was say 'hi' or something benign, but they'd almost always scream and nearly faint.

Natalie smiles at me when I set her coffee down and lean on the counter, waiting. Predictably, Natalie flat out refuses to make a 'mute button' for the boys since if something bad happened, it would prevent them from shouting for help. She finally convinces the kids' mother to accept a bracelet *she* can wear to prevent her from hearing the boys yell. Or maybe tone them down to normal volume. She requests a bit of hair from each child to work into the enchantment, which the mother obligingly provides.

The woman pays a deposit, buys a couple ever-bouncing balls for the boys, and leaves.

Natalie side-eyes the door. "I'm going to build in a strong zap."

"Zap?" I raise both eyebrows.

"Yeah. The bracelet's going to shock the crap out of her if the boys are in danger. She freakin' wanted me to make lockable bracelets the boys couldn't take off to keep them silent. Seriously. What is wrong with people?"

"Too much to talk about. Oh, consider yourself the recipient of a long, hot lesbian kiss."

She blinks, then laughs. "Umm, okay."

"That's how grateful I am for this necklace. Since we're not in romantic love with each other, my gesture of overwhelming appreciation is imaginary."

"Right. I thought you messed around?"

"You should know by now the scope of things I'd do on a whim 'just to see what it's like' is vast."

She blinks. "You've fooled around with another girl?"

"No, but you know me. I'd probably give it a whirl at least once for the hell of it."

"Umm, Brook, there are other ways to show gratitude. Like covering dinner."

I wave her off. "Told you, I'm already going to do that."

"So you'd try *anything* once?"

"More or less." I sip my coffee. "What are you thinking?"

She leans back, eyebrows up. "Only theoretically. You'd try like bestiality?"

"Nah." I am a master at keeping my revulsion out of my facial expression. In truth, there are many things I won't try. Bestiality is one of them. "Closest to it I'd be willing to attempt is a puck... but I'm in a committed relationship now, so goat boy has to wait."

Natalie laughs.

"Hey, question?"

She takes the lid off her coffee, sips it, and ends up with a spot of whip cream on her nose. "What's up?"

"How much do you know about thunderbirds?"

"Umm. Not too much. Why?"

After hopping up to sit on the counter, I tell her about the fire in Jersey.

"Whoa. I didn't think they got so large. Sec." She sets her coffee down and runs into the back room.

I gaze around at shelves full of random enchanted objects she's made to sell. The store is the sort of place my mother would've regretted bringing me to as a small kid. I'd have touched *everything*… and probably tried to steal something. No, not the remote-control magic faeries. Femmy-cute was never my thing. Maybe one of the illusory toy laser guns. Still think those are asking for trouble. Sure they look ridiculous and nothing like any real weapon, but they create fake energy bolts—totally unrealistic as lasers go—convincing enough to scare a high-strung cop. Of course, the beams don't do anything, being illusions. Actually, I probably would have stolen one of the prank items. She's got trinkets to create fart sounds at a distance, trip charms, a sack of marbles enchanted to return to the bag on command. Perfect for throwing into a crowded hallway, making a whole bunch of people fall, and pulling them out of sight before anyone notices what happened.

Maybe Nat has a bit more of a mischievous streak than her 'good girl' personality lets on.

"Found it," singsongs Natalie. She emerges from the office—whip cream no longer on her nose—carrying a large book, sets it on the counter next to me, and opens to a drawing of a thunderbird.

"They're native to the American Southwest. Some traditions believe they are guardians of an 'upper world' responsible for protecting humans from an entity known as the Great Horned Serpent who dwells in the lower world. They attributed thunder to these birds flapping their wings, and lightning storms meant the birds were at war against these serpents."

"So they're a myth?" I ask. "A story made up to explain weather? I freakin' saw one."

"No… they exist, but they're not celestial guardians as far as this says." She points at a passage. "Here, it describes the Ojibwe people as believing they punish humans for being evil."

I chuckle. "Blowing up chemical plants, lumber mills, petroleum refineries... someone might argue they *are* punishing us."

"Hmm. Maybe, but it's one legend from one group. The AMS regards them as a class 3 dangerous entity, but yellow-coded since they aren't believed to initiate aggression against people."

"AMS?"

"American Magizoological Society. You went to high school, right?"

"If you mean physically occupying space in one for four years, yeah."

She nudges me. "You couldn't have been too big a failure. You got into college—and graduated."

"How dangerous is 'class 3?' Doesn't mean much to me."

"Most stuff really capable of causing destruction ends up there. Dragons are the only creatures in class 2."

"Hmm. Do I want to know what they consider 'class 1' threats?"

Natalie makes 'ticking off' gestures on her fingers. "One Direction, Justin Beiber..."

I laugh, setting her off into giggles.

"Okay, but seriously? What's a class 1 magical threat?"

She wipes laugh tears from her face. "Nothing anyone has seen yet. City-destroying stuff like forty-foot-tall fire giants or maybe demigods."

"Godzilla?"

"If it existed, yeah, probably."

"Okay so..." I lean over to read the page a bit. Looks like the thunderbirds are usually about ten feet long from nose to tail, not counting the trailing ribbon feathers. "The one in Jersey was significantly bigger."

"Yeah, you said Leer jet sized?" She taps a finger to her chin. "The one you saw is either a never-before-observed giant thunderbird, or a conjuration. Since these creatures don't usually live in the northeast, my money's on a conjuration."

"Is there anything in there about the birds being able to teleport or go through wormholes?"

"No. I guess if you want to believe in the Native folklore, they'd be able to gate themselves back and forth between the 'upper world' and our world, but the way you described it sounds to me like a conjured creature running out of time."

"Running out of time?" I slug a few gulps of coffee.

She nods. "Yeah. Every spell lasts only so long before it's done. Spells aren't like enchanted items. Cast a firebolt, it exists for a second or three and it's gone. A conjuration is similar, but they hang around for quite a bit longer than a few seconds. Maybe an hour, two? Depends on the skill and power of the mage. A conjuration would also not be limited by reality. Someone could conjure a mouse as big as a car. Your giant thunderbird could be huge because the person who conjured it has never seen a real one or wanted it to be extra impressive."

"Hmm. So you think the douche on TV is right?"

She laughs. "Can you be more specific? There's a lot of douches on television."

"Uhh, that Sidney Stafford guy."

"Oh." She snarls. "He is such an asshole. He and his pack of bigots are constantly trying to make life difficult for mages. You know more people every year are hurt or killed by technological inventions than enchantments? Something like two percent of fatalities and seven percent of injuries are from enchanted objects, compared to machines. And most of those cases are from people deliberately using the item incorrectly. It's more likely a person is going to die to an 'otter related fatality' than an enchanted item, yet this moron wants to regulate and tax enchanters into the ground. They're not going to be happy until they make magic illegal."

I laugh. "Wait, there's seriously a category for 'otter related fatalities?'"

She nods. "Yeah. I'm being serious."

"Wow."

"Cows, too. They kill more humans than enchanted items." She grabs her hair in both hands. "Do you have any idea how much effort I put into making sure the stuff I make is safe? *Especially* any item a kid's going to be near."

"Don't worry about it. Magic has been around since way before technology. Everyone knows FRUM are fringe lunatics."

"Hope so." She folds her arms, looking down.

"Aww." I rub her shoulder. "So, basically, we've got an eco-terrorist mage conjuring these thunderbirds as a war on the oil industry and shit?"

"Yeah. Kinda sounds like it to me. Or we're dealing with a worm-hole-diving giant thunderbird no one has ever seen or documented before."

I exhale hard. "Hearing it in those words does make it sound kind of unlikely. You're right. It's probably a mage conjuring them."

She nods while sipping her mocha.

"Any idea how to find this mage?"

"Umm..." Natalie gives me side eye. "When did you decide to go vigilante?"

"Heh." I tilt my head back, gazing at the ceiling while swinging my feet side to side. "This limp little thing inside me masquerading as a conscience is Mom's doing. And I'm not 'going vigilante.' You can't blow up oil refineries or chemical plants and not eventually kill people. I'm supposed to put out fires, right? Slapping an arsonist around *before* he starts another blaze is technically fighting fires."

"Not sure the police would agree with you, even if you're techni-cally correct." She grins.

I look over at her. "So, can you find this mage?"

"I'm an enchanter, Brook." She huffs. "I don't really do immediate magic."

"I know, I know... but you're an actual mage. Way closer than I am to this stuff."

She paces, tapping her fingers on the coffee cup. "Not really sure how to go about tracing the origin of a summoned creature. It's nothing I've ever even thought about doing before."

"Do you *have* to do the scrying thing or cast a spell in real time?

Maybe you could enchant your way through it. Make an item to track the source?"

"Huh… possible. Can you give me a couple days to see if I can come up with something?"

"You are awesome."

She faces me and bows, smiling broadly. "At least you think so."

"Psh. You are. Oh, did I tell you? Ashley found out the hard way why not to put Chinese food in a rune oven."

"Oh, no!" Natalie cringes. "Is she okay? Please tell me they let a Lifemage fix her and she doesn't have to endure skin grafts."

"No… only lo mein, not General Tso's."

"Whew…" Natalie slouches.

"Her rune oven, too. Not mine."

"She *obviously* didn't use your oven. Pennsylvania still exists." Natalie biffs herself in the forehead. "I keep forgetting to get over there and fix it for you."

I raise an eyebrow. "So you think it's a sketchy oven and not merely proximity to my messed up aura? Didn't you like call me a vortex magnet for screwy energy?"

"It's a theory. You *do* have a cheap rune oven. Might be more susceptible to interference from your unique nature than a good one."

"Came with the apartment." I shrug. "Everything about the place is cheap except the rent."

An agitated man in his mid-forties runs in the door and rushes up to the counter, gives me a passing glance, then points at Natalie. "There's something wrong with it."

I glance at his crotch. "You're not in the right place, dude."

Natalie picks up her Augur tablet—a slab of pinkish crystal framed in decorative gold filigree, basically the enchanted version of an iPad. It emits faint bell chimes and puffs of light as she taps the 'screen.' "One second…"

The man fidgets, glancing at me again.

"Nat, when did you start making sex toys?"

The guy coughs. "Uhh… no. Not here about that."

"Could've fooled me. Why are you so embarrassed?" I ask.

"Dabbled with them a couple months ago," says Natalie, completely serious. Not sure if she's messing with me or actually *is* making enchanted bedroom products. "Aha, Mr. Gates?"

"Yeah," says the man.

"Oh, you got the paperless self-cleaning commode. What's the problem?"

He twitches. "It *licked* me."

Ack. "Right. I'm out." I slide off the counter. "Got stuff to do. Call ya later, Nat."

Natalie blinks at him. "It's supposed to. Why do you think it's paperless?"

Fingers in my ears, I hurry out the door.

15

FAMILIAR HAUNT

I t's tempting to fly around aimlessly searching for Mini-Me, but
also probably futile.

No idea why she's gnawing on the back of my mind. I've
never had the least bit of interest in Zen or meditation. Why do I have
this sudden urge to find myself? By now, the kid has to have been
picked up by the cops, caught by the warmongers, or something. If a
creep who wanted to harm her had the misfortune of trying to grab
her, the news would surely have run a story about a mangled corpse
found somewhere near small bloody footprints.

But, nothing.

It's as though Philadelphia merely swallowed her and any memory
of her ever existing.

On one hand, it's amusing to picture Melisandre storming around
pissed off about another plan failing. But I can't stop worrying maybe
they *did* catch her and simply decided to leave Ashley and me trapped
in the warehouse for a while. They likely wouldn't mistreat Mini-Me
beyond the cruelty of bringing her up to hate the physical world. My
mother always used to say no child is born bad; they're a product of
their environment.

I kinda disagree. At least to a point. Brooklyn Amari—hi, me—was definitely born highly mischievous, if not 'bad' per se. Guess Mom had a point, though. If not for her, I'd surely be in prison by now. Without her influence, I'd be indifferent to human life and a complete slave to my impulsiveness. It's doubtful I'd have turned into a psycho killer, but if someone got in my way, it wouldn't bug me to off them.

Okay, admittedly, it *still* doesn't really bother me to kill people, but at least I make an effort to only throw assholes under literal buses. Mom got me to be selective in my indifference. It's also completely her fault I'm chasing thunderbirds. She's a big proponent of signs and patterns. Her 'second life' working as an author, mystic, and fortune-teller is a weird experience. She's a legit mage, if only a luminare. Her ability to see visions or get insight into people's lives and circumstances is real. No charlatanry here for money. No, the weird part comes into play in her devotion to mythology. She thinks 'god' is real. Buys into the whole angels, demons, God and Satan thing completely. I'd say the trappings of her mysticism look like the occultist-slash-Satanic stuff she's supposed to hate, but there's a reason they look alike.

Awhile back, the mages and the Church got into a spat. Talking like the year 1200 or so. So some of them started regarding magical symbols and practices as 'the tools of the Devil' in an attempt to make war on the mages. Reminds me a lot of Sidney Stafford and his 'Foundation for the Responsible Use of Magic.' If you ask me, both the Church and ol' Sid are totally jealous.

Anyway, Mom somehow has no problem blending supposedly 'evil' practices into her religious outlook. She blames a schism in the Church for creating a 'false evil' meaning to symbols once used for good reasons. My mother sees cosmic patterns and, in her opinion, the way I keep happening to walk into rooms right as the news cuts to a story about these fires means 'god' wants me to do something about it.

No, I didn't talk to her about this. Merely imagining how she'd react.

The reason I haven't talked to her is mostly because she'd say something about the 'man upstairs,' and I'd be too tempted to ask why a being like her god with supposedly unlimited power needs people to do anything at all. Requiring human agents to act on his behalf is the exact opposite of limitless power. Unless he simply wants to watch us jump through hoops like pet hamsters. Either way, as far as I know, no greater powers exist. And if they do, they have much better things to worry about than the goings-on down here.

I end up deciding against going on a random, fruitless flight in search of Mini-Me and spend the night flopped on the couch nursing vague feelings of guilt and resentment.

Tonight feels like a PlayStation night. *Gods of War* time.

Whoever invented video games must have had a kid like me. The only thing more effective than a holding cell at the police station to keep me out of trouble was a PlayStation 2. Totally ironic I stole it, right? Not this one. My PS4 is paid for honestly. No way in hell could my mother have afforded to buy me a PS2 back then. Like I said, telekinesis was the absolute bomb for shoplifting.

Wham!

A heavy thud comes from Tracy's apartment. Great. Please tell me she doesn't have another asshole boyfriend. I'd almost gotten used to the lack of MMA tournaments every night.

"Ashley Marie!" shouts Tracy, sounding exasperated.

I know I'm twenty-three, an adult, living on my own, and in possession of a legit job. I also know Tracy Harper is only four years older than me. Nowhere near old enough to be my mother. However, hearing her use Ashley's middle name makes me tense up. My mother never raised her voice at me in anger, but whenever she used my middle name, Hope, I knew I'd crossed a line.

"Sorry!" yells Ashley. Rapid thudding of a small person running across the next door apartment follows.

"Why is there ketchup all over the kitchen floor?" yells Tracy.

"I was trying to summon the little Brooklyn back here. Big Brooklyn's worried about her."

I simultaneously choke up a bit and chuckle. Aww.

Tracy emits a resigned groan. "You made a ritual circle out of ketchup? Why?"

"Umm. 'Cause we don't have any strawberry pancake syrup left."

Hah!

Okay, Tracy merely slipped and landed on her ass. No domestic violence is going on. Whew.

Courtesy of this place's super thin walls, I eavesdrop on Ashley explaining her reasons for making a ten-foot-wide circle of condiments on the kitchen floor. She found some how-to guides online for basic summoning and figured she could get Mini-Me to appear 'so she didn't have to be out there in the cold all alone.'

Again, aww.

She's not still out there. She can't be.

Even a half Shaar'Nath kid couldn't spend days on their own outside. No matter if she managed to find food and protect herself, eventually someone's going to call the police about a kid streaking around. Philly people are notoriously good at minding their own business, but some situations invite action. Car accidents, burning buildings, street mimes, and so on.

Unless... could she be doing the 'don't notice me' trick? Mental powers are as intrinsic to Shaar'Nath as greed is to humans. At her age, the simple desire not to be found might automatically translate to action. The only reason I need to actively concentrate on using a mental power is newness. A child first learning to walk thinks about where to put their feet. I don't have to focus on walking anymore... unless I've had a few too many. To her, 'inconspicuousness' might be reflexive and she doesn't even realize she's doing it. And heck, it probably *did* work for me as a kid in a much less obvious way than now.

Makes me feel a little better.

I burn the night playing video games and trying to convince myself I don't feel bad for sitting here doing nothing. A little after ten, I get a weird craving for a donut. Guess it means I'm anxious about something. Drat. Going to Kwan's requires moving off the couch. And dammit, I need to go back to the DMV, too. Hopefully, my paperwork didn't get destroyed. The woman who took it spent about forty-nine minutes polymorphed into a cockatrice. Knowing my luck, my documents ended up in an enormous pile of bird droppings. If some dickhead in a polo shirt insists on me retaking the test, they are getting mentally toyed with.

Not one to ignore random impulses, I pause *Gods of War*. While I could 'inconspicuous' my way to Kwan's half dressed, it's mentally tiring and I'm already a little dazed. Need a bit more than a long T-shirt to go outside, so I throw on a skirt and flip-flops. The convenience store is only three blocks away, so I end up walking past the usual assortment of locals, most going on about their night. A few 'tough guys' at the corner check me out, but keep quiet. They still haven't figured out I'm responsible for smashing the one guy's car and starting a fight a few weeks ago, but Marco has seen me let the crazy out once or twice. Donny, our local source for various recreational substances, gives me a dirty look. Apparently, working for the fire department is almost as good as being a cop to him. Would probably blow his mind if I hit him up for some pot or E, but doing so would guarantee Sims announces a random screening the next day.

One guy at the first corner looks at me. The instant we make eye contact, his intention to rush me, knock me into the street, and run off with my purse is as obvious as a billboard sign. As soon as he pushes away from the wall to start his attack run, I casually use telekinesis to redirect him—adding a little speed—into the path of an oncoming, somewhat battered, Impala.

The car's only doing like thirty-five, so the collision doesn't kill the guy. He bounces off the hood, rolls over a few times, and lays there moaning.

A pudgy middle-aged man with slicked-back thinning hair jumps out and yells, "You stupid bastard! The hell you doin' jumping the fuck out inta traffic?"

Whistling, I do the Philly thing and mind my own business, continuing right on by as though I had nothing whatsoever to do with it.

Two blocks later, I near Kwan's Market, but stop short at the sight of a police car parked right in front of the place. Chill, Brook. I'm not up to anything. I'm a respectable—lol—firefighter and no longer a juvenile delinquent. No reason at all for me to have a flinch reaction to the sight of cops.

I take another few steps before I notice the bottom panel of the glass door is missing. Aha. Someone must have broken into Kwan's while it was closed. Explains the cops. Still, kinda weird they're here so late in the day. I'd assume the break-in happened hours ago at like three in the morning. This place is open super early, like five or so. Then again, lots of bad shit happens around here, so if he called it in to get a police report, they'd have taken their sweet time showing up. No one's life is in actual danger.

Acting casual, I walk into the store past a pile of swept-up glass shards and go over to the coffee station. Kwan's old school. He doesn't believe in any of the sissy, hipster 'fresh coffee every twenty minutes' nonsense. This pot's been sitting here for at least an hour. Coffee isn't coffee without the essence of scorched souls.

Not wanting to be up all damn night, I grab a small cup. It's a bit late for coffee, but I'm going to have a donut and there are cops here. If I try to eat a donut without java, they'll ticket me for breaking the law. Speaking of the police, they're in the process of taking a statement from Mr. Kwan about the break-in. Sounds like a weird robbery.

The window apparently broke itself. Some of the cooler case doors opened and shut on their own as a plastic bag floated around the store collecting sandwiches, microwave chicken sandwiches, and snacks. When the bag went toward the door, a box of Hostess cupcakes floated up off the shelf and followed it.

No money, cigarettes, or any 'high value' items walked away.

Something tells me *I* robbed Kwan's. Or at least the small version of me running around the city did. Seems our ability to remove ourselves from awareness works on cameras, too. Hmm. When the cops ask Mr. Kwan to show them the surveillance video, I get curious.

He shouts in Korean. A moment later, his wife hurries out from a back room to watch the register. As Mr. Kwan leads the police through the same door, I concentrate on wanting to be inconspicuous... and slow walk after them.

Mrs. Kwan doesn't look up at me or notice the swinging door

squeaking open. Three steps into a hallway heavy with the fragrance of cleaning products, I slip partially into the world's tiniest office. One green steel desk in the corner is stacked high with manila folders and paperwork around a computer. A file cabinet against the white cinderblocks behind him is also piled almost to the ceiling with papers. Above the desk, a wooden shelf bows under the weight of multiple three-ring binders, as if it's inches from collapse. Three adult men take up all the unused space in there, forcing me to remain in the doorway.

However, none of them notice me.

Alas, I am five-foot-nothing.

I plant my left foot on a stack of bottled water cases, grab the doorjamb on either side, and pull myself up to peer over the cops' shoulders.

Mr. Kwan opens the security feed on the computer. It takes him a moment to pull up the file from last night, fast-forward to 2:27 a.m., and hit play. A minute into the video, Mini-Me walks up to the door. She's still wearing only her wings, horns, and tail—plus a coating of dirt—but appears to be unhurt and calm. Neither Mr. Kwan nor the police show any sign of having noticed her on the video. The cops are still staring at the monitor like they're watching a ghost recording, waiting for the subtle weird thing to happen.

"Four seconds," whispers Mr. Kwan.

Mini-Me tugs on the door handle, finding it locked. She frowns, makes the same face I always make when an inanimate object pisses me off, then stabs her tail into the lower glass panel, shattering it. The cops jump. The kid version of me swishes her tail blade around the opening to clear away glass before ducking through, careful not to step on anything sharp. She goes straight for the register area to swipe an empty plastic bag before running around filling it with sandwiches from the refrigerated cabinets as well as a few bags of snack chips. On her way out, she casually impales a box of cupcakes from a shelf, lifting and carrying it on the end of her tail out the door.

"Crap," says the older cop. "Guess poltergeists are real."

"Why would ghosts steal food?" The other cop scratches his forehead. "Thought poltergeists just toss shit around randomly to make a mess. Someone or something wanted food."

"Gremlin? Shield's been iffy lately. Had a cockatrice on a city bus not too long ago."

"Hell if I know." The younger cop looks at Mr. Kwan. "How much money are we talkin' about here?"

"Thirty-two forty-eight." The elder smiles. "I not so much worried they steal food. But someone do this to me, they can do worse for big money somewhere else. You guys ought to see."

"Right…" The older cop sighs.

"And, I need police report for insurance." Mr. Kwan smiles.

"You're making an insurance claim on a couple of chicken sandwiches?" asks the younger cop.

"No, on the door. Glass expensive."

I can't help myself and chuckle.

Mr. Kwan looks sorta at me. "You hear that? Something laugh."

Time for me to move.

I scurry out to the store and head to the donut case. As long as I'm radiating inconspicuousness, I take the liberty of squeeze testing donuts until finding one not stale enough to use as a hammer. Usually, Mr. Kwan gets upset if people touch the donuts they're not buying. Getting fresh or stale is basically a sugary version of Russian roulette. Not tonight.

The freshest available donut is a pink-frosted glazed. Ugh. Really? Whatever. Pink, blue, brown, they all taste the same. It'll be in a bag for the walk home anyway.

Mr. Kwan and the two cops emerge from the back room, debating the idea of the thief being a goblin. Young Cop thinks it's impossible for magical creatures to get into the city limits due to the ward, an opinion his partner finds hilarious. Heh. Goblin. I'm laughing at the cuteness of picturing Mini-Me's reaction. Six-year-old me would've punched anyone who called me a goblin. Except Mom.

I approach Mrs. Kwan, set the donut bag and coffee on the counter, and fish out my AATM crystal. She doesn't speak much

English, or pretends not to, merely smiling and nodding at me while ringing up the order.

"All units, keep an eye out for a potential unaccompanied Caucasian minor, approximately five to seven years of age, wandering naked in the vicinity of Wharton Square. Last reported seen on the 23rd Street side. No further information at this time," says a woman's voice from both cops' radios.

The men exchange a 'what the hell is wrong with people?' glance.

Sigh. I stuff the AATM crystal back in my purse and nod at Mrs. Kwan before picking up my donut and coffee.

Fine, universe. You're not exactly being subtle. Okay, maybe I had been thinking about Mini-Me all damn night. Maybe the urge to come to Kwan's came from clairvoyance rather than the universe whispering in my ear, but dammit, I want to yell at the cosmos.

Wharton Square Playground is only a few blocks from here.

16

OUTER CHILD

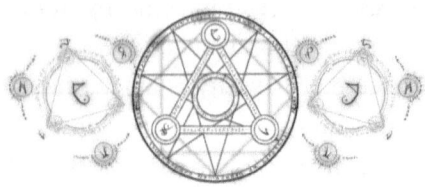

You know how they say even hardened convicts hate kid-touchers?

The vast majority of society's miscreants have something of a soft spot for children, sociopaths notwithstanding—not to lump myself in with the sort of people who belong in penitentiaries, even though I suppose some might call me a bit of a miscreant. Anyway, my jaded nature appears to have a child-shaped crack in it. The same limp fragment of a conscience I have tends to swell up when kids are involved. Same reason I couldn't ignore the Tracy/Ashley/Frank situation next door.

I'm not sure what to expect from a child clone of myself or why I'm feeling drawn to get involved. Maybe it's self-preservation. Yeah, good excuse. If someone finds her and figures out what she-slash-I am, it could cause problems for me. So I'm really helping myself. Wait, technically she is me so even if I wasn't trying to reframe this whole thing into a self-serving light to avoid feeling like an emotional sap… I'm still helping myself in a way.

Argh.

I'm going to kick Melisandre in the balls again for baking my brain.

Yanno, not too long ago, I debated what might happen if Jason and I had a kid. My imagination presented me with the image of a clawed, fanged, winged little monster zooming around my apartment, shredding the furniture like a cat on amphetamines. I absolutely do *not* have my mother's limitless patience. Spending too much time in the company of a kid like me is going to end badly. I really shouldn't be doing this.

Fate will find a way. She'll be fine. Not my problem.

Yet, I keep walking.

Point Breeze, despite the pretty name, isn't what one would call the nicest place in the world. I'm okay with it, though the neighborhood is nibbling on the edge of shithole so to speak. There have been some attempts to clean stuff up, but the violence is tenacious... like debt collectors or Jehovah Witnesses.

Oh, holy shit. I *totally* have to go horns/fangs out and snarl the next time one of those cult wackadoos shows up at my door. Yes. Plans made. Set in stone. Totally happening.

Anyway, back to Point Breeze. It's no surprise people around here are a little worried about a child running around alone. Frank aside, we don't really have all that much of a creep problem here. The biggest worries for an unsupervised street kid are catching stray bullets or getting mowed down by a car fleeing from the police. This is the kind of area where the cops *might* stop to help if someone has a garden variety car accident, but they'd probably roll right on by because they're going to investigate a shooting or robbery. Triage, and all.

A handful of cops and three or four ordinary citizens wander the edges of the playground at Wharton Square. It's actually a nice spot. A whole city block turned into a park with swings, a slide, trees, even a tennis court—though the only balls being knocked around there involve prostitutes. Can't remember ever seeing anyone legit play tennis on these courts. Then again, I'm not usually here in the middle of the day.

Munching on my donut, I wander as casually as possible into the playground. I get a glance or two from cops who think anyone wearing a small skirt must be a prostitute, though working girls don't generally rock goth couture or eat donuts on the job. Could be they're envious of the donut and not making a judgement call on my worth to society. Looking them over one by one gives me the sense they're all focused on worry about a kid, except for one guy who's also worrying about his mortgage.

Were I a naughty sort of demon, he'd be the one I approached to tempt into nefarious deeds.

Good thing for him demons aren't real and I'm not into messing with cops.

One woman talking to an officer insists she saw a little kid dart across the road, coming out of an alley across the street. Sounds like she's the one who called the police. I follow the walkpath toward the center of the park, looking around for any signs of Mini-Me. Not far past the actual center, where beige and red paver stones create a small courtyard bearing a butterfly pattern, I spot a pale white noodle dangling straight down from a tree, an onyx dagger at the end.

Aha.

Dammit. I shouldn't feel relief and happiness. Relief and happiness at finding her means I've somehow already developed an emotional attachment. How the heck is it even possible so fast? Not good. Totally not good. Nope. Totally imagining it.

Pretending not to have noticed her tail, I meander in the direction of the tree, then look up.

Mini-Me squats on a branch almost directly above me, her jet-black toe claws biting into the wood. She's got one hand on another branch overhead for stability, her wings tucked up behind her, horns out, and a chocolate cupcake in her other hand. More chocolate smears her face. Her ink black hair's waist length, the way Mom liked me to wear it at the same age. She's a scrap of a thing, short and thin, again exactly like I used to be.

Her eyes aren't shifted to Shaar'Nath form... and son of a bitch. Kids kinda have large eyes already. Mine were always a little over-sized. Not like anime girl big, more like a perpetually surprised French waif. This kid is *obnoxiously* cute, and her 'why is the world so mean to me' expression is unbearable. The instant I look at those big sapphire pity orbs, the only thing I want to do is wrap her in a blanket and take her home. It's exactly like Natalie going anywhere near an animal shelter. She instantly wants to bring a kitten or puppy home without any consideration for all the work taking care of it will involve.

Gah. No wonder Mom didn't abandon me at a fire house after all the stuff I did—well, she also believed she'd been charged by 'angels' to watch over a special child.

Of course, the kid isn't drowning in self-pity or even in a bad mood.

Kid me had 'resting tragic face.'

Despite the sorrowful expression, I'm ninety-nine percent sure her thoughts are something like 'what the fuck do you want?' Well, maybe not exactly. Mini-Me is six. She's probably thinking 'what the crap do you want?'

"Hey. So, umm. There you are."

She keeps chewing cupcake.

At least she's not running away. Right. When Tracy asked me what the heck I planned to do if I found her, it never really occurred to me success would be an option. Philly is a huge city and even a child version of me would be *damn* hard to catch if they didn't want to be found—or the person doing the hunting wasn't psychic. I'd been pretty freakin' sneaky even without using powers. Again, now that I think about it, I'd probably been using mental stuff and not realizing it. Sure would explain how I got away with so much.

Whatever. Point is, I didn't rehearse this.

"C'mon down. We need to figure out what's going on. Those buttheads are going to come after us both. We should stick together."

She takes another bite of cupcake.

"It's easier to hide if you put the wings and horns away."

The girl chews cupcake.

"I know you can talk. I'm not working with those morons. You know that."

She shifts her glance to the left.

A cop wanders down the path heading toward us. I look away from the kid, hoping he didn't see me talking to her and think to peer into the tree.

"Hey," says the cop. "You see a kid around here? Got a couple calls about a possible abandoned child or maybe a kid who got away from an abductor."

I force myself not to glance sideways at the tail dagger hanging inches away. "Nah. I haven't seen any children around here."

He scans the area. "Thought I heard you talking to someone."

"Just talking to myself." I hold up the third of a donut. "Always feel guilty when I eat junk like this. One donut isn't a big deal, right?"

"Heh, yeah. But one always leads to two. And two leads to three. Then three leads to an exercise activity management plan." He laughs.

Dude doesn't look like he's got a donut problem. Maybe he's completed the management plan.

"I've reached the next level. Eating the donut while walking it off."

He snickers. "Bit late for a girl to be out alone. You okay? Don't mind escorting you somewhere if you're uncomfortable."

"Yeah, I live around here. It's fine. The local idiots know me." I give him a tiny prod to settle his worries and send him on his way.

"All right. Stay safe." He waves before walking off.

See? Resting tragic face. Cops always were kinda nice to me even when they knew I'd done something bad. I peer back up at Mini-Me. Her cupcake is gone and she's now licking chocolate frosting off her fingers.

"So, you working on being a gargoyle?" I ask.

"No," says Mini-Me. "I'm hiding from idiots. Why can you see me?"

"I'm not an idiot."

"Debatable," mutters the child, before gripping the branch over her head in both hands.

Yeah, it's me. "Look, kiddo. Most people have an inner child, but they don't usually jump out and start causing trouble."

"I'm not causing trouble." She stares at me with this 'how could you accuse me of being bad' face for a few seconds before grinning. "Yet."

"Do you understand what the buttheads did?"

"You're too big to call anyone a butthead. You should call them shitheads or assholes."

I blink. "How do you know words like that?"

"We're in Philly."

"Hah. Okay. Fair point."

She watches me for a while, not saying anything.

I reach up and tap a finger to her big toe claw. "Probably not a great idea to sink these into the trees. Leaves marks people will find and start wondering what made them."

"They won't find me."

"I did."

"You're not people."

"Gee, thanks." I chuckle.

"No... I mean you're like me." She tilts her head left, then right. "Am I part of you? Are you trying to eat me so I go back inside?"

"Nah."

"Are you my mother?"

"There's a question I don't have a good answer for. Guess it depends on how you think of 'mother.' Mom is technically both of our mothers. But in some way, they kinda made you from me, so I suppose an argument could be made. We can talk about whatever you want... but why don't we go home first? I wouldn't like sleeping outside, so you can't be happy out here."

She shakes her head. "No. It sucks."

"We should stick together for a bit until we figure out what's going on."

The kid stares down at me for a few seconds. "I can't feel your head."

I almost blurt 'what?' but catch myself. She's six. Gotta be talking about our ability to read intention. "You're wondering why, when you look at me, you don't just know what I want to do?"

She nods.

"Because we're the same sort of, umm, being. Half of us is human. Half something else."

"Demon?"

"Nope." I chuckle. "Some people mistake us for demons though."

"Yeah. This man did. He wanted to hurt me. Called me a demon and threw water on me."

"Ugh." I roll my eyes.

"I bit his arm and stuck my tail in his leg." She grins. "He screamed."

Wow, okay. Mom never had to deal with this. Of course, biting would have been an understandable response to a jackass throwing holy water on me. I chuckle. "Nice. Idiot."

"Okay." Mini-Me lets go of the overhead branch and parachutes on her wings to the ground beside me. As soon as she lands, she shifts fully human, concealing all extra body parts. "I don't wanna sleep outside again."

Wow, she's so tiny. Was I really ever this small?

I pull my top off, activate the amulet for illusion clothes, and offer her the shirt. "Here. You can put this on."

"Why?" She tilts her head.

We can argue about clothing later. Best to get her off the street fast. "Okay, whatever." I put it back on and turn the amulet off.

"You're not gonna make me wear it?"

"Nope. You are basically me. I'd take the shirt and toss it in the bushes for no reason other than my mother demanded I wear it."

She giggles.

"C'mon." I take her hand. "It's not too far."

"If you're just gonna toss it, why are you wearing it?"

"Because I'm too old for people to think it's cute to run around outside with nothing on. Once you grow up, people get kinda stupid about it."

"Sucks."

"Yeah. I thought about going to live in the Amazon jungle, but they don't have internet there."

"Huh?" asks Mini-Me.

"Forget it."

She walks along beside me, tolerating holding my hand.

People in the area are still looking for her, so *I* radiate inconspicuousness. Hey it worked for stealing coffee. Maybe I can cloak a kid, too?

"We're gonna get in trouble, aren't we?" asks Mini-Me.

"Trouble?"

"'Cause I'm naked."

"Yeah, probably. If anyone sees us, they'll cause trouble. Humans are really uptight about clothing."

"Okay. Fine. I'll put it on."

I start to remove my shirt.

"Wait." She holds a 'stop' hand up at me. "Not yet."

"Now what?" I ask.

Mini-Me points ahead of us and full-shifts into a tiny armored form. "Buttheads approach."

17

BUTTHEADS

Doesn't matter who you are, the sight of a little kid wearing custom-fit body armor (or at least appearing to be wearing custom fit-body armor) is cute. Her 'I'm going to kick your ass' expression is also cute. Am I damaged in the head for finding a little kid in 'demonic' armor with wings, tail, and horns adorable?

I look from the child to where she points.

The six warmongers from the warehouse—everyone except Melisandre, guess he's too busy for simple things like searching—have appeared out of thin air in front of us. The three Shaar'Nath look like normal humans in street clothes, while the three Elestari appear as impossibly beautiful humans in slutty street clothes. Yes, I just referred to two men's attire as 'slutty.' Baal'Omun and Ralea, the Elestari, hold a glass-and-silver box about the size of a kennel crate supported on two poles like a litter. It's rather obviously a cage meant for Mini-Me.

Ralea leans back, spreading her beautiful feathery wings and arms to either side. A pulse of faint blue magic radiates outward from her in a sphere. Nothing noticeable occurs, so I assume she's hiding us from ordinary humans.

I shake my head at Asztirian and Jenathri. "You two guys are lost.

1980s' Fire Island is a few hundred miles east, and like forty years ago."

The guys scrunch their noses at me in confusion.

"Will you start making sense?" says Jenathri.

"Those outfits. *No* normal people would ever wear anything like that except in satirical porn movies making fun of gay pimps."

Baal'Omun throws his head back and laughs.

Both Elestari men snarl and shift forms, growing a foot or so taller. Their garments change into the typical white toga-wraps they love so much.

"You have something of ours," says Na'az.

"The only thing I'm giving you idiots"—I full shift—"is an ass kicking."

"Resistance is pointless," says Xir. As a 'human,' her hair is crimson.

I shake my head. "Hon, the line is 'resistance is futile.' Are you guys messing up on purpose? If you're going to pretend to be humans, at least watch some television."

Mini-Me snarls. Aww. "I'm not getting in there. You're a bunch of stupid-heads."

"So precious," says Baal'Omun in a ridiculously deep voice.

"Look. Why don't you guys just save everyone the trouble and fudge off."

Mini-Me gives me side eye. "Since when do *you* not curse? I'm small, not delicate."

"It doesn't work that way." Asztirian summons a gleaming silver broadsword. Glowing runes etched along both sides of the blade give off dark orange light.

"Wow, you guys are dense. No matter what you do, neither one of us is ever going to be willing to destroy the Armistice. You copied me. Meaning, she and I think and feel the same way."

"For now." Ralea narrows her eyes and fly-hops over to us, great white wings kicking up a storm of air. "The young one is still malleable. By the time she comes of age, she will see the necessity in it. Glory awaits."

"You guys take the dumbshit trophy away from the guy who tried to clear floodwaters off his driveway by scooping buckets over a chain link fence."

"Silence, failure!" roars Ralea.

Mini-Me launches herself at the Elestari woman, shrieking, clawing, biting, and flailing her tail blade around.

Ralea mostly catches the child by the chest, backpedaling while suffering dozens of little slashing wounds. "I have her! Bring the vessel."

The three Shaar'Nath shift up into their armored forms and rush at me. Baal'Omun, despite being the biggest, reaches me first. I duck his grab. Ralea screams in pain behind me. I swipe my tail at Na'az to keep her at bay while catching Xir's wrists. Claws to the face are bad. She's surprised as hell when I none-too-slowly overpower her, pushing her back and pivot to check on the kid. Mini-Me sank her tail blade into Ralea's gut. Bright red blood gushes down over perfect pale skin.

Damn, now I want cherry vanilla ice cream.

Ralea shrieks in pain as the girl tries to twist the tail blade in the wound. Her hands glow in shrouds of gold light. Magical chains appear around Mini-Me, shrinking amid a clatter of metal into a tight, mummifying bundle.

Baal'Omun lunges at me, going for a bear hug. I swing Xir off her feet, hurl her into him, and leap into a punch, driving my armored knuckles into Ralea's mouth. A meaty *thud* precedes the skinny faux angel flying headfirst in a backward arc. The forming gold chains burst into clouds of loose magical energy.

Mini-Me breaks loose of the strands encircling her, springs to her feet, arms up in a pose like a WWE wrestler, and roars.

Something hits me in the right ankle, knocking my legs out from under me and dumping me flat on the ground, eating grass. Mini-Me leaps in my direction, crashes into Jenathri's face, biting and clawing at him in a fair impression of a Looney Tunes Tasmanian Devil. The Elestari must have kicked my feet out from under me. He shrieks, spinning in circles, trying to fling her to the ground, but her claws are in his cheeks. Baal'Omun, snarling, grabs at me with two hands' worth of claws.

I roll away, giving the big Shaar'Nath a telekinetic shove. His toe claws rip gouges in the grass as he slides backward. Ralea, covered in tiny scratches, runs over and grabs Mini-Me from behind, plucking her off Jenathri. The child rams an elbow backward into the side of the woman's head hard enough to stun her, then spins and resumes her electrocuted chihuahua attack routine. Screaming, Ralea backpedals. It's unclear if she's trying to hold onto the child or failing to throw her off.

A faint hiss warns me of Na'az swinging her tail blade for my face. I TK-yank her feet out from under her, causing her tail slice to pass over my head. As soon as she lands on her back, I pounce on top of her, hammering her repeatedly in the face with a closed fist—until a flying mailbox hits me broadside and knocks me rolling. Jenathri looks around for something else to hurl at me. He plucks a stop sign off a pole and ninja-star chucks it.

Eep!

I fling myself to the side, but didn't even have to. The flimsy sign swerves hard, totally missing where I was, and embeds in the side of a tree.

"Careful," shouts Xir, glaring at Na'az. "Don't destroy—"

Mini-Me flies into my field of view butt first, her arms and legs thrust out, face almost touching her shins. The child crashes into Xir, back to back, their heads clonking together. Ralea, even bloodier than before, bounces on one leg like a pitcher after throwing a fastball. Not missing a moment, the kid spins around and begins chewing on Xir's wing. She's clawing with both hands and feet, too, but her little needles aren't much of a threat to an adult's armor plating.

Baal'Omun bull-charges at me. A telekinetic shove to his shins trips him into sliding on his face. I jump over him, snickering at the stream of obscenities rumbling out of his mouth. Ralea conjures a handful of yellow-white light and focuses it into her stomach. Most of the scratches, and her gut wound, disappear.

Ignoring the child, Xir raises her tail in a stabbing orientation toward me.

Mini-Me covers the woman's eyes.

"Gah! Brat!" yells Xir.

I grab Xir's tail in both hands and yank her into the air, swinging her around in a hammer throw a few times. Right as Baal'Omun stands back up, I hurl her at him. The two crash together; she stops cold as though she'd collided with a tree trunk, the big guy not giving an inch.

Mini-Me, having lost her grip on Xir, swerves around and attacks Ralea again, who screams and runs in circles, trying to swat the biting child away. Damn this kid loves wings. I'm gonna have to buy hot sauce in gallon jugs.

Jenathri chases them, seeming unsure if he should whack the kid using his sword or risk grabbing her. It's like they tried to play catch using a hedgehog for a ball and are wondering why they've ended up bleeding from a dozen different places.

Asztirian comes out of nowhere, catching me off guard with a right cross. I don't notice him until four perfectly sculpted knuckles mash into my cheek. Elestari aren't as strong as Shaar'Nath, though he is significantly stronger than an ordinary human. Armor or not, I don't weigh a ridiculous amount. Yeah, I go stumbling back, seeing stars. Baal'Omun trips me, but yields to Asztirian, who jumps on top of me as soon as my back hits the ground. He struggles to grab my arms and force my wrists together.

Baal'Omun holds his right hand out toward me, muttering in a low, repetitive chant. Red light forms around my wrists, hinting at the shape of manacles, rapidly darkening into some kind of black rock or metal.

Mini-Me flies into him, wrapping her arms and legs around his head. She koala-clings tight, mushing his face into her chest, blind-folding him and muffling his speech in one move. I ram my tail all the way through Asztirian's left arm and partially into his chest. Gasping, he falls off me to the side. Luckily, the force binding my wrists together is still rubbery. Grunting, I pull my arms apart, causing the spell energy to burst in a crimson flash.

Baal'Omun grabs at the kid. She leaps away in a blur, superhuman strength flinging her teeny body clear so fast he ends up smacking himself in the face. Xir snags the kid's tail. Mini-Me screams, flapping her wings and trying to climb higher. For a few seconds, Xir flies a child-shaped balloon until I hack her hand off at the wrist with my tail.

She staggers into a retreat, screaming.

Ralea runs after her.

Both male Elestari rush at me. They're not expecting me to charge right at them instead of ducking or going sideways. Surprise lets me get inside their sword reach and sink my claws into their necks before they can bring their blades down. They feebly swat at me, their blades nicking my armored sides, as I lift them off their feet and smash their heads together.

Na'az jumps on me from behind, grabbing my wings and dragging me back. I toss the men in a dazed heap to free my hands. Her tail slips between my legs, curving up to stab me in the stomach. I grab the blade before she can jab it into me, and hurl all my weight backward. We both crash to the ground, but I land on top of her and roll off to the side.

Baal'Omun rips a 'no parking' signpost out of the ground and raises it to hurl like a spear. The instant he throws it, I grab Na'az by her wing, dragging her in front of me as a shield. The steel signpost punches through her chest below the left breast, comes out her back, and cracks the armor over my stomach.

"Damn, boy," I say. "You've got one hell of an arm."

He grumbles.

Na'az gurgles.

I throw her aside and stand, bracing the cracked spot.

Xir, once again in possession of two hands, dive-tackles me from a blind angle. I eat grass for the second time, the woman on my back. She wrenches down on my left wing spar, breaking it halfway between my back and the joint. Oh, shit this hurts. Asztirian chimes in by stabbing his sword through my right shoulder into the ground beneath me. Dark red blood rolls down the silvery blade to the grass.

I'm screaming in pain before I realize it. Xir scrambles to gather my arms behind me, pretending to be a cop about to handcuff a suspect.

Fuck you. Despite the blinding pain in my wing and shoulder, I ram my head backward into her face, powered by a boost of complete *nope*. I freakin' hate it bad enough when cops cuff me, and they're legally allowed to. This bitch can go straight to Imbreleth.

Mini-Me lands on Xir's right wing while simultaneously spearing her tail blade into the back of Asztirian's left knee. He howls and crumples to the ground, dragging his sword out of me. Ever see a cat slide down curtains, shredding them? Yeah, the kid does the same thing to Xir's wing membrane. The bitch wails in agony. I cringe in sympathetic pain. Baal'Omun and Na'az both gasp. I think he's got a tear in his eye. Know how when guys see other guys take it in the balls, they all groan? Same deal. A Shaar'Nath watching membrane damage is like a dude witnessing another dude have his sack smashed in a car door, and then the car drives away with the poor bastard clinging to the side.

Jenathri raises his left hand, projecting a golden beam into Na'az, who rips the impaling signpost out, the wound closing behind it. After a second to breathe, she javelins the sign right at me. I dive to the ground. The blunt-tipped spear strikes Xir in the forehead, bouncing off her armor with a dull *clank* and diverting into the air. Her pink-hued energy eyes appear to cross for a second.

Lost to pain-rage, Xir grabs Mini-Me by one ankle, tearing the child off her wing and swinging her into a throw. The child yowls in pain, catching herself on her wings before going face-first into a parked car at the edge of the playground. Snarling, Mini-Me pulls a 180 and zooms at Na'az—who happened to be closest to her—flying into a frenzy of clawing.

Jenathri conjures golden light, mending Xir's wing membrane.

Na'az grabs for the girl's tiny neck.

I telekinetically yank Mini-Me away from her into my arms. Along with a broken wing strut, I've suffered a few minor cuts from their swords—which sting—but feel mostly tired. These six don't appear too winded, and none are still wounded. Shit, this is a lopsided fight.

One-on-one, I could totally own them, except maybe Baal'Omun. He'd be a challenge. Somewhat. I've still got the advantage in the physical world. But six on one plus they have healers? Maybe it's time I consider running.

Mini-Me wriggles in my grip like she wants to rip faces off.

Baal'Omun charges at me, doing a passable impression of an NFL linebacker with anger management issues. I squeeze Mini-Me tight and jump sideways, screaming again as my mangled wing flops around. A dark orange energy beam streaks down from overhead into Baal'Omun's chest, stopping him cold as though he'd run into the corner of a skyscraper.

"The heck?" I mutter. Damn my broken wing and shoulder throb like fuck.

Laniah swoops down and lands near me, her body surrounded in a faint golden aura. Her wings crackle with similar energy, brighter, in the form of sparks. She's barefoot, in the same white ribbon 'wrap' garment as the other Elestari. Her attempt to look intimidating feels more like the thirteen-year-old vegetarian kid sister making pouty faces at someone for eating meat. No, she isn't a child, but she absolutely sucks at being commanding. The girl's way too sweet... and having blonde hair so long she can sit on it doesn't really say 'war maiden.'

A golden flash bursts to my right, out of which steps a tall male Elestari. Also blonde, he's part Nordic god and part sanctimonious jackass. It would normally annoy me for Ezriel—a.k.a. Daniel Graf—to show up and give me grief, but at the moment, I don't mind him being here so much. The reason the dude's an asshole is he does *not* want the Armistice to be destroyed, and he refuses to believe me about having zero interest in destroying it.

"What in the nine sanctums of Arboz is going on here?" bellows Ezriel, raising a large silver broadsword.

The warmongers hesitate, as if unsure what to make of two more Elestari showing up.

"You want the long version or the short version?" I rasp.

"Considering the situation, I'll settle for short."

I twist to show him Mini-Me—who is still squirming to get loose and clawing at the air—"Melisandre tricked me into a barrier ward. These guys cloned me and think if they raise her differently, she'll be willing to blow up the world when she's my age. This right here is your basic kidnapping attempt with a side order of penis measuring."

Ezriel blinks in a flutter, then turns his head to look at me. "Penis measuring?"

Sigh. "Not literally. They're trying to pretend they're stronger than me."

Laniah raises a hand and bathes me in magic. My left wing spar emits a *snap* as it un-breaks. Burning pain in my shoulder goes away. The crack in my stomach armor seals. All the little sword dings disappear as well, though they still kinda ache. In seconds, I'm unhurt—still tired—but unhurt.

"Warmongers?" she asks.

"Who else would want to break the Armistice?" I wiggle my wing, grateful the pain has stopped. Can't pick on her for asking a dumb question after healing me. "Yes. All six of them are morons."

"Buttheads!" yells Mini-Me.

"I suggest you all leave this place," says Ezriel. "None of you will threaten the Armistice while I yet stand."

Ralea, Asztirian, and Jenathri appear somewhat hesitant.

I glance at Laniah. "Hey, didn't you once tell me wounds from Elestari swords can't be healed by your magic?"

"Yes. But I was talking about Elestari and Shaar'Nath. *You* belong in this world. Restorative magic is also my focus."

"Come, little Elestari." Baal'Omun raises his arm at Ezriel, curling his claws in a beckoning gesture. "Let me show you the true meaning of war. I have longed for millennia to spill the energy of your pathetic kind."

I look around.

"What are you searching for?" whispers Laniah.

"The cameras. He's trying *way* too hard."

Baal'Omun snarls.

"Don't tell me it's a compensation thing?" I ask. "You're not hung like an Elestari are you?"

Ezriel, Asztirian, and Jenathri all stare at me. If 'offended' had a picture in the dictionary, they'd be it.

"What? Don't lie." I smile. "You're the ones who didn't bother with loincloths the other day. And hey, it's nothing to be ashamed of. Nature is nature. Can't control how you were born."

"I am not 'compensating'." Baal'Omun glances at me. "Another time, I would be happy to prove it."

"Wait… are you hitting on me or are you like talking about just showing it off in an alley somewhere for verification purposes?"

"Kill the pacifists!" shouts Asztirian—before he runs at Laniah.

Wow, brave man.

Mini-Me rams her elbow into my gut and slips loose. Ooh, brat! She goes psycho-death-hamster all over Asztirian, ruining his charge. Xir rushes at Mini-Me. Laniah spins into a graceful attack, wielding a relatively thin sword like an elven fencer, deftly maneuvering around Xir's defenses and striking her in the thigh and shoulder.

Baal'Omun charges Ezriel, swinging his enormous arms in wide, sweeping claw strikes. Ezriel leans out of the way, his expression as calm as a bored karate teacher evaluating a new student—until the third dodge. He whirls under the big Shaar'Nath's arm and wallops him in the chest. His blade strikes armor, giving off a brilliant golden flash, the *clang* echoing over the playground. Baal'Omun sails backward, flying a few feet before crashing to the ground and slide-spinning to a stop some ten yards away. Smoke peels up from a glowing magmatic crack splitting his armor open from shoulder to hip.

Ezriel smirks, reaching to pluck Mini-Me off Asztirian—who's shrieking in pain and covered in hundreds of small scratches. The kid leaps off him and starts savaging Ezriel.

"No! He's on our side!" I yell. "Mostly."

Ralea begins focusing a healing beam on Baal'Omun.

Xir pounces, trying to grab me as Na'az cheap-shots Ezriel from behind, stabbing her tail blade into his back while he's covered in pissed-off child. He grunts and flings Mini-Me straight up. I lunge forward, smashing Xir in the face with my forearm. She staggers. I press, ramming my knee into her stomach hard enough to launch her like twenty feet.

"Look out!" shouts Mini-Me.

I turn toward her voice in time to eat a flying mailbox, compliments of Asztirian. Same mailbox, different tosser. Doesn't hurt *too* much, but it knocks me on my ass. A snarling Baal'Omun pushes himself back to his feet. The gaping hole in his chest armor has partially healed, a long, angry line of molten armor still spanning it. He raises a hand at Laniah and summons a stream of Imbreleth fire.

She screams in terror, launching herself straight up, avoiding the deadly blast by a fraction of a second. Mini-Me zooms in a figure-eight, harassing Xir and Na'az. Baal'Omun laughs, turning to chase Laniah with the fire stream as she flies overhead. Imbreleth fire is an express ticket back to Aesinor for any Elestari it hits.

Realizing his back's to me, I run and jump on him from behind, grabbing at his face. He mostly ignores me, too fixated on the screaming Laniah—and his fire stream being only inches from her legs—to pay much attention to me. In seconds, she's going to be taking a break for decades.

"You wouldn't be too bad a guy if you weren't a warmonger moron." I swing my tail around his side and ram the blade into the middle of the scar.

Oopsie. Overconfident dumbass forgot his armor had a big compromise. My fourteen-inch tail blade penetrates the half-thickness armor deep enough to destroy his heart. The roaring stream of dark crimson flames peters out to a faint puff, then stops entirely. He wheezes, jaw open in an expression of utter shock.

"Seriously. Re-think your priorities. Put yourself back together, and maybe we'll talk. See you soon." I pat him on the head, and spring away from him.

He wheezes again and falls over forward, stiff as a felled tree. In seconds, his entire form evaporates into a low-hanging grey fog.

Na'az slams into me from behind, wrapping her arms around and pinning mine to my sides. "Bitch!"

"Re-freaking-lax. All I did was give him a vacation."

A high-pitched war cry from overhead precedes Mini-Me falling on Na'az. Having seen the kid wantonly go for wing membrane earlier, she throws me aside and spins to face the dive-bombing child. I catch my balance before eating grass for a third time, and spin around to face her.

Nearby on the left, Ezriel trades sword strokes with Asztirian and Jenathri. I think he's playing with them... both warmonger Elestari really seem to be going for broke. Ezriel calmly defends himself in a choreographed looking series of parries and slight leans, allowing their blades to whistle past his body.

"Fools," says Ezriel, "You do not comprehend the true meaning of what you so thoughtlessly pursue. Everything we have built will be destroyed if the Armistice fails. We are enlightened and no longer seek the vacuous thrill of endless war."

A tiny high-pitched scream of rage draws my attention back to Na'az. Mini-Me crashes into my face, thrown with enough force to knock me stumbling. She ends up draped over my shoulder.

"Oof!" yells the child. "Bitch!"

I grunt.

"Not you," chirps Mini-Me. "Her."

"I know what you meant."

Laniah lands next to me, rests a hand on the child's right wing, and repairs a break.

Ezriel howls in pain.

Enraged at the bitch breaking the child's wing, I lunge and pound Na'az in the nose, then glance toward Ezriel as she flies over backward.

Xir's tail blade sticks out of his chest, stuck into the middle of his back. A slight deflection off his spine appears to be the reason he hasn't disintegrated. Asztirian, staggering from a recent strike, isn't in any position to take advantage, but Jenathri rears back to behead Ezriel. I toss Mini-Me straight up, jump onto my wings, and accelerate as fast as I can manage in only about forty yards.

A bright golden energy beam flies past me on the right, striking

Xir in the side above her left hip. I crash into Jenathri, tackling him before his sword comes around and strikes Ezriel. Jenathri grunts, his feathered wings scraping over the ground as we slide across grass then sidewalk before crashing into the door of a parked van with a loud *boom*, making a big-ass dent. A rain of shattered automotive glass falls like snow over us.

"More trouble than you're worth," snarls Jenathri. He thrusts his left hand out in a shoving motion at me.

Yellow light bursts between us, punting me back like I'd been fired out of a cannon.

Xir cries out in a demonically low-pitched feminine roar, the searing golden light from Laniah's spell rapidly spreading throughout her body, disintegrating her into a flutter of black ash. Watching it hurts. Dad told me the Elestari have magic specifically designed to destroy us... and I think I've just seen it. Some kind of 'sun-beam' spell.

"Ezriel!" shouts Laniah.

The force of Jenathri's magic hurtles me halfway across the park. I crash into the ground, tumbling in a backward somersault until a nice, helpful tree catches me. My body more or less hits it like a thrown knife, both horns stuck in the trunk. Feels as though I've been hit over the head with a baseball bat. I end up trapped in a sort of push-up position, my head too low to the ground to get my knees under me, but too high off the ground to lay flat on my stomach.

Grr.

Bracing my hands on the tree, I struggle to pull the horns out and not break my neck.

Jenathri appears behind me in a golden flicker, sword raised.

"Jena!" shouts Na'az. "Do not kill her. She is no use to us on the other side."

"*Rawr!*" shouts Mini-Me. She jumps on Jenathri's back, bites him on the wing edge, and shreds his tender non-armored skin—hand claws in his armpits, toe claws ripping at his lower back.

He shrieks in agony.

While he's distracted, I spear my tail into his abdomen, impaling it straight up into his heart. I also stop being a moron and unsummon my horns for a second to free them from the tree. Jenathri's physical body bursts into a flickering cloud of golden light, his essence drawn away to Aesinor. Mini-Me flops on top of me.

"Bye, bye dickhead. Hope it was painful," I mutter.

"You okay?" asks Mini-Me.

"This is gonna hurt in the morning."

Mini-Me hops off me as I pull myself upright, holding onto the tree for balance until my skull stops throbbing. Asztirian's war cry gets my attention. I spin, raising an arm to defend, but he's a distance away, charging at Laniah.

Gold light flashes beside me. Mini-Me falls to the ground, wrapped up in glowing gold chains.

"Naughty, naughty," says Ralea. "Child, you need to learn who your friends are."

"Poop," mutters Mini-Me, squirming. "Will you please go ask her to let me out?"

Huh? 'Ask her to let me out' is a way too tame reaction for me in such a situation. I *hate* being tied up. Granted, cops hadn't started using handcuffs on me until I was past ten, so maybe Mini-Me hasn't developed a rage reaction to being immobilized. But she sounds too placid.

Ezriel pulls a charred onyx blade out of his back—Xir's former tail —and throws it at Asztirian. He misses, but not by much. It distracts him enough for Laniah to block his swing. I run at Ralea, growling. Her haughtiness evaporates to a 'perhaps I should not have done that' stare.

Mini-Me grunts, wriggling. "Peace chains suck!"

I glare at Ralea, speaking in a voice part growl. "Those chains disappear if I send you back to Aesinor, right?"

Ralea briefly raises her sword, but decides to run. Bah. She's probably like Laniah, more of a healer than a fighter. I chase her for a moment, nearly getting my claws on her before she remembers at the last second Elestari can fly faster than us. She leaps into the air, rapidly pulling ahead out of claw reach.

Laniah surprises the shit out of Asztirian—and me—with a series of three masterful parries and a disarming maneuver, tossing the man's broadsword off to the side and placing the tip of her blade under his chin. "Stand down. Your violence serves no purpose other than to beget more violence. You claim the nobility of the Elestari, yet display the same savagery you hold the Shaar'Nath in contempt for."

I don't even bother trying to keep up with Ralea in the air, slamming on the metaphorical brakes. Hovering, I shift my focus to telekinesis, making a minor adjustment to her flight path—straight into the ground. Mini-Me stares at her, a vapid, intense expression on her face. It's as if she took cocaine and 'shrooms at the same time. Hyper excited and simultaneously super-mellow.

Peace chains… the spell is preventing her from having violent thoughts—but she *really* wants to.

Ezriel, having healed himself, walks toward Asztirian, his expression absolutely one of 'play time is over. I am going to kick your ass.'

Asztirian runs to his blade, picks it up, and disappears in a golden flash. I spot Na'az hiding behind a tree only because she gates herself out in a flicker of dull red light. Black-armored Shaar'Nath are pretty difficult to spot at night. Ralea appears to have zero interest in taking on the three of us herself, and also gates out. Laniah gestures at Mini-Me, dispelling the peace chains.

The child stands, dusts herself off, and walks over next to me. "Stupid buttheads."

Ezriel emits an annoyed, hard sigh. "This will only continue. We need to destroy the doppelganger."

"Fuck you," says Mini-Me.

I point at her. "What she said."

Laniah gasps at him. "What? No. We can't kill her. She's a child!"

Ezriel faces me, trying to be imperious, but hesitation is all over him. "She is a copy."

"You're lying to yourself," says Laniah. "No."

"If she is an exact copy of me, then there's no chance she's ever going to want to break the Armistice. I don't. I like it here."

The kid points at me. "What she said."

"We cannot hurt her." Laniah's sword vanishes in a golden flash. She grasps his hand in both of hers. "She might be a second Brooklyn, but she is still a child."

I raise a hand. "Hang on. Might be a second Brooklyn *but* she's a child? That implies a second Brooklyn needs to die, just not as a child. Or implies you think I need to die."

"Umm. No." Laniah blushes. "I'm sometimes confused by English. Not what I meant at all."

"No problem." I chuckle. "English confuses the shit out of me sometimes, too. And I went to school for it."

Ezriel dispels his sword, setting his hands on his hips.

"See?" I smile. "You don't really want to hurt a child. Those idiots thought they'd be able to mold her into what they want, but she's already giving them the finger."

Mini-Me flips Ezriel off.

"Such a charming little tyke," mumbles Ezriel.

"You did suggest murdering her." I fold my arms. "She hoofed Melisandre right in the nuts, punched him in the nose, and took off. Even those assholes aren't so stupid as to think copying me is going to work after she gave them such an obvious 'go to hell' answer."

He sighs up at the clouds. "Fine. I still do not trust either one of you, and not necessarily because of what you may knowingly do. You —and now this child—are still susceptible to being manipulated."

"I'll tell you the same thing I said last time. If I can't stop myself from doing it, go right ahead and send me to Imbreleth. Better we roll the dice and see what happens when my human half dies than every-thing goes away. Not only will every human—and whatever alien life might be out there—die, but both your people and mine will start slaughtering each other, maybe even wipe themselves out. I don't want that to happen either."

He doesn't look at all happy, but nods.

I rest a hand on his shoulder. "Thanks for the assist."

"Are you hurt?" Laniah looks me over.

"Not anymore… only sore."

Mini-Me shifts down to human form.

"Oh my... she is *adorable*," coos Laniah.

The kid peers up at her. "Is she always like this? I'm not a kitten. She's going to hug me, isn't she?"

Laniah laughs. "Only if you want to."

"I've never been much of a hug person, except for my mother." I press my knuckles to Laniah's shoulder, giving a light, friendly push. "Don't take it personally."

"She did fix your boos, my boo, and help us not get kidnapped." Mini-Me tolerates a hug.

Laniah's gone to full adorable kitten mode and would stand there squeezing the kid all night if she could, but doesn't.

I look at the child once the hug ends. "Still want the shirt?"

Mini-Me shrugs in a 'whatever' way. "Only because I'm too tired to wait while you argue with a bunch of nosy people on the way to wherever you're taking me."

"Just home. Hell with it. It's not far. Think real hard about not wanting anyone to see you. And, we might as well fly."

The kid thrusts her wings out to full extension with a leathery *fwoof* like a mini collapsible umbrella opening. "Cool."

I sorta salute Laniah. "Thanks for the help."

"Happy to. I like this world, too."

She gates out in a golden flash.

"Ready?" I shift back to human form, but leave the wings out. My clothes reappear in a magical flicker. Oh, there's a thought. Natalie could make the kid an amulet so she at least *looks* like she's dressed. One way to solve the lazy problem.

"Sure. Knock yourself out."

I take her hand.

"Really?" She smirks. "I'm not four."

As a kid, I *always* complained about Mom holding my hand in public—but never pulled away because, in truth, it didn't bother me. Only being seen doing it bothered me. I keep holding her hand as we leap into the air and fly toward my apartment.

18

IMMEDIATE PLANS

We land on my apartment building's roof and pull our wings in.

Or at least, I do.

"Gonna leave those out all night?" I ask.

"I like them. They make me look tough."

Meaning, she's scared. Fair enough. I would be too, in her place. Okay, I *am* in her place. Technically.

"All right. Try not to knock stuff over. Wings are a little unwieldy inside."

I pull open the beat-up brown steel door to the stairs. She ducks past me and heads down. One of the reasons I keep referring to 'the universe' doing stuff as though it had sentience is my apartment. I'm in unit sixty-six on the sixth floor. Totally did *not* request it on purpose, just sorta happened. Didn't complain about it either. Hilarious. My Catholic mother doesn't like it, go figure.

Mini-Me doesn't understand why the number is funny/ironic, which she really shouldn't at her age. But, she somehow found her way to Point Breeze and even Kwan's store—my routine haunt. She must have some kind of subconscious version of my more recent memories.

She walks into my apartment, looks around, and peers up at me. "Wow. Straight home? Didn't drag me somewhere to buy clothes?"

"I've got plenty of clothes here already you can leave on the floor."

She laughs.

"If you're anything like me at that age… why waste money on stuff you won't bother wearing?"

The kid tilts her head. "Are you being serious or trying to make me feel bad?"

I walk toward the kitchen. "Hungry? And mostly serious. Maybe exaggerating a little. If Mom didn't make sure I got dressed, I'd go right out the door in whatever I slept in… or nothing."

She holds her arms high, wings out. "I'm a powerful creature from another realm! Pants are for lesser mortals."

I pull open the fridge.

She pads in behind me. "Not really hungry. I had cupcakes."

"Okay." I shove the fridge closed and head to the living room.

Mini-Me flops on the couch next to me, watching as I resume playing *Gods of War*. She seems calm, content, perhaps a little confused. Probably wondering why I'm not telling her to go to sleep given it's almost midnight.

Not sure where I'm going with the clothing thing. Obviously, I need to get her to want to be dressed… at least when we leave the apartment. Mom finally convinced me not to be so indifferent to it after much tearful begging. She'd been afraid the state would take me away from her if I got caught too many times. But how do you over-write thousands of years of instinct? Shaar'Nath—and even Elestari—largely ignore clothing as a concept. They don't possess any sense of shame about their bodies.

If it's any indication how completely stupid the warmongers are, the Elestari guys had the nerve to act offended at me making fun of their size despite their bodies being completely products of their desire in this world. Vanity regarding 'length' is entirely a human flaw. Not sure if they've been spending too much time in the physical world, but they have no reason to care. For one reason, they can change themselves to look however they want. For another reason they shouldn't be ashamed of—oh, I get it. They hadn't been upset I pointed out tiny dicks... merely I failed to find their physical appearance amazingly beautiful and flawless. Pointing out *any* perceived flaw would have elicited the same 'offense.'

And honestly, Imbreleth is like 300 degrees in the coldest parts. Humans couldn't survive there without magic. Fabric wouldn't last more than a few seconds. Besides, our armor plating is kinda like clothes. Hides the naughty bits humans are so uptight about. I suppose convincing Mini-Me to wear her armor outside might be a compromise. Can always tell people it's a costume she's obsessed with.

"Aren't you going to send me to bed?" asks Mini-Me.

"You ate a box of cupcakes and got into a fight against a bunch of buttheads. You're too wound up and high on sugar. I could tell you to go to bed since it's midnight, but you probably wouldn't sleep."

"Are you always cold?"

"Yeah."

She brushes a hand down the sleeve of my top. "Is that why you like this stuff?"

"Not really. Clothing doesn't help us feel warm."

"Why do you wear it then? Won't your wings rip it?"

"Yeah. I wear it because humans are weird. For some reason, they freak out if people go naked. Except in certain situations."

"Certain situations?"

"They have special beaches where it's not considered bad. And other stuff I'm not talking about yet. Humans are overly fixated on shame."

"Oh." She sticks her tongue out. "See? We're smarter than them."

"Yep."

The girl squirms a bit in an attempt to get comfortable on the sofa. Finally, she decides to put her wings away and lean against my side. She thinks she's being slick, trying to endear herself to me. I'm wise to her since it's what I'd do. At least, it's what I think I'd do if Mom died and an orphan version of me found someone they felt safe with.

"However," I say, "I did have to get dressed for school."

"Blech. Been there, done that." She waves dismissively. "No thanks."

I laugh. "You're like what, six? Even if you somehow have all of my memories—which I doubt—you're a kid and need to go to school."

She flicks her hair back off her shoulder. "I don't have your memories, just your attitude."

"Hah. Okay, so why the 'been there done that' if you don't remember finishing school?"

"*Hello.* It's called lying. School's for losers."

I pause the video game. "You're looking at it the wrong way."

"Oh?" She folds her arms. "Being made to do work and not getting paid for it is being a loser."

"There's two reasons why you should go to school."

The girl taps her foot on air. "You're not going to convince me, but go ahead and try."

Wow. Her toenails look normal. It's been a long time since I had nails *not* painted black. My claws are black and I usually paint my nails black, so it kinda worked. The fire department is a bit funny about nail polish, so I had to give it up on my fingers. Still paint my toenails, though. Claws are murder on shoes.

"Okay, reason one: it's the law. If you don't go to school, they're going to take you away, put you with a foster family, and those people will try to make you go to school. If you still don't, you'll end up going through a gauntlet of psychiatrists and therapists, probably getting so frustrated you shred someone and then end up classified as a dangerous magical creature they put in a box."

The girl stares at me.

"Second, and better reason—"

"I get to learn stuff?" she asks with an eye roll.

"Nope." I grin. "It's kinda fun if you approach it right. Think of all the mischief you can cause with telekinesis."

"Huh? What's tell-e-whatever?"

"Oh, wow you are new."

She sticks her tongue out at me again.

I point at the small pillow on the far end of the couch, then levitate it.

"Whoa."

"You can do that, too."

She smirks. "Obviously. I'm you. Just younger and cuter."

I stick my tongue out at her.

"So how's it work?"

"Pretty easy. I figured it out... Aha! Yeah. You're only six. Found TK at like seven or eight when I got mad at a ball."

Mini-Me scrunches up her face. "You got mad at a ball?"

"It hit me in the face. Some other kids at the trailer park were kicking it around, and a stray shot hit me. I launched the damn thing."

She laughs.

"Okay..." I set the pillow down on the rug in front of us and start explaining the necessary means of concentrating on an object, picturing invisible threads of energy connecting my mind to the target like remote control hands.

It only takes her ten minutes to get the hang of it and make the pillow float around.

"See? Now picture being in school with like thirty other kids and a teacher. All the opportunity there to mess with people."

Mini-Me does weasel hands while attempting an evil mastermind laugh.

"One important thing to remember."

She drops the pillow and peers up at me. "Don't kill anyone?"

"Okay, two important things to remember. I was going to say never do anything so obvious everyone knows where it came from."

She nods.

"The trick to getting away with stuff is for people to think you're just a normal kid."

"Ugh. So I gotta hide my wings and stuff, and wear clothes."

"When you're out in public, yeah. But the mischief is worth it. Trust me."

"I'll think about it." She pauses, then raises one eyebrow. "Wait a minute. Are you saying I won't get in trouble for killing people?"

"Sort of. Under certain conditions." I hold up a finger. "Only people who are trying to hurt you. And I mean like seriously hurt you. A school bully punching you isn't cause for killing them. And I know you can tell what someone's intention toward you is."

"Duh. I'd punch them back."

I'm not too worried. She is me after all. I know where my lines are drawn. "Good. So basically, don't seriously injure anyone and don't get caught."

"Pff. Get caught. Hah. Who are you talking to here?"

I laugh. Wow, my mother had the patience of a saint. "Rule three—don't get overconfident. I got caught plenty of times."

"How?"

"By getting overconfident."

She laughs.

I whistle. "Guess we need to hit Walmart after all."

"They're closed now." She yawns. "Did your mom make you hide your wings, too?"

"Not exactly. I didn't know I had them until only a few months ago."

Mini-Me gasps. "Seriously?"

"Yeah." I tell her about growing up thinking myself normal, how my—our—father lurked in the shadows, forbidden to make contact because the stupid warmongers hoped my overly religious and sweet mother would 'tame' the evil demon enough to the point they could convince me destroying the world was the 'just and noble' thing to do.

"What a bunch of freakin' buttheads," mutters the child.

"Exactly."

She yawns again.

Ugh. This kid is too much. I totally get why the cops went so easy on me now. It's going to bite me in the ass, but I kinda want her to stick around. No, this isn't the 'I don't want a cat. Oh, look a kitten, we'll just warm her up and bring her to a shelter tomorrow—and the cat lives with me for twenty years' situation. Really. It isn't. She hasn't gotten her claws into me. I'm purely thinking about being the best person on Earth to protect her from the warmongers as well as humans. I'm not emotionally attached to her. Not at all. It only makes sense from a tactical point of view. Not attached in the least. Nope. Not me.

Sigh.

Hello. It's called lying.

19

PICKING UP A FEW THINGS

I walk the kid to the bathroom and run a tub for her—naturally, 100% hot water.

Can't put her to bed covered in dirt, leaves, and blood, right? After cleaning her up and drying her off, I break open a new toothbrush and turn into my freakin' mother, teaching her how to brush. Oy. What's wrong with me now?

On the way to the bedroom, I send Lieutenant Sims a text message informing him of 'family issues' I need to deal with and am 'calling out sick' tomorrow unless the shit hits the fan fire wise and I'll show up if he calls me.

The kid and I crawl in bed. It's a queen, so plenty of room. She does the cat thing, taking up way more space than her size dictates she ought to.

"This is *so* much nicer than concrete." She rolls over, snuggling into the pillow and generally adoring the softness of an actual bed.

"It sure is." This is why I put up with the whole day job and society thing.

I WAKE UP WITH A SMALL PERSON DRAPED HALF ON TOP OF ME.

Mini-Me is curled into a ball tucked under my right arm, her head resting on my shoulder, knee on my stomach, tail coiled around my leg like an emotionally needy python. This gets me wondering how things are for Shaar'Nath. Do they routinely co-sleep with their kids? Do tails and wings normally get involved in hugs or is Mini-Me way more insecure and frightened than she appears to be. Her tail's got a death grip on my thigh. Getting attached to someone is supposed to be metaphorical.

Well, you know what they say. If you can't love yourself, you can't be loved.

I grab the phone and check messages.

Sims wants more info.

How to explain this one? Umm... I send him a text explaining I've ended up unexpectedly responsible for a little kid no one else can adequately care for, and a little time is needed for me to make life adjustments.

Drat. I shouldn't have sent it. Makes it sound like I'm planning to keep her permanently.

Mini-Me emits a soft sigh, fidgeting slightly and cuddling a little more tightly against my side.

Really. I'm not planning to keep her. Honest?

I stare at the ceiling.

Fuck.

I'm so screwed.

We lay there for a while. Eventually, the kid wakes. She hastily uncurls her tail from my leg, the slightest hint of pink appearing in her cheeks.

I pat her on the head. "It's okay. No shame in being scared as long as no one notices. I was scared plenty as a kid. Fortunately, I had Mom. It's not so bad to have one person you can trust with the truth."

She sits on the bed next to me, making a series of faces across a range of emotions: embarrassment, worry, relief, indignation, and 'maybe I can trust you.' Hmm. This girl might not *exactly* be me after all. Not sure I'd have warmed up to me so fast in the same situation. But then again, I never ended up on the street alone as a six-year-old. Nor did I understand my supernatural nature so young. Something tells me we're going to be quite alike but not exact copies, at least, beyond physical appearance. Someday, years in the future when we stop growing older, we're going to be twins. Actually, I might already be 'mature' in the sense my outward appearance won't change with time. Mom didn't get a user's manual with me.

Because we'll eventually look like identical twins, it might be better to be big sister instead of mom here. It'll be less awkward. Then again, this one girl who lived in my dorm during college had a mother who everyone mistook for her older sister. Of course, they didn't appear to be *exactly* the same age.

Anyway… time for breakfast.

We head to the kitchen by way of the bathroom. The first breakfast burrito I subject to the rune oven leaps out at my face after it's done 'cooking.' It's sprouted little wings and a harmless mouth of teeth apparently made from cheddar cheese shreds. Mini-Me leaps after it, also spreading her wings and flying in circles around the room. She hits a few cabinet doors, jumping off them and leaving tiny claw marks.

Around and around they go for a minute or two in a scene of absolute chaos, the child claw-swiping at the runaway burrito like a demon-possessed cat on cocaine. Maybe my ears are playing tricks on me, but the eggs could be screaming in fear. I wonder if there's any connection with my apartment being number sixty-six on the sixth floor and me having the rune oven from Hell?

Finally, the child lands a claw swipe, tearing the burrito in half. Both pieces fall out of the air, inert. She pounces on one, kneeling while eating it.

"That was on the floor…"

She looks up at me. "Is touching the floor worse than it flying around? Still tastes okay."

Shaking my head, I put another burrito in the oven, lean back, and poke the purple gem. In a total miracle, the second one comes out normal. I offer it to her, but she's content to eat the formerly alive one. However, I do relocate her to a chair at the table with a plate.

Soon after breakfast is done, my phone rings.

Probably Lieutenant Sims wanting a real explanation. I hurry back to the bedroom and grab it. Oh, it's Natalie.

"Hey, what's up?" I ask, answering.

"Made some progress about your bird problem. I think there's a way for me to trace the origin of a summoned creature. It's going to require a part of it though. Like a feather maybe."

"Umm, won't a feather taken from a conjured creature disappear when the spell ends?"

"Yeah. I didn't say it would be easy."

Sigh. "How long do these birds exist?"

"I'm not a conjurer. No idea."

"You're a mage at least. Take a guess."

"Some of them can last until they're killed. Others, a couple hours. Depends entirely on the nature of the spell and how much focus the mage puts into it. Oh, idea."

I cringe. "So we're stuck unless I can manage to get to an attack scene before the bird leaves again. The chances aren't too good... and a feather? This is gonna hurt, isn't it?"

"No. Don't be silly." She laughs. "What we really need for a trace is a scrap of magical energy. A feather or piece of the summoned creature is the ideal source, but it could be too difficult for you to find. Another option would be a piece of debris the magic affected. There might be enough energy left in it to detect the magic responsible. You'd have to get something it either clawed, bit, or melted using lightning. Something burned by the fire it started won't work. The magic would have had to touch the object directly."

I pace around the bedroom, thinking. "Hmm. I can probably come up with something. Give me a couple hours."

"Okay. See you soon."

"Yep. And thank you."

"Anytime."

I hang up and return to the living room.

The kid's on the sofa playing *Gears of War.*

"C'mon. Get dressed. We need to go out for a bit."

"I don't have any clothes. Does it matter?"

"Damn," I mutter.

Could maybe borrow something from Ashley, but they're already gone for the day. I'd have to let myself into their apartment and grab something. Also, ninety-eight percent of Ashley's wardrobe is girly. Mini-Me would somehow manage to experience a wardrobe malfunction on purpose. I'd have been more embarrassed to be seen in a pink dress than streaking. Okay, doesn't say much about my feelings for pink since streaking didn't embarrass me at all.

I jog to the bedroom, grab my black ankh T-shirt and pull it on over her.

She peers down at it, stands, and nearly slips entirely through the neck opening. Wow, I was a *small* kid. I mean, it's not falling off her, but it wouldn't take much of a downward tug to stretch the fabric enough to get it past her shoulders. People are going to give us weird looks, but it's better than nothing. But flying… Oh, hell.

"Were you making people not notice you on purpose?" I ask.

"Yeah. Duh."

"Okay, good. Do it again for a little while longer. We're gonna go get you some stuff to wear. Need you to stay out of sight until you have something on."

"What's wrong with this?"

"It's too big on you. And we have to fly."

Mini-Me shrugs and pulls it off. "Okay. Let's go."

I grab the shirt, put it on, then head to my room for jeans and boots. When I return to the living room, I pretend not to see her standing beside the couch and start looking around.

"Lame. I'm not even doing it yet. And I know you can still see me."

"Heh. C'mon."

We go out, up to the roof, and pop wings at the same time. Having her along is kinda cool, actually. Good practice as well. The kid has no trouble keeping up with me. Seems our flight speed is constant regardless of age. She keeps close formation, but doesn't appear interested in holding hands out in public. Yeah, it's a bit too mushy.

As we near the Walmart, I also concentrate on my desire not to be noticed. We land in the parking lot about halfway between the edge and the storefront. No one pays us any attention. Okay, this is pretty damn cool. Hell, we could probably walk in and take whatever we wanted. Heh. It worked at Starbucks. A shopping cart would be pushing it since the wheels rattle. Someone would hear it. Mr. Kwan heard me laugh. But as much as I can carry could float out the door with me and no one would notice.

Grr. It would be my luck they have magic cameras or some bull-shit. I'm still getting used to exerting power over my surroundings so people don't see me. Not worth losing my job over a few items of kid clothing I can easily pay for.

Dammit. I'm getting old.

What's this foresight bullshit and where did it come from?

I put my wings away. The kid does as well.

On the way into the store, I attract a few of the usual looks. Older people get their disdainful frowns on—look at the goth punk. Middle-aged and thirtysomethings mostly only look at me long enough to process my existence so they don't walk into me. A few guys check me out. A girl or two check me out as well. Two guys in Iron Maiden shirts make metal horns at me. I return them.

Nobody appears to notice the kid beside me streaking around.

I lead her straight to the children's clothing section and proceed to pick out a few items: two fairly plain dresses with cutout backs so wings aren't an issue, plus a bunch of tops and skirts. I'm eyeballing size, erring on the slightly large so they last a while. Mini-Me watches in silence the entire time until I feel satisfied and head toward the shoe section.

"Umm. You're just grabbing stuff and not asking me if I like any of it," says Mini-Me.

I stop, face her, and hold up each item one by one so she can see them. Walmart's selection isn't exactly amazing, but I've grabbed the 'blackest' least girly stuff they have.

"Hrm. Okay." She folds her arms, seeming pissed. "It's fine."

"Not ignoring your opinion. I already know it."

Her mood brightens. "Huh?"

"I'm you, remember? Well, mostly. I know what I like."

"Oh..." She scratches her toe claw at the floor. "Are we gonna stay clones?"

"Expecting to randomly change into someone else?"

"No, silly." She sighs. "I mean... are we always gonna be like the same person inside?"

I gaze into space, confused. "Huh. I dunno. Didn't pay much attention in psych 101. Still kinda blurry on the nature vs. nurture deal. You'll probably be a little different if you stick around me instead of going to live with our—I mean my mother."

"She's not my mom?"

"Well, technically... I suppose she is in a biological sense. She's only forty-four now. Not impossible to have a six-year-old. But she's not the one who endured the pain of childbirth for you."

"I wasn't born. They tore me whole from the very fabric of your being."

"That, too. Here." I toss one of the dresses over her head.

She pulls it on, no protest. Sounds about right. My overly casual relationship with clothing as a kid came from two main reasons: laziness and loving how it made adults freak out. Nowadays, it's only laziness. People would still flip out if I streaked, only, it wouldn't end well. Cops are real killjoys.

The dress is a bit loose on her, but fits way better than my T-shirt. She examines it, twists side to side, seeming neither to like nor hate it.

"Dresses are girly."

"Yep. Used to think the same at your age. But, I've changed my opinion."

"Why?" She stares up at me.

"Dresses and skirts don't get in the way of the tail."

"Oh." Mini-Me twists around to look at her rear end. Her little tail drops down out of the dress and swishes side to side. "Yeah. But if the blade has to come out, we already have bigger problems than a hole in pants."

Chuckling, I take her hand and lead her to the shoe aisle. She hisses like a vampire seeing crosses. "Do I have to?"

"Not right away, but the school is going to give us a hard time if you keep showing up barefoot. Ask me how I know."

"Don't have to. I'm you, remember?"

"Brat," I say past a grin.

"I know." She smiles, satisfied.

Between our collective disinterest in shoes, potential for claw destruction, and growing out of stuff, no reason to go crazy here. I can't even comprehend how some girls get all fired up about shoe fashion. Never made sense to me at all. I wore shoes as a kid/teen for two reasons only, and neither of them were to keep warm or earn style points. First reason was Mom or society ordered me to. Had to wear them to school, for example, since I didn't go to a one-room schoolhouse in turn-of-the-century Kansas. My second reason—and driver of fashion choice—for footwear involved more practical concerns, like not having my toes smashed in a fight or the need to stomp a bitch in the face.

Hopefully, Mini-Me doesn't need shit-kickers for a few years at least, even though they'd be ridiculously adorable in her size. Argh. Why do I keep thinking the A word? Gah. Kids are evil. Little me is evil. She's already in my head. I shouldn't be thinking this way at all.

I grab her a pair of ordinary sneakers—*not* the ones with pink trim, though I do go for them first as a joke to tease her. Also, on impulse, I grab a set of tough-looking black synthetic sandals. Best of both worlds. These shoes, toe claws won't destroy. Of course, if she full shifts, the straps would probably break from the size increase, but whatever. They're six bucks.

We head to the registers. A woman does a double take at Mini-Me's tail, twisting to keep watching us as we pass. The kid retracts the wayward appendage before the woman finishes turning. Stunned, the woman blinks a few times, then shakes her head while muttering about not getting enough sleep.

Hah. Messing with people already. Awesome.

The dress she's wearing mysteriously loses its tags before we reach the register. Weird how they spontaneously detach and float away. What's their loss prevention going to do? Accuse her of walking into the store with no clothes? Obviously, someone would've noticed.

So, stealing a $12 dress isn't exactly my greatest thrill, but it's a matter of principle. Gotta teach the kid right after all.

We walk out carrying a few plastic bags, heading around to the side of the store where they have the dumpsters. Fewer people there, so it's easier to hide wings. A few minutes later, we land on the roof of our apartment building. It's only a short stop to leave the shopping bags. Going to head back to the tank farm in Jersey and look for something Natalie can use to locate the source of the conjurations.

Mini-Me seems excited by the idea of taking a long high-speed flight. We're a couple minutes away from Philly when I notice she isn't wearing shoes.

"What happened to your sandals?"

"Umm. Forgot them in the shopping bag."

"Okay." No point saying I told her twice. She knows. I know she knows. She knows I know she knows.

"Didn't know you wanted me to wear them," she replies in a tone making her lie more of a joke than a serious attempt to deceive me.

"All right."

She looks down at her feet and splays her toes apart. "Oops."

I laugh, remembering saying almost the same things to Mom when she showed up at school to drop off the shoes I 'forgot' for the third time in a week. Hey, tying laces took precious time away from more fun things.

"Just be careful where you step when we get there. Could be sharp crap all over the place."

"You're not gonna turn around?"

"Small cuts will heal before you even look at them."

"You're not like worried about me getting hurt?"

"Are you worried about getting hurt?"

CONTENTS

1. A Waste of a Fine Afternoon 1
2. Meltdown 18
3. Here We Go Again 23
4. Kinda Lazy 31
5. A Little Extreme 42
6. Territorial 51
7. Mostly Harmless 60
8. My Problem Now 68
9. The Front Street Bastards 74
10. Plan-B 83
11. Circle of Binding 89
12. Saving the World 96
13. Mother's Guilt 108
14. Wild Thunderbird Chase 121
15. Familiar Haunt 133
16. Outer Child 142
17. Buttheads 150
18. Immediate Plans 167
19. Picking Up a Few Things 174
20. Hitting the Leaf 187
21. The Third Eye 191
22. Thunder Hawk 199
23. It's Going to be Interesting 208
24. The Power of Names 215
Acknowledgments 223
About the Author 224
Other books by Matthew S. Cox 225

The Queen of Discord
Temporal Armistice Book 4
© 2020 Matthew S. Cox
All Rights Reserved

Cover & interior art by: Alexandria Thompson

ISBN (ebook): 978-1-950738-22-9

ISBN (paperback): 978-1-950738-23-6

THE QUEEN OF DISCORD

TEMPORAL ARMISTICE BOOK 4

MATTHEW S. COX

DIVISION ZERO PRESS

She shrugs. "No, but I'm only six. You're supposed to be the responsible one."

This is probably the kind of shit I'd have said to Mom if she hadn't been the most amazing parent in the world.

"If I'm the responsible one here, we're both in big trouble."

Mini-Me giggles.

"We're ballsy, not stupid. I trust you not to do anything too dangerous."

"Okay."

She spends most of the hour-long flight ogling the scenery below. If her existing memories are based on me at six, flying wouldn't be part of it. This is the first time she's been up at a couple thousand feet. The view is pretty cool, even if it is New Jersey.

The tank facility is, predictably, a mess. The middle group of six tanks lay in ruins, but it appears the Hydromancers managed to save the rest of them. Impressively, they've also managed to put the fire out already. Gotta love mages.

A handful of cops stand guard at the facility's road entrance. To avoid them, we dive in low over the Raritan River, maybe six feet above the water, and cruise past a dock loaded with pipes and hoses for ships to transfer or take on liquid cargo. Obviously, the storage facility isn't operating at the moment. Probably won't be for weeks.

Undetected by the police, we slip into the center of the burned area. Thick black sludge striated in a rainbow sheen coats the ground, oil, plus fire retardant foam, plus whatever effect being magically frozen had. The stench of petroleum and gasoline is eye watering. I elect *not* to land, instead hovering over the morass, as does Mini-Me. This gunk would be an absolute chore to wash off... and we'd reek for days.

She scrunches her face at me. "It smells bad here."

"That's just New Jersey."

The kid gives me a 'seriously?' stare.

"No, I'm kidding. Helped out once for a giant fire a couple miles north of here. The whole area smelled like diapers."

"Eww."

"Yeah, I still don't know if it was the water, mud from low tide, or something else." I look around. "See if you can find a piece of metal that looks like lightning hit it."

"Okay." She eagerly glides off to the right.

The strange things I find fun. Mom never took me to a burned petroleum storage facility as a child. I feel deprived. We spend about an hour picking around before finding a spot on one of the tanks where the thick steel outer shell is ripped a bit like the fondant on a huge cake where the knife went in. It melted more in the resulting fire, but I'm almost certain this is the damage caused by the initial lightning bolt breaching the tank.

I land in a gargoyle crouch atop the remains of the metal wall. The child alights on the other side of the breach in the side wall, in a similar pose. Hmm. Yanno, maybe medieval stonemasons invented gargoyles based on Shaar'Nath. Obviously, they way exaggerated the ugly, but the pose is right. Or this is merely the natural arrangement of limbs for a biped perching like a cat on a narrow surface. Whatever. I extend my tail and chop at the steel, slicing off a nice-sized fragment.

"Cops!" whispers Mini-Me. They heard you hit the metal."

"Yeah figured. They're not going to walk back here and go knee-deep in sludge. Just stay quiet."

She nods.

We hide behind the wreckage of the tank, listening to the cops walk as close as they can. The only creatures lazier than me are—no not cops—mall security guards. Cops are a few notches higher on the lazy scale. The main difference between mall security guards and cops in terms of laziness is cops have triggers where they get really *un*-lazy. Stuff like speeding, stealing cars, giving them the finger, and so on. And when cops are forced to become un-lazy, they are mad at you for it.

However, a pair of cops presently reduced to the functional equivalent of mall security guards aren't too motivated to investigate a random *clank* in a burned out tank farm, especially when doing so would require they step in knee-deep sludge.

"Probably something falling apart," says a man.

"Wanna go check it out?" asks a woman.

"How desperately do you want to smell like the engine of a '78 Buick Skylark for the rest of the month?"

"Umm." The woman pauses. "That is a strangely specific reference."

He laughs. "My granddad's car. Damn thing always smelled like burning oil. Nah, screw it. You're right. Just a rock or some shit. Maybe a seagull."

They walk back to the gate.

I look at Mini-Me. "Are you thinking what I'm thinking?"

"Probably. I'm you."

I grin.

She grins wider.

We spend another hour or so teasing the cops by making random noises while 'inconspicuous.' The cops start to get nervous when the woman asks her partner if he believes in ghosts.

Mini-Me sticks her head into the burst-open, empty tank at the northwest corner and calls, "Mommy?"

The woman cop jumps. "Did you hear a kid, Ray?"

Her partner's like a hundred feet off on the right of the burned area. He looks in her direction. "Hear what?"

"Sounded like a little kid yelling for their mother."

"You been watchin' too damn many movies, El."

I chuck a small rock to the ground behind him.

He spins. "Jesus freakin' Christmas. If someone's in here, you better show yourself right goddamn now."

The woman cop screams.

Her partner jumps again, spinning toward her and drawing his gun. "Ellen?"

She runs over to him, looking more white than Puerto Rican. In rapid-fire Spanish, she rambles about a sensation like a little kid grabbing her hand. She's so scared she's lost command of English.

Mini-Me's hiding and watching her from too far away to touch her, so I suspect the 'hand hold' came from telekinesis. Heh. She's learning.

I give her an 'okay, that's enough' nod. Don't want these two to end up in psychiatric care.

She responds with a thumbs-up, then leaps off the tank, gliding out over the water. I fly after her and we climb together up to about 2,000 feet.

Once we're out of earshot from the cops, we both erupt in laughter. It's been way too long since I wantonly dicked around with people. All my 'friends' are too grown up to do this kind of shit anymore. But... Mini-Me isn't.

Oh, boy. This is potentially bad.

I love it.

20

HITTING THE LEAF

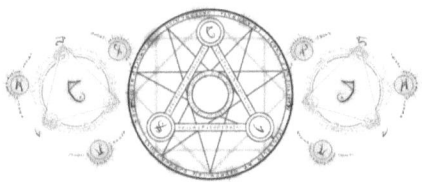

N atalie's sitting behind the counter of her enchanting shop, reading her Scry when we walk in.

Of course, being a mage, it's like obligatory or something for her to use one of those instead of a tech e-reader. She looks up only briefly as we walk in. I approach the counter, Mini-Me at my left.

"Hey, Brook. Hey, Ash."

"Who's Ash?" asks Mini-Me.

"The human girl the buttheads put in the dog cage at the warehouse," I say.

"Oh." Mini-Me nods. "She was really angry."

Natalie peels her attention off the Scry and stares at us. "Whoa. Who's that? Are you starting like a child-walking service or something? Don't they have leash laws?"

"Ha. No. It's a strange situation." I set the tank fragment on the counter, then pick Mini-Me up so our faces are side by side. "Notice anything?"

Natalie squints at us. I can practically feel her subconscious mind screaming the obvious answer at her, but her conscious mind is presently occupied by the plot of the fiction novel she'd been reading.

I set the child on her feet, pull out my phone, and bring up a picture of me and my mother when I was about eight. Closest I have. "Does this help?"

She looks at the picture, at us, back at the picture. "Holy shit, you found a time fold?"

"No."

"Aren't mages supposed to be smart?" asks Mini-Me.

"They are, but she's an enchanter," I say.

Natalie gives me the finger, pretending to pick her eye.

We laugh.

"So, what's going on here?" Natalie leans over the counter. "She looks just like you."

"Only smaller and cuter," adds Mini-Me.

I playfully swat at her. "Warmongers."

"I'm going to need more than one word to explain this." She whistles.

"Natalie, meet Mini-Me. The idiots magically cloned me hoping to raise her differently enough to end the world."

"Nope." The child shakes her head. "I kicked him in his stupid balls."

"Wait…" Natalie stands there a second, open-mouthed. "So she's basically you?"

"Mostly," I say. "Physically, totally identical. But she already knows about the Shaar'Nath stuff. Figuring we'll be slightly different personalities but close."

"If she's even 'close' to you as a child, keep her away from the toys." Natalie pretend-panics. "I think I still have a kennel in the back room."

"Toys?" Mini-Me raises both eyebrows. She turns, spots the kid section, and twitches.

"Oh, shit," mutters Natalie, in a teasing voice like she's not really worried.

Mini-Me walks over to the little wall surrounding the play area. It's an inch or two higher than her chin, so she does a pull-up to see inside. "Ooh."

"Didn't ask permission?" whispers Natalie.

"She's me. Easier to ask forgiveness. Besides, she knows I'd say yes." I twist around to look at the kid. "Be careful with the doorbell on the dollhouse. It will shrink you."

"Pff. Dolls," says Mini-Me. "As if."

I look back to Natalie and explain getting stuck in the barrier, the horribly painful magic, and waking up to find them talking to the kid.

"Hard to believe. Lifemages have been trying to clone people and make them young again for… as long as magic existed. Very few have come close to success."

"You're forgetting Elestari are involved. Human mages are like chimpanzees using grass to get ants out of anthills. Elestari are neurosurgeons doing nanobot surgery."

"We're not *that* far behind."

I laugh. "Still. They made the Armistice a really damn long time ago. I think they can figure out how to Xerox me."

"Fair."

"Oh, Nat, can you maybe make her an amulet like mine? She has the same 'frequently destroys clothes' problem."

Mini-Me leaps onto the top of a tall shelf of toys inside the play area, wings, horns, and tail out. "Like, rawr or something."

"Backless dress. Good thinking. And yeah, no problem." Natalie picks up the steel fragment. "Hmm. What's this?"

"Part of the tank the bird zapped. Should be right where the lightning made contact. Will it work?"

"Only one way to find out. Give me a bit to scry it."

I raise both eyebrows. "If you're going to light up, let me in on that action."

"What about the department drug tests?"

"Not like I'm planning to do this every day, and I can probably make Sims just mark me down as passing without even going."

"Me too!" yells Mini-Me. She jumps off the shelf, gliding across the store to land atop the counter on all fours like a cat with wings.

"Not yet, kiddo." I poke her in the side. "I didn't touch pot until twelve."

She stands and taps her foot on the glass. "And look how you turned out."

Natalie laughs. "This kid is great."

Smirking, I mutter, "I'm my own worst critic."

"What are you gonna do with her?" asks Natalie.

Mini-Me frowns. "I'm not 'something to be dealt with.'"

"No, not what I mean." Natalie ruffles the kid's hair. "I mean are you gonna bring her to your mom? Keep her? Is she even real?"

"Don't be a bitch," says Mini-Me. "I'm real. And I am *totally* hitting the leaf with you guys."

"You're way too small for pot." I pluck a scrunchie out of a bin on the counter and toss it, trying to get it to land on one of her little horns.

The pink fabric circle goes right where I wanted—thank you, telekinesis. The horn it landed on, plus half of the child's hair, turns hot pink.

She stares at me, unamused. "Since when do you care about rules?"

"It's not rules. It's caring about not doing stupid things. Your body isn't ready for weed yet."

"And yours was at twelve?" She taps her foot again.

"Kid's got a point." Natalie laughs.

"Well, more ready than six. Besides"—I take the scrunchie off her horn, which promptly returns to being jet black—"I had zero interest in smoking weed at six, so I know you don't. But I would've totally messed with my mother about it."

"Damn." Mini-Me snaps her fingers. "You got me."

"Would have messed with your mom?" asks Natalie.

"Yeah. *If* Mom smoked weed. Which she doesn't. Devil's lettuce and all that."

"Ugh." Natalie rolls her eyes. "Okay, to the scrying room!" She runs to the front door, switches the sign to 'ring bell for service,' locks the door, and hurries into the back.

I point at Mini-Me. "You aren't toking up."

She sticks her tongue out at me before jumping off the counter and returning to the play area.

21

THE THIRD EYE

Whoa.

I needed that.

All throughout college, Natalie always did manage to get the *good* stuff. I haven't felt this relaxed in at least a year. In fact, pretty sure the nap faerie came to visit me unexpectedly as I don't remember Mini-Me laying across me.

We're in Natalie's 'meditation chamber,' which is merely a fancy way of saying pot lounge. Sure, she sometimes does actual magical scrying in here, but when you have a nice little room where the floor is covered in pillows around a giant hookah, it can't sit there doing nothing when no magic needs to happen.

A small table in the middle holds her enchanted bong. I'm not sure if it counts as a bong or hookah since it has extension hoses. The room is also enchanted to keep the smoke from seeping into the store. No, we're not stewing in it... much. She's got a rope to pull in order to vent the happy fumes outside. A police drug dog could walk right up to the doorway in the hall outside this room, but unless it stuck its nose past the threshold, wouldn't smell anything.

Of course, the local cops don't really care too much about pot. It's still technically illegal here, but there's so much national pressure to legalize they've kinda forgotten it in favor of going after heroin, coke, e-meth and stuff.

Crap. What's Mini-Me doing in here?

I lift my head off the pillow.

All three of us are sacked out on the floor. I don't remember taking my boots off, but they're gone. Wow. It's been too long. Weed doesn't usually make me lose time. Mini-Me is awake, merely using me as a living pillow. Her eyes are slightly red around the edges.

"I told you not to."

She smiles dazedly. "I didn't. Just sat in the room watching you and Natalie. Secondary buzz is weaksauce."

Ugh. Poor Mom. Is this what she had to go through with me? My kid got a contact high. Wait. Did I just think *my* kid?

"Crap!" I yell.

Mini-Me jumps. "What?"

Natalie moans. "Ooh. Little stronger than I intended."

"Fell asleep," I say with the speed of a practiced liar. "If Sims called me, I would've missed it."

"Oh." Mini-Me nods, oblivious.

It's easy to lie to myself. Seem to be doing it rather often lately.

Natalie sits up, eyes half-lidded. "Wharton State Forest."

I look over at her and crack up. 'Someone' drew a third eye on her forehead in eyeliner pencil. Mini-Me also laughs.

"Ugh, my head." Natalie shifts to sit cross-legged, face in both hands. "Feels like a rock."

"What the heck did we smoke?"

"Dispensary-grade 'midnight oil' with a couple pinches of dediscaria, witchwood leaf, and ginger added."

"Dediscaria... no wonder I can't remember the past twenty minutes." I grasp the child's head in both hands and study her eyes. Hmm. She doesn't look *too* high.

"You probably have to go to the forest," says Mini-Me. "Natalie will watch me while you go rip this guy's head off."

"Hah. It's going to take me a few minutes to find the desire to stand. I've been wound way too tight lately and my spring's unwound all over the floor now."

"Good shit," says Natalie, grinning. "The magic this steel touched came from Wharton State Forest."

"Wherever that is." I keep rubbing my forehead.

The bell rings out in the store.

Natalie drags herself upright and plods out of the meditation room. A few minutes later, traces of conversation leak back down the corridor. Sounds like a couple of parents interested in a rideable toy unicorn. A polite little girl voice asks if it can 'pleeeease' have rainbow colored hair. Mini-Me looks physically ill at the concept. By the time I manage to find the desire to part ways with the lovely pillow-covered floor, the deal's been signed and the couple plus daughter are on their way out the door.

I stumble past a bead curtain into the area behind the front counter, where Natalie is scribbling in her logbook. Mini-Me follows, oddly quiet.

"Hey," she says, not looking back. "You okay?"

"Fine, just super relaxed."

She smiles over her shoulder at me. "So you're not going to race out there and rip this guy's head off?"

"No." I yawn. "You know I don't casually kill people for the lols. Don't even know for sure if it's a guy."

"It is." Natalie writes more in her notebook. "Pretty sure of it."

"Any idea where the hell Wharton State Forest is?" I ask.

"Probably somewhere with trees," says Mini-Me.

"Hah."

"Not a clue. The words came to me." Natalie closes the book. "Just sold a Rainbow Unicorn. And wow, what a pleasant change of pace."

"Change of pace?" I ask.

"The little girl was *so* damn polite and nice compared to most."

Mini-Me gives her the finger.

Natalie laughs. "Wasn't talking about you. Most of the time when parents come in here to buy the high-end magic toys, they're well…

rich or close to it and the kids are total brats. This girl was so sweet and polite."

"Nice. And sure, of course. Deal with it before Mini's necklace. You need income." I borrow Natalie's cash register computer and check Google maps for Wharton State Forest. Hmm. Southern New Jersey. Not too far away from Philly. It's a lot of ground to cover with no idea what exactly I'm looking for, but definitely more information than I had before.

The door opens, setting off the melodic magical chimes. A late-thirties guy in a brown raincoat, unshaven, combover, and dark glasses walks in. He totally looks like the sort of dude who chloroforms little girls and drags them off never to be seen again.

He approaches the counter, staring at the assortment of wands. "Hi. I'm looking for something in a self-defense wand. What sort of combat spells do you have?"

I narrow my eyes at him. The guy senses me staring at him and looks up. As soon as we make eye contact, I read him. Much to my surprise, he's not at all interested in kids despite having 'the look'. However, I'm absolutely sure he's going to kill someone. Wait, not *someone*, his wife and little son. He already tried to buy a gun, but didn't want to deal with the waiting period.

Mini-Me bumps a plastic cup off a shelf, sending shiny baubles scattering all over the floor behind the counter.

Natalie groans. "Excuse me."

The moment she crouches to start picking stuff up, I send my tail over my shoulder and ram the blade into the guy's face. A few inches of sharp onyx poke out the back of his skull. He gawks, emitting a faint raspy wheeze. I give the blade a twist and yank it out.

"Nice shot," says Mini-Me.

"Huh, what?" Natalie starts to stand.

The kid jumps on her back. "Stay down. You don't want to see."

Natalie peers through the glass wand cabinet at the guy lying flat on his back. "Baked fucking cockatrice! Did you just freakin..."

"Yeah."

"Why! Not two minutes ago, you told me you didn't kill people randomly for the lols." She sits on the floor rubbing her hands up over her head, faintly trembling.

"Don't freak out, 'kay? I saved you a giant headache. The guy was looking for a murder weapon to kill his wife and little son."

"Brook?" asks Mini-Me.

"Yeah?"

"How did I know it, too? And how did I know you were gonna kill him?"

I jump over the counter, landing beside the dead guy. "You knew what he was going to do because you're half Shaar'Nath. Well, more than half. Demon genes are supercharged. We can look at humans and tell their deepest desires or outward intent in any moment. You knew I was going to end him because you're me and it's what you'd do if you were older."

"Since when do you care about other people committing crimes?" asks Natalie.

Mini-Me and I say, "Soft spot for kids," simultaneously.

"And this guy planned to use a wand he bought from you to murder his family because he didn't like the waiting period for guns. The cops would've been up your ass sideways. Trust me." I pick the body up. "Everyone involved here wins."

"Except the dead guy," says Mini-Me.

"But there's still a Federal Arcane Controlled Enchantments background check," says Natalie.

I point at the corpse. "Which this idiot probably would have passed. They check past criminal activity, not future intent. And how long does it take?"

"Like fifteen minutes," mumbles Natalie. "I'm not sure what freaks me out more. That you just killed a guy right in front of me, or this child watched you do it and doesn't seem bothered."

"How about neither?" Mini-Me smiles. "Sorry about the shiny rocks. I'll help you pick them up. Only knocked it over so you didn't watch her stab him."

I drag the guy out to the alley behind the store, lay him on the paving, and fish his wallet out of his pants, plus car keys. Then, I incinerate the remains with Imbreleth fire. After a minute, not even bones remain… and the blacktop kinda glows like lava. No one will even find DNA in there. Perfect. The alley's going to smell like burned steak for a few hours, but only a mage or psychic will ever be able to figure out anything happened here. It's on me to make sure no one has any reason to be on this spot searching for paranormal information.

Time to relocate the car. Can't have it being found close to Natalie's store. I go in the back door, cross the shop while telling Mini-Me to wait here, and head out the front door. The registration in the wallet has an address in Wynnewood, out in the suburbs. It plus the keys point at a later-model BMW parked a few spaces to my right. Wynnewood's a hell of a drive from Kensington, far more time than I'm willing to invest. I could ditch the Beemer in Strawberry Mansion and it'll vanish in an hour. Meh, the almost-murdered wife might want it.

I am enough of a wiseass…

Concentrating on being inconspicuous, I hop in the Beemer and drive it over to East Girard Ave and park it in sight of the police station. After giving it a quick wipe-down, well-practiced after a few good years of joyriding, I drop the keys on the floor and walk away. It's fairly unlikely anyone will steal it there, and I'm sure the cops will find it soon after the wife reports it missing. Two blocks away, I corner onto Fletcher Street and leap into the air.

Natalie's scrubbing the floor when I walk back in.

By that, I mean she's watching an enchanted mop and two brushes do the work. She looks a bit rattled still, but nowhere near as bad as she'd have been if she witnessed my blade nail the guy.

"You okay?" I ask.

"Not really, but I guess I'll deal with it. You did basically save two lives."

"If it makes you feel better, the dude planned to off himself, too. Just gave him what he wanted faster, without collateral casualties." I'm lying out my ass. Well, maybe not. The guy might have been intending to end himself after the murders, but suicide hadn't been obvious in his intent at the moment I read him.

"I guess. At least you stopped a double murder, and spared me the guilt of being involved. Ugh. Maybe I shouldn't sell combat wands."

"Sell them or don't sell them. Up to you. It's not your responsibility what people do with them. Some people really do need them for protection against beasties. The suburbs aren't warded and no handgun in the world is going to bother a basilisk."

She exhales. "Yeah, true. So, umm, next time, maybe take them outside first? Now I'm going to have to put up a ward against pissed off ghosts."

"Sorry. Anyway, car's nowhere near here." I set the wallet on the counter. "License in here if you feel like pretending to be a psychic and contacting the wife, telling her not to go crazy hunting for the guy and she shouldn't feel sad over it. Gonna go see what's in the park now."

She eyes the wallet. "You know I'm going to crack and admit the truth if she pushes."

"You are too honest." I grab a fistful of her sweater and pull her close enough to kiss her atop the head. "Adorable."

She shoves at me. "So creepy."

"What?"

"You're acting like you didn't just stab a guy."

"Sorry. I can pretend to be upset if it helps."

She sighs. "No, no… it's okay. I just have to keep in mind you have a different frame of reference."

"Think about the douchebag from the city trying to shut you down for selling wands. He would have used this guy killing his family to metaphorically burn you at the stake."

Natalie grumbles. "I hate him. And you know me. I don't hate anyone."

"Except that guy," says Mini-Me.

"Okay. Off to the park. Guess the kid's gonna stay here."

"Yeah. Surprised she didn't insist on going with you."

Mini-Me shrugs. "I'm not scared. Just lazy. And, not even Brooklyn is crazy enough to bring a six-year-old along to fight someone for real. I'll go if you want me to, but I am kinda small."

I pat her on the head. "Nah. Stay here and have fun. You're not allowed to murder anyone until you're at least twenty-five."

"Aww! No fair."

"Sorry kid." I grin. "Them's the breaks."

"But you're only twenty-three."

I stare at the ceiling. "Fine. You're not allowed to kill anyone until you're twenty-three."

She pouts.

"Unless they're trying to kill you first."

The kid smiles. "Deal."

"Okay..." Natalie gives her side eye. "That's disturbing as hell."

"Relax. She's only acting creepy to tease you."

"Brook!" Mini-Me flails her arms. "Stop ruining it!"

22

THUNDER HAWK

Natalie may or may not regret babysitting a child version of me.

She's about as sweet and good natured as my mother, but nowhere near as resilient. Nat does, however, have something Mom did not: a store with a section of enchanted toys. It should be enough to occupy my escaped inner child for a few hours. Fortunately, I wasn't a hellion—no apology for the pun—as a kid. Never did anything malicious like setting fires, torturing animals, or attacking people. I was merely a free spirit who didn't accept 'against the law' as a reason not to have fun.

Up until the dude in the enchanting shop, every human I've ended had tried to kill me first. Note I said 'human.' Frank doesn't count as a person. He hadn't tried to kill me, but I caught him ripping Ashley's dress off her. The only thing I regret about tearing him apart is not being in the room twenty seconds earlier before he got his hands on her.

Anyway.

Wand man was imminently about to kill his wife and son. Again, no guilt.

The thunderbird conjurer, as far as I know, hasn't *deliberately* killed anyone. Conjured creatures are less precise than fire bolts. Several men died during an attack on a logging camp. However, based on what I've learned, I suspect they might have been armed and shot at the thunderbird. Multiple people have been hurt, though, including a few firefighters. It's pretty likely more people somewhere else have died as a result of his war against industrialization. Going to find this guy annoys me in the same way it annoyed me when my mother demanded I take the garbage out to the curb or cleaned the bathroom. It's a chore I don't really want to do and have only taken to begrudgingly out of guilt.

My mother didn't even nag me to do it this time.

A phantom, imaginary version of Mom sitting inside my head kept giving me the look. The 'I'm exhausted as hell, but if you don't want to clean the bathroom, I'll do it, *cariña'* look. My mother never had to yell or nag me. She's Catholic. The woman wields guilt like a two-handed sword. She's so good at guilt-fu, she's sending me to stop this guy from setting fires without even knowing she's doing it.

It doesn't take me long to reach Wharton State Forest, or at least the enormous swath of green southeast of Cherry Hill. Okay, it's *way* southeast of Cherry Hill, like twenty miles or so. A good chunk of southern New Jersey is green. Who'd have ever thought?

According to the app on my phone, Wharton State Forest is northeast from a pale spot labeled Hammonton. Looks like miles and miles of undisturbed woodlands. Basically, the perfect place for someone who doesn't want to be found and has no need of the modern world to hide.

Nothing else to do other than begin circling. Several small rivers squiggle through the woods, obvious from the air. Someone living out here would probably want to be fairly close to a water source, so I start my search by overflying them, favoring the northern one as it doesn't have roads surrounding it. According to my phone, I'm cruising over Springer's Brook and the Mullica River, two parallel tracts running north-south.

No signs of human habitation leap out at me right away. The navigation app shows a small lake a ways east of me called Mannis Duck

Pond. I veer toward it, flying in a gradually expanding circle. West of the pond and a little north, I spot a clearing containing a scorch mark in the general shape of a small airplane—or an enormous bird. Calling it a bird shape requires a certain degree of artistic license. Not quite as much as one needs to regard anything auto-tuned as 'music,' but almost. It's the first bit of anything to stand out as potentially unusual, so worth checking out.

I land at the edge of the char mark. It's pretty close to the same size as the bird I saw attacking the storage tanks. Kinda worries me the guy is reckless enough to attack stuff so close to where he lives, but maybe he's thinking a failure to do so would make his location obvious.

It's quiet here. Way quieter than even the trailer park. I consider myself a city girl even if most people from Philly or New York would laugh at the idea of referring to Quakertown or Allentown where I grew up as 'cities' in the same sense. Still, I'm accustomed to having lots of people around, plus endless noise from traffic and civilization.

In a way, the serenity is nice... but I wouldn't want to live here.

Less than a minute in this clearing, and already, boredom is starting. Okay, time to cheat. Or at least try. I am psychic, right? Normal people don't touch magical crystals used to start fires and end up getting hit over the head with a vision of the arsonist. Crouching, I grab a handful of charred dirt. What burned here? Who did this? Am I even in the right place?

No vision comes, but a mild, nagging urge to walk comes out of nowhere. Beats nothing.

I pull my wings in and begin wandering, not paying much conscious attention to where I'm going other than 'kinda feels right.' Outdoors is so not my element. I consider myself maybe an eight on a scale of one to ten in terms of being sneaky, ten being a movie-magic ninja. I used to sneak past mall cops, teachers, real cops, and normal citizens all the time. Okay, so maybe supernatural phenomena had been involved the same way Mini-Me made herself 'inconspicuous' without consciously wanting to activate special powers. My subconscious mind wouldn't have needed to know the truth in order to tap an instinctual talent. Maybe my score of eight is underselling myself.

Regardless, out here in the woods, I feel about as quiet and graceful as an army of donut-munching mall cops trying to roller skate through a warehouse full of smashed light bulbs. It's like every twig in two square miles has a suicide wish and races to get under my boots. If this conjurer is a real nature person, they've probably heard me already.

Of course, I look like a city kid who had a car problem and got lost in the woods. No one to be afraid of. By appearance, I'm the victim in every cheap horror movie ever made where a girl gets lost in the woods and the creep drags her into a cabin. People like forty-five or older assume I'm eighteen. Probably my slightly oversized eyes. Well, they do tend to cast blondes in those roles, not a half-Latina in a goth skirt. Normally, I find it irritating to get carded when people don't believe I'm over twenty-one. Here, it might come in handy. This guy won't think of me as a threat. Maybe he won't run.

I'm still not entirely sure if I *am* a threat to him. Killing the dude will take effort. More effort than tying shoes or putting on pants, two things I skip frequently due to their being too much work. And honestly, other than the fire hurting innocent people thing, I can't say my inner anarchist objects to his campaign against corporate entities. I'm no environmentalist hippie, but sticking it to big business is something I can root for.

For the better part of a half hour, I stumble through the underbrush, crunching twigs, ripping vines, getting branches across the face.

Total fun.

Finally, I catch a whiff of wood smoke, so I stop and listen. Sizzling. Maybe.

I head toward the sound, up a mild incline. A group of close-standing trees encircles an area about the size of an average single-story house. There appears to be a small dwelling inside, a hut made of branches, vines, and animal hides. Five fish hang from a wooden frame, perhaps drying out. A fallen tree cut into three sections forms a triangle around a fire pit, where a single man sits, tending a frying pan.

He's maybe forty with long black hair, wearing an ordinary windbreaker and jeans. At first, I figure him for Mexican, but a few steps closer, I change my mind. He's probably Native American. Really shouldn't surprise me considering he's been summoning thunderbirds. Well, making conjured copies of them. Speaking of, a thunderbird sits on a branch overlooking the campsite, farther away from me than the guy. Thankfully, this one's nowhere near as big as the last one I saw. If it stood on the ground, its head would about come up to my chest. A lightning bolt from this one wouldn't instantly vaporize me and slice a bunch of big rig trailers in half... but it would certainly suck.

"You may as well come closer," calls the man, not looking up from his pot.

Wow. I'm like sixty feet away, hiding behind a tree. Drat. Wasn't thinking about being inconspicuous. Oh, well. Busted. In my many years of nefarious deeds, I've learned one truth about being sneaky. When cops talk like they know where you are, they generally do, so there's no point pretending not to exist. It only makes them angry when you force them to come and drag you out of marshy weeds. Mall security guards, on the other hand, don't actually know where you are when they say they see you.

I'm not sure where on the scale of actual cop to mall guard conjurers fall, but considering the bird is looking right at me, I'm going to err on the side of busted. I stand out from behind the tree and casually walk the rest of the way up the incline and past the ring of trees. No way do I think they naturally grew in this formation.

"Please, sit. Are you hungry?" He gestures at one of the other logs.

"Thank you, but I can't take your food. I can get my own easily enough." I do, however, sit.

The man looks up from a hunk of fish in his frying pan, smiling at me. "I have been wondering when you would arrive."

"You knew?"

"Not exactly when, but yes. Though I expected your arrival, I do not understand your purpose. The spirits did not warn me of danger. However, you wear death like a shadowy cloak."

A brief mental image of Death—the Grim Reaper—being unwillingly crafted into a cloak, his head sticking out with a 'help me' expression, almost makes me laugh. Something about this guy keeps me quiet, like laughing at or near him is somehow disrespectful. "Wear death like a shadowy cloak... sounds cool."

He chuckles. "Most fear death. Few see it as a necessary part of the cycle. No world is permanent, but our greatest responsibility is to care for the world we inhabit. You are the first visitor to wander here and see me. How did the smoke not fog your vision?"

"This oval of trees"—I glance around—"it's somehow supposed to confuse people into not seeing you?"

He nods once.

"I've got a few tricks. Not exactly what you'd call normal."

"This, I knew when you walked through the flames at the natural gas pumping station, and grasped the valve wheel so hot it melted in your hands."

"Yeah. I can see through smoke."

"It is not literal smoke surrounding me. Smoke within the mind."

I lean forward, elbows on my knees, gazing into the fire. Even a small one like this is mesmerizing, a taste of a home my ancestry remembers but I've never seen. "Magic's not really my thing. I don't understand. Maybe because I'm kinda supernatural."

"You're no skinwalker."

"Thanks. Nope."

"Are you what *they* refer to as a demon?"

"Heh." Can't help but smile. "I could technically answer your question with both yes and no and not be lying."

"I am interested in understanding how the answer can simultaneously be true as well as false." He turns the slab of frying fish over.

"Simple. There aren't any such things as demons. I'm one of the beings ancient humans mistook for demons. Before you ask, no, I'm not here to kill you."

"Mistook for demons?" He tilts his head at me. "*They* constantly tell stories of how they wish the world to be. *They* speak of demons, angels, and a savior, yet insult our spirits. You bring different stories."

I let my horns and wings out. "Has anyone telling you stories ever *proved* what they say?"

He leans back.

The bird watches me more intently, its sapphire beak opening slightly—likely the thunderbird version of pulling the hammer on a gun back. Hope the shock chicken doesn't have wing envy. I've got him beat for span.

"My mother's human. Dad's one of these guys,"—I flutter my wings. "He told me humans saw us thousands of years ago and made up demons. As far as I know, there are no such things as true demons the way humans think of them. Of course, it's impossible to prove something doesn't exist, so maybe they're out there. I only know for certain I'm not a minion of Hell."

"What are you then?"

"A firefighter."

He blinks.

"Yeah, I know. Female firefighters are all six-foot bull lesbians, right?"

"I wouldn't imagine so. Why would you say that?"

"It's what people I've run into always assume. Gets old fast. Really, I'm just Brooklyn Amari." I retract the wings and horns, then offer a hand.

"I am sometimes known as Thunder Hawk, but you may call me Allen Machcote." He shakes. "What brings you all the way here to find me? You would not come without purpose."

"Well, to be completely blunt with you, I was kinda hoping you'd stop blowing up chemical plants, factories, and petroleum facilities."

"They are killing the Earth Mother, and it needs to stop before we perish. *They* have greed which knows no boundaries. I sense you are not one of them."

"If the 'they' you keep referring to is white people, then yeah. I'm not one of them. My mother's side of the family is from Puerto Rico. My father's side of the family is slightly less local. Look, I'm totally with you about giving it to 'the man,' but the big boom needs to stop."

He regards me with an unreadable expression.

"You're into the whole spirit whispering thing. What if I told you... ugh. I don't mean to sound like the Matrix guy. Sorry. Normally, I'm like the laziest person in the world. I'm not a cop. There's no reason for me to really get off my ass and do anything about someone like you doing your thing. But, I am psychic. Over and over again, I'd walk into a room *just* as the news showed a fire one of your birds started. Or I'd walk in on people talking about a fire at a chemical plant. It's like the universe kept throwing you in my face. I couldn't get away from it, and believe me, I wanted to ignore you."

Allen rubs his chin, staring *through* me.

"I'm completely guessing here, but it's possible if you keep doing what you're doing the way you're doing it, something *really* bad is going to happen. Might only be bad in the sense me or someone I love is going to get killed. Might be bad in a bigger way. I don't know. People who had nothing to do with the 'white man's greed' have been hurt. Ninety percent of the workers at these places are as much victims of the companies' greed as the planet. They're only trying to do what they can to feed their families or not end up homeless. If you ask me, it would be more effective for you to selectively target the real problem. CEOs. Bigwigs. Or better yet, instead of blowing stuff up, overrun the facilities with out-of-control plant growth."

"The spirits have sent you." Allen pulls his fish off the fire, setting the pan on the log beside him. "You who are cloaked in death come as a warning of what is to come."

"Umm. Are you saying I'm going to end up having to kill you?"

He laughs. "No. The spirits sent one like you here as a message. Perhaps you are right. I thought to make war on those who would kill the Earth Mother, but these men thrive on war. Making war on poison only spreads it farther. Those who do not participate in war directly suffer the most."

"So... you'll stop lighting places on fire?"

"The message you bring may mean my actions release a great death into the world, death with wings."

I furrow my brow, thinking. "Like gas? You hit the wrong tank and set loose a cloud of methyl isocyanate or something? Kill thousands?"

"Such a disaster would be one way to interpret the notion of death on wings, yes." He bows to me. "Tell the spirits their message is received. I will not continue as I have been."

"Cool. Then, I'll leave you be. I'm sure you've got a lot of meditating or something to do. And your dinner's getting cold."

"City woman, you are leaving in peace?"

I stand. "Yep. Not a cop. My job is putting out fires… and apparently being psychically badgered into finding you and delivering a warning. Can't say I disagree with your opinions, only the methods."

"Walk with the spirits, young one." Allen smiles at me, then picks up his frying pan to use as a plate.

The bird emits a faint squawk, also slightly bowing its head at me.

"Thanks." Now, maybe the universe will ease back on me a bit.

Leaving Allen to his fish dinner, I stretch my wings and jump into the air, trying to be 'inconspicuous.' Time to go back home and deal with something far scarier than leer-jet-sized lightning birds: a six-year-old version of me.

23

IT'S GOING TO BE INTERESTING

Considering I'm already out here and my meeting with Allen went *way* better than expected, I decide to pay a visit to the wife of the man who wanted to kill her.

I haul ass to Wynnewood, then slow to a hover a couple thousand feet over the ground to fish the guy's wallet out of my hip bag. The driver's license of one Brad Akers—grr, I still need to go back to the DMV—gives me the address to a nice suburban home with an Acura in a two-car driveway. Lights on the back side of the house draw me around to the yard, where I land, leaning hard on my urge to stay unnoticed. A mid-thirties white chick with dye-blonde hair overdue for a reapplication of color is in the kitchen, evidently preparing dinner. She's got an 'I need to talk to your manager' haircut, but not the imperious facial expression. Matter of fact, she looks scared.

It's a few minutes after six, no surprise the wife is home.

Even without making eye contact, I pick up a sense of despondent dread from her. The mood makes the half inch of brown roots in her hair feel like she hates being blonde and does it for him. This woman is on edge. However, I can't tell if she's worried about Brad or frightened at what his absence might mean. It doesn't seem possible to me that a woman whose husband is ready to buy a gun/wand to murder her would be totally clueless of the danger she's in. I'm gonna assume she's reacting to his unexplained absence by expecting tonight's the night he tries to kill her.

I walk up onto the back deck, approaching the door. While talking to her might work out, it's better for everyone concerned if Natalie and I remain as far removed from this as possible. I set the wallet on the doormat—keeping the cash as I do have some standards—and raise my hand to knock.

Wait. Let's get a bit more creative.

I extend my claws and lightly scratch them down the door, not enough to damage it, only make noise. As soon as the woman inside starts to walk over, I scoot to the right, concentrating *hard* on not wanting her to be aware of me.

She peers out the window, shrugs, and turns around.

Dammit.

I stick my tail out and scrape the blade down the door.

"Brad?" asks the woman, sounding nervous. She moves up to the door and peers out. I use my tail to scrape it again. Finally, she opens the door, looking down as if suspecting a raccoon or other animal. Upon seeing the wallet, she gets paler, whispering, "What kind of sick game are you up to this time?"

"Do not mourn him," I whisper.

The woman jumps, looks around rapidly, then presses a hand to her face. "Voices now? Really?"

"Not voices," I whisper.

"Who's there?" She leans out, looking right, then left—straight at me, only she doesn't appear to see me. "Hello?"

"A messenger," I rasp, barely managing not to break into giggles at the cheese. "Brad intended to take your life tonight, and harm your son as well."

She swallows hard, falling to her knees in the doorway. Shaking, she gingerly reaches out and picks up the wallet, opening it, gasping when she sees his license. Hope and relief radiate from her. Yeah, figured she knew the score.

"Brad Akers is dead," I whisper. "Do not mourn."

"He's gone..."

"Yes," I whisper, trying to sound spooky.

Okay, any more of this melodramatic horror movie bullshit and I'm going to crack up laughing. Yeah, it's serious as hell and she's in a really bad place, but I can't keep pretending to be some messenger of the dead with a straight face. Also can't reveal myself and create any possible route for the cops to trace things back to Natalie. Before she says anything else, I leap into the air. My ability to force people not to notice me doesn't stop the wind from my sudden departure. No big deal. Adds to the ghostly effect.

I smile the whole way back to Kensington.

As soon as I walk into Natalie's shop, Mini-Me pops up over the wall around the play area.

"This place is cool, but all these toys are like medieval and stuff. Where are the video games?"

"Back home," I say. "We'll be there soon enough."

The kid grins. "Did you kill the chicken guy?"

"Colonel Sanders?" I ask, eyebrow raised.

She smirks. "Funny."

Natalie emerges from the bead curtain behind the counter. She looks... exhausted, but okay.

"Yeah, 'chicken guy' is handled. Didn't have to kill him or even threaten." I lean on the counter and tell them about my meeting with Allen Machcote. "So, Nat, you think I really did get a precognitive worry about a giant poison gas disaster?"

"No idea. I'm into magic. Psychic stuff is your thing." She winks.

I gaze around at the store. "Glad to see she didn't burn it down. Please tell me you didn't put her in the cage."

Mini-Me gasps.

"I don't really have a cage." Natalie throws an enchanted scrunchie at me. "Though, I have been worrying. Hate to say it, but she's kinda dangerous to the world. Have you considered undoing the spell?"

The child goes platter-eyed, lip quivering. "What? I-is she saying she wants to kill me?"

Wow. I can't tell if she's overacting or actually scared.

"Nope." I shake my head. "Haven't considered undoing anything. If she's me, it's not going to be a problem. I don't think she's 'magic in progress' either. She can't be 'dispelled.'"

"What the heck were they thinking?" asks Natalie.

"Already said. They wanted to raise her evil. Also, I can't kill myself."

Natalie exhales. "It's not killing her. If she's a conjuration from a spell, it would only be reversing the magic so she never existed in the first place."

"Still." I put a hand on Mini-Me's shoulder, defensiveness rising as well as a bit of anger at Nat. "Feels wrong to even talk about this. We're not hurting her."

Natalie swallows hard, aware of the edge in my voice, and averts her eyes from Mini-Me's pathetic stare. "No, no… I don't want to hurt her. Only saying the forces of evil could use her to end the world. If she's not a truly real person, we'd be taking a big risk is all."

"I'm real," whispers Mini-Me.

"*Is* she an apparition or real?" I ask.

"Hmm." Natalie looks at the kid and raises a hand as if to invoke magic.

Mini-Me sprouts claws, then ducks behind me, growling. "Stay away!"

"It's okay," says Natalie.

"This bitch wants to kill me." Mini-Me points around me at her.

"That bitch is my best friend. She won't hurt you." I really don't mean to sound like I'm adding a nonverbal 'or else' at the end, but it's possible one leapt on there by itself.

"Only a sensing spell. Honest." Natalie mumbles something in quasi-Latin. Her eyes glow amber for an instant and fade back to normal. "Hmm again." She ducks into the back room.

"What is your crazy friend doing?" asks Mini-Me.

"Not sure. But she isn't going to hurt you. She's overly cautious."

"She just wanted to *undo* me." The girl hides behind me.

I twist to look her in the eye. "Undoing isn't the same as killing."

Mini-Me furrows her brows. "It's technically true to say murder is 'undoing' having a baby."

Natalie returns with the Aznian crystal. She sets it in a bowl on the counter. "Hey, kiddo. Would you mind touching this?"

"It's not going to blow me up, is it?"

"No." Natalie smiles. "I promise."

I touch the crystal. It glows crimson in response. "See? Just light."

Mini-Me reaches up and puts a finger on it. The crystal glows crimson.

"Okay. She's real." Natalie exhales, lips flapping. "No active magic and the crystal identifies her as Shaar'Nath."

"Well there we go." I raise my arms and let them fall against my sides. "She's real. We can't destroy her."

"Oh, great." Mini-Me rolls her eyes. "Just what every kid wants to hear from their mother. 'I can't destroy you' is *so* much more epic than 'I love you.'"

Mother? I blink. She called me her mother?

Natalie glances back and forth between us.

"How much like me is she going to be?" I ask, forcing my voice past a tiny lump in my throat.

"Sec." Natalie runs the Aznian crystal into the back room again, returning with two amethyst wands, a white marble rod, and a book.

She spends a few minutes invoking the wands and rod at Mini-Me, making wisps of green, pink, and rose-colored light. They must do something she can see, as each time she finishes using an item, she reads a few lines in the book as if referencing a chart. Reminds me of a mechanic looking up diagnostic codes from a car's computer. Other than a bit of glowing vapor, nothing appears to happen to her or the child.

"All right." Natalie closes the book. "I think it's going to be similar to diverging time streams. You two will be a lot alike, but the experiences in her life going forward from now on will make her into a slightly different person by the time she's your age. The only way she will turn into exactly you would be to recreate the exact set of life experiences you had. Everything you lived through would need to be recreated for her to come out as the same person you are mentally."

"Way too much work," I say.

"You going to leave her with your mother?"

Mini-Me bites her lip, glancing down for a second before catching herself and acting casual.

"Hah." I laugh. It would be like one of those Mob movies where the hitman finally thinks he's free and clear of obligations only to have the kingpin come calling again. "She'd drop dead. And the idiots will never leave Mom alone. They're probably going to try to kidnap Mini-Me at least once or twice more before they get it through their thick damn heads she's not going to end the world for them. I have to keep her."

Mini-Me's body language brightens. She tries not to smile, but I notice.

Even Natalie is giving me this 'I know you want her but won't admit it for some stupid reason' face.

Sigh.

"Ugh," mutters Mini-Me. "Kidnapping is so overdone. Why can't they leave me alone?"

"You don't look upset," says Natalie.

The kid and I both ask, "Me or her?" at the same time.

"Brook."

"Why should I be upset?" I tilt my head at her.

"Because." Natalie fights to stop from snickering. "You're standing here beside yourself."

Mini-Me holds up her tail blade. "Can I stab her?"

"No."

"Aww, please?"

"No. Bad puns are not justification for homicide."

Mini-Me overacts a sigh and lowers the tail. "I wasn't going to kill her. Just stab her."

I grasp the kid's shoulders, looking at Natalie. "Thanks for watching her. Gonna head home. Gotta feed the little beast."

"Grr," deadpans the kid.

"No problem. She was surprisingly well behaved. More so than I expected."

Mini-Me shrugs. "You're Brook's best friend. It would be rude of me to unleash my full powers of destruction on your shop."

Natalie and I laugh.

"Thanks. Whenever you and Jason want some alone time, feel free to drop her off here."

Shit. I never even thought of how having a kid around 24/7 is going to affect Jason time. Mom might be willing to watch her for a weekend now and then, but I can't do it until I'm totally sure the warmongers have given up on Mini-Me. "Great. You're a lifesaver."

I head for the back door, leading the kid out to the alley. "Ready to go home?"

"Yeah. Is it bad to steal from Natalie?"

"Yep."

"Is that a yeah it's bad but nice job, or yeah it's bad, don't do it?"

"Don't do it."

"Oops." She cringes, grinning.

I smirk.

"Just kidding." She straightens up. "I didn't take anything."

"Heh." I stretch my wings.

… and we fly away home.

24

THE POWER OF NAMES

My miniature doppelganger sits next to me on the sofa, a plate of chicken nuggets in her lap, wearing one of my black T-shirts as a dress.

I also have a plate of chicken nuggets in my lap, wearing a long T-shirt.

We're watching *Dead Like Me*, feet up on the coffee table in pretty much the exact same slouched pose. If anyone took our picture, it would kinda look like someone photoshopped me small next to myself. Eventually, we finish the nuggets, and telekinetically levitate the plates across the apartment to the kitchen. I'll wash them later.

Mini-Me fidgets at a small amulet around her neck on a silver chain. It's like a cartoony skull with way oversized eyes. Her shirt disappears off her. She sits there in her birthday suit for a moment, then the shirt reappears. Seconds later, the shirt vanishes. A super-frilly black sparkle-goth dress appears on her with lace sleeves, multi-tiered ruffles, and little black roses embroidered on the chest. She got the same illusion outfit as me, including miniature shit-kicker boots.

"Oh, wow. This is *so* extra."

I laugh. "Yeah, Natalie is extra all right. But amazing. The wings are murder on wardrobe. We still need to keep that stuff hidden."

"Yeah, I know. Easier to get away with having fun if people think we're normal."

"Exactly."

"Backless dress was a good idea. Almost like you know what you're doing," says Mini-Me. The extra goth dress—an illusion—poofs and the T-shirt returns.

"Heh. Thanks." I glance at her. "Hmm. Okay. Time to stop thinking of you as Mini-Me or 'kid.' You need a name."

"I have a name. Ungrateful Whelp."

"What?" I blink. "Are you messing with me?"

"It's what the asshole kept calling me."

"Are you being innocent or messing with me?"

She winces. "It's an insult, isn't it?"

"Yeah. Not the worst thing he could've called you though. Whelp is just an insulting term for child." Okay, wow. Guess there really is a child in there somewhere. "Hmm. Names."

"If you say Xerox..."

"No." I laugh. "How about Emma?"

"You might as well just name me Fourteen."

"Huh?" I ask.

She shrugs. "Because there'll be thirteen other girls named Emma in every class."

"Oh. Hmm." I think for a moment. "Ensley?"

Mini-Me gives me side eye. "Does it come with free avocado toast for life?"

I snicker. "What?"

"Too hipster."

"Wait, you know what hipster means but not 'ungrateful whelp'?"

"Do not question the mysteries of the magical universe," drones the kid.

I TK levitate my phone into my hand and go to a name website. "Aspen?"

"Ick. Too snooty."

"Aura?"

"Too space cadet-y."

Scroll... scroll... "Dharma?"

"Do I look enlightened or peaceful?"

Scroll... scroll... "Seraphina?"

She holds her tail up. "I will cut you."

Laughing, I keep scrolling. "What about Paisley?"

"I'm not a necktie."

"Clementine?"

She smirks. "Be serious."

"Pax?"

Mini-Me blinks. "Huh? Like Packs a box? Pass."

"No. P-a-x."

She scrunches her nose. "Is that even a word?"

"Yeah, it's right here on this baby name site. Exotic girl names. Means peace."

The child laughs so hard she falls over sideways.

Valid point.

"Harper?" I ask once she calms down.

"Nah, too bright and sweet."

"It's Ashley and Tracy's last name."

"Then don't. It'll get confusing."

"Hmm." Scrolling... "Emily?"

Mini-Me shakes her head. "Way too normal."

"Chloe?"

"Too fluffy."

"Zoey or Zooey?"

She ponders for a second. Ooh, progress? "Nah. I don't want to be last for everything. No Z names."

"You're gonna be nearly first. They go by last name. Amari."

She waves me off. "Still nah."

"Alexa?"

A double beep comes from the kitchen.

"Oh, maybe." Mini-Me grins. "Every time you start yelling at me, the Amazon thing will go crazy. The name's kinda snooty, but it might be worth it for the chaos."

"Uhh, better not then."

She snaps her fingers in fake disappointment.

"Heh." I grin at the phone. "Lilith?"

Mini-Me rolls her eyes. "Oh, come on!" Her T-shirt vanishes. She springs up to stand on the couch, sprouting wings, horns, tail, and glowing eyes. "Lilith? Seriously? A little too on the nose?"

"Okay. Fair point. Umm... Fable?"

She downshifts back to human and plops seated, tilting her hand. "Hmm. Not bad. On the short list."

"Pandora?"

Mini-Me perks up. "Ooh. Kinda neat. Also, short list."

"Tempest?"

She grins. "I like it... but people are gonna call me 'Temp.' How about as a middle name? Pandora Tempest?"

Hmm. I mull for a second or four. "I'm gonna regret this. Names have power, you know."

"Not *too* much power. You didn't turn into a city, *Brooklyn*."

I lean my head back, laughing. Oh, this kid... She might be a little more mentally adult than she looks, which could be good and bad. Good if it comes with greater self-control. Bad if it comes with increased deviousness.

"So you like Pandora?"

She nods, smiling. "Someone shortening it to Pan won't bother me like being called Temp. And if someone called me 'Tempy,' they'd need a new nose."

"Pandora Tempest Amari..."

The kid stares up at the ceiling as if listening for a distant voice.

"What?"

"I'm waiting for the ominous thunderclap."

I snicker. "No thunderclap means it's safe to call you that, I think."

"Aww, poop." She looks down, picking at her nails.

"Don't like the name now?"

"No, I like it." She stretches, then leans against me. "Just hoping for some more chaos."

Someone knocks at the door.

Pandora grasps her necklace and re-summons the T-shirt.

"Okay, tomorrow I'm going to start the process of charming everyone I need to in order to make everything about you being here legal. This is gonna mean school."

"I know. I know. Can't wait to mess with people." She grins.

"Brooklyn?" asks Tracy from outside.

"C'mon in."

Tracy walks in, Ashley in tow.

Ashley narrows her eyes at Pandora. "Are you cheating on me with some other babysitting gig?"

"Nope."

"Did I leave the summoning circle open?" asks Ashley.

"No. Come on, you know her."

Ashley runs over. "Oh… it's the mini you?"

"Yes. Ashley, this is Pandora. Pandora, Ashley."

"Hey." Pandora waves. "You look much happier out of the cage."

"Yeah," says Ashley. "I'm okay. Mostly angry about it."

Pandora looks up at me. "Why is she here?"

"They live next door. They are close friends and in on our secret. You don't have to hide from them." I pat the girls on the head and look at Tracy. "What's up?"

"Just going to work. Wondering if you could watch Ash for a couple hours."

"Yeah, no problem."

Pandora leans close to me and whispers, "Does she really think she summoned us?"

"Yeah, just go with it," I whisper back.

"So, who's this?" asks Tracy.

"Pandora. My… daughter."

Tracy stares at us for a moment. "There is no way in hell *you* have a… what is she five?"

"Six," grumbles Pandora.

"A six-year-old? Did you get knocked up at thirteen?" Tracy whistles. "Wow, she looks so much like you."

"Magic happened." I twirl a finger around in the air. "Evil plot, but it failed. And you know damn well I'm not eighteen."

"Cool. If you need help redoing the small room you're not using into a bedroom for her, let me know." Tracy waves.

"Sure, will do. Have fun at work. Oh, Trace... here."

She skids to a stop halfway to the door.

While the girls flop on the floor in front of the TV for PlayStation time, I run to the bedroom and fish the $50 gift card I 'acquired' from Sanjay out of my purse, running back over to Tracy with it. "Here."

"Oh... you didn't have to..."

"Don't worry about it. Food is food. Don't question where it comes from."

She hugs me. "Thanks."

Ack. Hugs. I tolerate it though. She means well and doesn't squeeze too tight or too long.

Tracy hurries out. I flop on the couch watching two children play video games. Dammit. Kids are like cats. One leads to two. I better not have a litter by the end of next year. What the hell am I even doing? Oh, right. Suppose there's no point lying to myself anymore. From the instant we first made eye contact, I really did want her. Besides, I'm her best chance at *not* turning into the world-ender as well as protecting her from Melisandre and his idiot brigade. Ugh, Mom's going to laugh at me. She always said 'I hope you grow up one day and have a kid who's just as much trouble as you are.'

Wow, she had no idea how literally it would come true.

Worse, Dad's going to freak the hell out. He's totally going to be all over us when he learns about her. He couldn't interact with me as a child due to the stupid Elestari threatening to kill me if he revealed himself, so now, grandpa's going to overcompensate with her.

Oh, well. Things could be worse. Melisandre could've turned *me* back into a child, or done something truly evil like resurrect the career of the New Kids on the Block. I should be happy all he did was make a mini-me.

Some people are worried having kids will destroy their social life or get in the way of them doing fun things like breaking into abandoned places, shoplifting, getting high with their friends, or having the occasional random swordfight against dangerous extraplanar beings. Not this girl.

I'll just bring my daughter with me.

---

fin

ACKNOWLEDGMENTS

Thank you for reading *The Queen of Discord!* I hope you enjoyed the story and will take the time to leave a review.

Thanks to Lee Sheridan for editing! Additional thanks to Alexandria Thompson for the cover design.

ABOUT THE AUTHOR

Originally from South Amboy NJ, Matthew has been creating science fiction and fantasy worlds for most of his reasoning life. Since 1996, he has developed the "Divergent Fates" world, in which *Division Zero*, *Virtual Immortality*, *The Awakened Series*, *The Harmony Paradox*, and the *Daughter of Mars series* take place. Along with being an editor at Curiosity Quills press, he has worked in IT and technical support.

Matthew is an avid gamer, a recovered WoW addict, Gamemaster for two custom RPG systems, and a fan of anime, British humour, and intellectual science fiction that questions the nature of reality, life, and what happens after it.

He is also fond of cats.

Visit me online at:
  Facebook: https://www.facebook.com/MatthewSCoxAuthor
  Amazon: https://www.amazon.com/author/mscox
  Pinterest: https://www.pinterest.com/matthewcox10420/
  Goodreads: https://www.goodreads.com/author/show/
7712730.Matthew_S_Cox
  Email: mcox2112@gmail.com

OTHER BOOKS BY MATTHEW S. COX

Divergent Fates Universe Novels

Division Zero series

- Division Zero
- Lex De Mortuis
- Thrall
- Guardian
- Harbinger

The Awakened series

- Prophet of the Badlands
- Archon's Queen
- Grey Ronin
- Daughter of Ash
- Zero Rogue
- Angel Descended

Daughter of Mars series

- The Hand of Raziel
- Araphel
- Ghost Black

Virtual Immortality series

- Virtual Immortality
- The Harmony Paradox

Prophet of the Badlands Series

- Prophet's Journey

Divergent Fates Anthology

(Fiction Novels - Adult)

The Roadhouse Chronicles Series

- One More Run
- The Redeemed
- Dead Man's Number

Faded Skies series

- Heir Ascendant
- Ascendant Unrest
- Ascendant Revolution

Temporal Armistice Series

- Nascent Shadow
- The Shadow Collector
- The Gate to Oblivion
- The Queen of Discord

Vampire Innocent series

- A Nighttime of Forever
- A Beginner's Guide to Fangs
- The Artist of Ruin
- The Last Family Road Trip
- The Phantom Oracle
- How Not to Summon Demons
- Ordinary Problems of a College Vampire

- A Vampire's Guide to Surviving Holidays
- An Introduction to Paranormal Diplomacy

Standalones

- Wayfarer: AV494
- Axillon99
- Chiaroscuro: The Mouse and the Candle
- The Spirits of Six Minstrel Run
- Sophie's Light
- The Far Side of Promise anthology
- Operation: Chimera (with Tony Healey)
- The Dysfunctional Conspiracy (with Christopher Veltmann)
- Of Myth and Shadow
- The Girl Who Found the Sun

Winter Solstice series (with J.R. Rain)

- Convergence
- Containment
- Catalyst

Alexis Silver series (with J.R. Rain)

- Silver Light
- Deep Silver
- Silver Quarrel

Samantha Moon Origins series (with J.R. Rain)

- New Moon Rising
- Moon Mourning

Vampire For Hire series (with J.R. Rain)

- Moon Master
- Dead Moon
- Lost Moon

Maddy Wimsey series (with J.R. Rain)

- The Devil's Eye
- The Drifting Gloom
- Dark Mercy

Samantha Moon Case Files series (with J.R. Rain)

- Blood Moon

Immortal Operative series (with J.R. Rain)

- Broken Ice

Four Elements series (with J.R. Rain)

- The Elementalist
- The Black Rose
- The Wakefield Curse

Young Adult Novels

The Eldritch Heart Series

- The Eldritch Heart
- The Cursed Crown

Evergreen Series

- Evergreen

- The World That Remains
- The Lucky Ones
- Nuclear Summer

Standalones

- Caller 107
- The Summer the World Ended
- Nine Candles of Deepest Black
- The Forest Beyond the Earth
- Out of Sight

Middle Grade Novels

The Adventures of Ubergirl series

- My Dad is a Mad Scientist
- Aliens Ate My Homework
- The End of all Halloweens

Tales of Widowswood series

- Emma and the Banderwigh
- Emma and the Silk Thieves
- Emma and the Silverbell Faeries
- Emma and the Elixir of Madness
- Emma and the Weeping Spirit

Standalones

- Citadel: The Concordant Sequence
- The Cursed Codex
- The Menagerie of Jenkins Bailey

www.ingramcontent.com/pod-product-compliance
Lightning Source LLC
Chambersburg PA
CBHW020608180626
46810CB00007B/2688